THE PEASANTS

AUTUMN

FROM THE POLISH OF

LADISLAS REYMONT

ALFRED · A · KNOPF
NEW YORK MCMXXV

PUBLISHED, JANUARY, 1925, BY ALFRED A. KNOPF, INC.

SECOND PRINTING, DECEMBER, 1924.
THIRD PRINTING, DECEMBER, 1924.
FOURTH PRINTING, DECEMBER, 1924.
FIFTH PRINTING, DECEMBER, 1924.
SIXTH PRINTING, FEBRUARY, 1925.
SEVENTH PRINTING, MAY, 1925.
EIGHTH PRINTING, JULY, 1925.
NINTH PRINTING, SEPTEMBER, 1925.

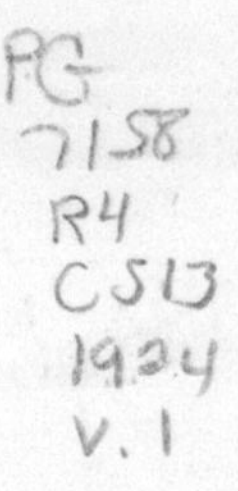

MANUFACTURED IN THE UNITED STATES OF AMERICA

PUBLISHER'S NOTE

The Peasants has been translated from the original Polish by Michael H. Dziewicki, Reader of English Literature at the University of Cracow. I wish to make special acknowledgment to Dr. A. M. Nawench of Columbia University for his invaluable assistance in seeing the work through the press.

A. A. K.

THE PEASANTS

AUTUMN

CHAPTER I

"PRAISED be Jesus Christ!"

"World without end!—What, my good Agatha? And whither be you wandering now?"

"Out into the world, please your Reverence, into the wide world!" she answered, with a wave of her staff from east to west.

The priest mechanically turned his eyes in that direction, but closed them to the blinding sun in the western sky. Then he said, in a lower and somewhat hesitating tone:

"Have the Klembas turned you out? Or is it only a little bickering between you?"

She drew herself up a little and, before answering, cast her eyes around her upon the bare autumnal fields and the village roofs surrounded by fruit-gardens.

"No, they have not turned me out: how could they? They are good folk and my close kin. And as for bickering, there was none. I myself saw that I had better leave; that's all. 'Better to leap into the deep than cumber another man's wagon.' . . . So I had to go; there was no work for me. Winter is coming, but what of that? Are they to give me food and a corner to sleep in while I do nothing to earn it? Besides, they have just weaned their calf, and the goslings must be sheltered under their roof at night, for it is getting cold. I have to make room. Why, beasts are God's creatures, too. . . . But they are kind folk; they keep me in summer-time at least, and do not begrudge me a corner of their house and a morsel of their food. . . . And in winter I go out into the wide world, asking alms. . . . I need but little, and that little good people give me. With the help of the Lord Jesus, I shall pull through till spring, and put something by into the bargain.

Surely, the sweet, good Jesus will not forsake His poor."

"No, that He will not," the priest reassured her in earnest tones, quietly pressing a small silver coin into her hand.

"Thanks, thanks, and God bless your Reverence!"

She bowed her shaking head as low as his knees, while big tears trickled down her face, a face rugged and furrowed like newly-ploughed autumn fields.

The priest felt confused.

"Go, and God speed you on your way," he faltered, raising her up.

With trembling hands she crossed herself, took hold of her wallet and her sharp-pointed staff, and started off along the broad and deeply rutted road toward the forest, turning now and again to glance at the village, the fields where potatoes were then being dug, and the smoke from many a herdsman's fire, wafted low over the stubble.

The priest, who had previously been seated upon a plough-wheel, now returned to it, took a pinch of snuff, and opened his breviary; but his eyes would stray now and then from the red print and glance over the vast landscape slumbering in autumnal peace, or gaze into the pale blue sky, or wander to his men leaning over the plough he was guiding.

"Hey, Valek! That furrow is crooked!" he cried out, sitting up, with his eyes following every step of two sturdy grey plough-horses.

Once more he returned to his breviary, and his lips again moved, but his eyes soon unconsciously wandered to the horses, or to a flock of crows cautiously hopping, with outstretched beaks, in the newly-made furrow, and taking wing when even the whip cracked or the horses wheeled round: after which they would alight heavily in the wake of the plough, and sharpen their beaks on the hard, sun-baked clods just turned up.

"Valek, just flick the right-hand mare a bit; she is lagging behind."

He smiled to see her draw evenly after this correction and, when the horses came to the roadside, jumped up to pat their necks—a caress to which the animals responded by stretching their noses towards his face and sniffing complacently.

"Het—a—ah!" Valek then sang out. Pulling the silver bright share out of the furrow, he deftly lifted up the plough, swung the horses round, and thrust the shining steel into the earth again. At a crack of the whip, the horses set tugging till the cross-bar creaked again; and on they went, ploughing away at the great strip of land which, stretching out at right angles to the road, descended the slope, and, not unlike the woof of some coarse hempen stuff, ran down as far as the low-lying hamlet nestling amongst the red and yellow leaves of its orchards.

It was near the end of autumn, but the weather was still warm and rather drowsy. The sun was still hot enough and, hanging in the south-west above the woods, made the shrubs and the pear-trees, and even the hard, dry clods, cast strong, cold shadows.

Ineffable sweetness and serenity reigned in the air, full of a golden haze of sunlit dust over the fields lately harvested; while above in the azure heaven, enormous white clouds floated here and there like great wind-tormented snow-drifts.

Below, as far as the eye could see, lay the drab-hued fields, forming a sort of huge basin with a dark-blue rim of forest, a basin across which, like a silken skein glittering in the sunshine, a river coursed sparkling and winding among the alders and willows on its banks. In the midst of the hamlet, it spread out into a large oblong body of water, and then ran northward through a rift in the hills. At the bottom of the valley, skirting the lake, lay the village, with the sunlight playing on the many autumnal hues of its fruit gardens. Thence, even up to the very edge of the forest, ran the long bands of cultivated ground, stretches of grey fields with thread-like pathways between them, whereon pear-trees and blackthorns grew; the general ashen tint being in places variegated by patches of gold-yellow lupines with fragrant flowers, or by the dull silver of the dried-up bed of some torrent; or by quiet sandy roads, with rows of tall poplars overshadowing them, reaching upwards to the hills and woods.

The priest was suddenly roused from the contemplation of this scene. A long, mournful lowing was heard at no great distance, making the crows take wing and fly away obliquely to the potato-diggings, their dark fluttering shadows following them over the partly sown fields. Shading his eyes with his hand, he gazed in the direction of the sun and the forest, and beheld a little girl coming towards him and leading a large red cow by a rope. As she approached, she said: "Praised be Jesus Christ!" and would have gone out of her way to kiss the priest's hand, but the cow jerked her away and fell a-lowing anew.

"Are you taking it to market?" the priest asked.

"No, only to the steer at the miller's.—Be still, you pest! Are you possessed?" she cried, out of breath, and striving to master the animal, which, however, dragged her along till both disappeared in a cloud of dust.

Presently there came along the sandy road, trudging heavily, a Jewish ragpicker, who trundled a barrow so loaded down that he had to stop for breath every now and then.

"What news, Moshek?" cried the priest.

"What news? Good news to those it may concern. Potatoes, God be praised! are plentiful; there's a good crop of rye, and cabbages will be abundant. It's all very well for such as have potatoes and rye and cabbages." He kissed the priest's sleeve, adjusted the barrow-strap, and went on more lightly, his way now leading down a gentle slope. In his wake, along the middle of the road and in the haze of dust raised by his dragging feet, came a blind beggar, led by a well-fed dog at the end of a string. Then a lad carrying a bottle approached from the side of the wood. The latter, catching sight of the holy man on the road, gave him a wide berth and made for the village tavern by a short cut through the fields.

A peasant from the next hamlet, on his way to the mill, and a Jewess driving a flock of geese, then also passed by.

Each praised God; the priest exchanged some kind words and friendly looks with them, and they went on their way.

By this time the sun was low. The priest got up and called to Valek: "You will plough as far as the birches, then home. The poor beasts are quite tired out."

Going along the path between the fields, he said his Office under his breath, looking round from time to time at the scene with fond, glistening eyes. Working-women gleamed in red rows at the potato-diggings, and the contents of their baskets rumbled into the carts. Here and there, the ground was still being ploughed for sowing. On the fallows a herd of brindled cows was feeding. The ashen-grey hue of certain lands was beginning to take on a ruddy tint from the blades of corn already sprouting there. On the close-cropped, tawny grass of the meadows, the geese showed up like white snowflakes. A cow was heard lowing afar. Fires had been lit, and long blue clouds of smoke trailed over the cornfields. Elsewhere harrows were at work, a dim cloud of dust rising in the wake of each and settling down at the foot of the hills. From beneath it, coming as it were out of a cloud, a bareheaded, barefooted peasant, with a cloth full of corn tied round his waist, was pacing leisurely, taking handfuls of grain and scattering them all over the earth with a solemn gesture, as one bestowing a blessing. On reaching the end of the ploughed fields, he would turn and slowly ascend the slope, his shock of touzled hair first appearing above the sky-line, then his shoulders, and finally his whole body, still with the same solemn gesture, the sower's benediction, that shed forth upon the soil, a holy thing as it were—the golden seed which fell in a semicircle round him.

The priest's pace became more and more leisurely: now he would stop to take breath, now to look at his two grey horses, now to glance at a few boys who were throwing stones into a large pear-tree. They came running to him in a body, and, holding their hands behind them, all kissed the sleeve of his soutane.

He stroked their flaxen heads, but added a word of warning: "Have a care not to break the branches, or you will get no pears at all next year."

"We were not throwing stones at the pears," answered one boy, bolder than the rest; "there's a chough's nest up in the tree."

The priest passed on with a friendly smile and was presently among the potato-diggers.

"God speed your work!"

"May God reward you!" they replied in a chorus, and all came up to kiss their beloved pastor's hands.

"Our Lord has given us plenty of potatoes this year, I think," he said, offering his open snuff-box to the men, who respectfully accepted; refraining, however, from taking snuff in his presence.

"Aye, potatoes are as big as a cat's head, and plenty to each plant."

"Ah, then pigs will rise in price; you will all want to have some to fatten."

"They are dear enough as it is. There was a swine plague last summer, and we have to buy them even in Prussia."

"So there was, so there was. And whose potatoes are you digging here?"

"Why Boryna's, of course."

"I don't see him with you, so I wasn't sure."

"Father is only at the forest with my goodman."

"Oh, there you are, Hanka? How goes it?" he said, turning to a handsome young woman who wore a red kerchief round her head. She came forward, and, her hands being soiled, threw her apron over them as she took the priest's hand to kiss.

"Well, and how is your little boy whom I christened in harvest time?"

"God bless your Reverence, he is well and lively."

"The Lord be with you all!"

"And with your Reverence!"

He walked away to the right, where the burying-ground, near a road planted with poplars, lay on that side of the village. They gazed after him in silence for some time, and it was only when his thin and slightly bent figure had passed the low stone enclosure and entered the mortuary chapel, overshadowed with the yellowish and reddish foliage of birches and maples, that they found their tongues again.

"There is no better man in the whole world," said one of the women.

"Yes, indeed," chimed in Hanka, emptying her basketful on to a yellow heap conspicuous on the freshly furrowed soil and dry stalks. "They would have taken him away from us to town, but father went with the Voyt[1] to entreat the Bishop, and so they did not get him. But dig away, you, dig away: the day and the field are both drawing to a close."

They set again to work in silence. Only the crunching sound of the hoes in the hard ground, with now and then the sharp clink of steel upon stone, was to be heard.

Less than a score of workers were there, most of them old women and farm-labourers. At some distance were fixed two couples of crossed poles from which, swathed in cloths, a couple of babies were swinging as in hammocks, and wailing now and then.

"Well, and so the old woman has gone off a-wandering," Yagustynka said after some time.

"The old woman? Who?" asked Anna, straightening herself.

"Why, old Agatha."

"What, a-begging?"

"Of course a-begging! No, not for the pleasure of the thing. She has been working hard for her kinsfolk, serving them all summer long; and now they let her go—to get some fresh air! Next spring she will return, with baskets full of sugar and tea, and some money, besides. Oh, they will be fond enough of her then, and cover her up snugly in bed, and tell her that she must not work, but just rest up. Oh, yes! and they will call her 'Aunt,' till they have got the last bit of money out of her. But when autumn comes round again, there will again be no room for her—not even

[1] *Voyt*—the headman of the community.—*Translator's Note.*

in the passageway, not even in the pigsty. Oh, those blood-sucking kinsfolk! Those inhuman beasts!"

Yagustynka put such passion into her outburst that her face turned livid as she spoke.

An old farm-labourer—a wry-faced worn-out man—remarked: "Here you see how true is the saying: 'The wind is always blowing in the face of the poor.'"

"Now, good people, please dig away," interrupted Hanka hastily; she did not like the turn the conversation was taking. But Yagustynka, who could not hold her tongue, soon looked up and said:

"Those Pacheses,—they are getting on in years; the hair is thin upon their heads."

"And yet," another woman put in, "they still remain unmarried men."

"And there are so many girls growing old here, too, or forced to take service elsewhere!"

"Yet, they have a score of acres and more, besides a meadow beyond the mill."

"Aye, but will their mothers let them marry, do you think, or let them have anything if they do?"

"Yes, who would then milk the cows, or do the washing, or tend to the farm and the pigs?"

"They have to keep house for their mother and for Yagna. Else how could Yagna be the grand lady that she is? Quite a gentlewoman, always dressing up, and washing herself, and peering into her glass, and for ever braiding her hair!"

"And looking for someone to share her bed—any able-bodied young man will do," added Yagustynka with a malicious sneer.

"Joseph Bandech sent 'proposers'[1] to her with a gift of vodka, but she would not have him."

"A plague on her, the pampered minx!"

"And the old dame, too: always in church, and praying

[1] Two men go to the girl's family, offering vodka in the young man's name; if the girl drinks to him, she is regarded as affianced.—*Translator's Note.*

out of her prayer-book, and going wherever there's an indulgence!" [1]

"She's a witch, all the same. Who was it that made Vavrek's cows dry up, pray? And, ah! when Yashek's little boy stole plums from her orchard, and she muttered evil words against him, did he not get the *koltun* [2] at once, and shrivel up with crooked limbs?"

"Oh, how can God's blessings descend upon a place where such creatures dwell?"

"In former days," Yagustynka observed, "when I was still tending father's cattle, they used to drive such people out of our midst. . . . Aye, and it does them no harm, for they are not without protectors." Then, lowering her voice, and casting a side-glance at Hanka, then busily digging in the foremost row, Yagustynka whispered to her neighbours: "The first to defend her would be Hanka's goodman; he follows Yagna everywhere like a dog."

"For God's sake! Pray, hold your tongue. What awful things you are telling us! Why, that's an offence against God, a sin!" the gossips whispered to her, as they went on digging with bowed shoulders.

"Is he, then, the only one? Why, all the lads are after her, like cats after their kind."

"Indeed, she is good-looking: plump as a well-fed heifer, with a face as white as cream, and eyes even as the flax-flower. Strong, besides; many a man no stronger."

"For what does she do but eat and sleep? No wonder she is comely."

A long silence ensued while they emptied their baskets on to the heap. Afterwards the talk ran on other subjects, till Yuzka, Boryna's daughter, was seen coming at a run across the cornfields, from the village, and they stopped. She came, panting and all out of breath, shouting from a distance:

[1] An annual local festival held in every parish, where those who come to church may gain an indulgence.—*Translator's Note.*

[2] *Koltun*—a diseased, matted condition of the hair.—*Translator's Note.*

"Hanka, come home: there's something wrong with the cow!"

"Mercy on us! which cow?"

"White-and-Red."

Hanka heaved a sigh of relief. "Good God! how you frightened me! I thought it was mine."

"Vitek brought her in but now; the keeper had driven them out of the wood. She ran too fast—she is so very fat,—and fell just outside the byre. She neither eats nor drinks; only rolls about and bellows. Mercy on us!"

"Is father home yet?"

"No, he is not. Oh, good Lord! Such a cow, too! She gave more than a gallon at each milking. Oh, do come, quick!"

"Yes, yes, quick as thought—instantly!"

She at once took her child out of the cloth in which it hung hammock-like, and came away so alarmed at the news that she forgot to let down the apron with which she had tucked her dress up to the knees for work. And, as she followed Yuzka, her white legs twinkled across the fields.

The potato-diggers, working with their hoes between their feet, went on more slowly, having no one to hurry or to chide them any more.

Thc sun, now quite in the West, glowing red as if heated by its rapid course, hung like a huge crimson globe above the high, black woods. Twilight was deepening and spreading over the landscape; filling furrows, hiding in ditches, gathering under thickets, and slowly pouring over the land; deadening, blotting out and wiping away all colours, until the tree-tops and the churchroof and steeple alone glowed with gorgeous hues. Many labourers were already plodding homewards.

Shouts and neighings, and bellowings and the rattling of carts, growing ever louder and louder, filled the quiet evening air. But presently a tinkling from the belfry announced the Angelus; and at the bell's sonorous vibrations, these noises were all hushed, and only whispered prayers, like the faint sound of falling leaves, were audible.

And now the cattle, driven home with merry cries and songs in a confused multitude, came along the roads stirring up such a volume of dust that only now and then were their mighty, thickly-horned heads seen to emerge from it.

Sheep, too, bleated here and there, and flocks of geese, flying off the pasture lands, were lost in the Western glow, so that only their shrill, creaking cries betrayed the fact that they were on the wing.

"A pity that White-and-Red was with calf."

"It is a good thing that Boryna is not poor."

"A pity, all the same, to lose so fine an animal."

"Boryna has no wife, everything he has goes as through a sieve."

"Because Hanka is no sort of housekeeper, you know."

"Oh, but she is—for herself. They lodge with her father as if they were farm-labourers; each of them is on the lookout for what can be got out of him. As to Boryna's property, let the dog watch over it!"

"Yuzka is a child, and knows nothing. What can she do?"

"Well, Boryna might as well give up his land to Antek, might he not?"

"Yes, indeed, and live on the portion they will allow him?" Yagustynka returned hotly. "You are old, Vavrek, but a great fool for all that. Ho, ho! Boryna is still hale: he may marry again. If he gave all he had to his children, he would be an ass."

"Hale he is, but over sixty."

"Never fear, Vavrek; any girl would have him, if he only asked her."

"He has buried two wives already."

"May he bury a third, then, and, God help him! Never while he lives let him give his children the least bit of ground;—no, not so much as a foot of it. The carrion! They would give him a fine portion, they would! Force him to work on the farm, or starve, or go far off to beg! Yes, turn over what you have to your children; they will give you just enough, to buy a rope to hang yourself or to tie a stone round your neck with!"

"Well, it's getting dark; time to go home."

"Yes, it is time; the sun is going down."

So they quickly shouldered their hoes and, taking their baskets and dinner pails in hand, went off in single file along the path, old Yagustynka always passionately holding forth against her own and everybody else's children.

A girl was going home in the same direction, but by another path, driving a sow with its little ones and singing in a shrill voice:

"Oh, go not near the wagon,
Nor with its axle play,
Nor let a young man kiss thee,
Whatever he may say!"

"Listen to that idiot howling as if she was being skinned alive!"

CHAPTER II

A GOOD many people had gathered by this time in Boryna's yard, which, surrounded on three sides by farm buildings, was separated from the road by an orchard on the fourth. Several women were offering advice and eyeing with amazement the very large red-and-white cow that lay wallowing on a heap of manure just before the byre.

An old dog, somewhat lame and with hairless patches along its sides, was now sniffing at her and barking, now running to the fence and driving back into the road such boys and girls as had climbed up and were gazing curiously into the yard, and now approaching a sow that lay near the hut, suckling four white little pigs and gently grunting.

Hanka ran straight to the cow on arriving, and at once began to stroke her face and head.

"Poor, poor dear Red-and-White!" she cried, with copious tears and many lamentations.

From time to time the women would recommend her a new remedy for the sick animal. Now they would pour brine down its throat, now milk into which wax from a consecrated taper had been dropped. One advised soap dissolved in whey, and another suggested bleeding. But the cow did not benefit from any of these nostrums. At times she would lift up her head, and, as though imploring for help, low till her beautiful large eyes, with pink-tinged whites, grew dim and misty. Then, quite exhausted with pain, she would bow her horned head and put forth her tongue to lick Hanka's hand.

"May not Ambrose be able to do something?" was one woman's suggestions.

"Yes, yes, he knows a good deal about sicknesses."

"Run to him, Yuska. He has just rung the Angelus, so is likely to be somewhere about the church. Good God! when Father comes home, how furious he will be! And yet," Hanka sobbed, " 'tis no fault of ours!"

She then sat down on the threshold of the cow-house and bared her full white bosom to the babe that was wailing for food, meanwhile watching the suffering animal with keen apprehension and, expecting Boryna's arrival, casting uneasy glances past the fence.

In a few minutes Yuzka returned, announcing the arrival of Ambrose, who came almost as soon himself. He was close to a hundred years old, one-legged, and walked with the aid of a staff, but still as straight as an arrow. His face, dry and wrinkled as a potato in spring, was clean-shaven, but scarred; his hair as white as milk, with long wisps falling on his forehead and hanging down to his shoulders. He went straight to the cow and looked her over very carefully.

"Oho!" he said, "you will have fresh meat presently, I see."

"Oh, but pray do something to make her well!" cried Jozia. "A cow worth over three hundred *zloty*[1] . . . and just now with calf, besides! Do help us! Oh, dear! Oh dear!"

Ambrose produced a lancet, whetted it on his boot, looked at the edge against the sky, and then cut a blood-vessel in Red-and-White's belly. But no spurt of blood followed; only a few drops, black and foam-flecked, oozed out slowly.

All were standing about, their necks craned forward, breathless with attention.

"Too late!" he said mournfully. "Yes, the poor thing is near its last gasp. It must be cattle plague or something of the sort. You should have sent for me as soon as there was anything the matter. Those women! Peevish things they are, fit only to weep! When anything's to be done, they only fall a-bleating. A lot of ewes!"

[1] *Zloty.* A Polish coin, formerly worth about seven cents.

He spat contemptuously, looked once more at the cow's eyes and tongue, wiped his gory hands on her sleek hide, and prepared to go.

"I shall not ring for her funeral; your pots will clink instead."

"Here come Father and Antek!" exclaimed Yuzka, hastening to meet them as a rumbling sound came from the farther end of the pond and a long cart and horses appeared, looming dark against the red glow of dust blazing in the light of the setting sun.

"Father, Father! Red-and-White is dying!" she called out. He was just turning the pond. Antek had got down behind; the pine they had on the cart was a long one, and had to be held up.

"Don't waste your breath talking nonsense," he growled in reply, lashing the horses.

"Ambrose has bled it—in vain. Melted wax down her throat—in vain, too. Salt—no use. . . . 'Tis the cattle-plague, no doubt. Vitek says the forester drove them out of the grove, and all at once Red-and-White lay down and started to moan; and so he brought her back here."

"Red-and-White, our best cow! You foul beasts! The devil take you for the care you took of her!"

He threw the reins to his son and ran forward, whip in hand.

The women drew away. Vitek, who had all the time been very calmly doing things about the house, ran off, faint with fear, into the garden. Even Hanka stood up on the threshhold, bewildered and dismayed.

Old Boryna looked long at the cow and then cried out:

"Yes, she is gone, and because of them! The filthy sluts! Always ready to eat, but to watch—never! Such a splendid animal! One cannot stir from the house, but that some harm and evil must come of it."

Hanka murmured in excuse: "But I have been out potato-digging all afternoon."

He turned on her in a rage. "You! Do you ever see anything that goes wrong? Do you care one pin for the things that are mine? Such a cow as 'twould be hard to find—aye, even at a manor farm!"

He went on lamenting for some time, examined the cow, tried to make her stand up, and looked into her mouth. She was breathing heavily, with a rattle in her throat. Her blood had quite ceased to flow and formed hard, black clots like cinders.

"What's to be done? She must be killed: I'll save at least as much as that will bring us."

Thus making up his mind, he went into the barn for a scythe. After sharpening it with a few turns of a grindstone that stood under the eaves of the cow-house, he pulled off his coat, tucked up his shirt-sleeves, and set about his grim task.

Hanka and Yuzka began to weep as Red-and-White, as though feeling death close at hand, raised her heavy head and, moaning faintly, fell flat, with her throat cut. Her legs jerked convulsively once or twice.

The dog lapped the blood, which was already beginning to clot.

Antek, who had just arrived, angrily addressed his weeping wife:

"What have you to weep over, foolish one? Father's cow is father's loss, not ours!"

And he set to unharnessing the horses, which Vitek took to the stable.

"Is the potato crop good?" Boryna inquired as he was washing his hands by the well.

"Why shouldn't it be good? Twenty sacks or thereabouts," was the reply.

"They must be brought in this very day."

"Bring them in yourself, then," said Antek. "I am dead tired and ready to drop. The off-horse, too, is lame in one foreleg."

"Yuzka, go and tell Kuba to stop digging. Let him put the young mare to instead of the off-horse, and bring the potatoes home to-day. It may rain."

Boryna was boiling over with anger and mortification. Every now and then he went to gaze at the slaughtered cow and swore outrageously. Then he strode across the yard, looked into the byre, the barn, and all the sheds, being so confused by his loss that he did not know what he was doing.

"Vitek! Vitek!" he roared at length, unfastening the broad leather girdle round his waist. But Vitek did not answer his call.

All the neighbours had disappeared, feeling that such sorrow for so great a loss was likely to end in blows, and Boryna was at no time indisposed for a fight. To-day, however, he did nothing but curse and swear.

Going toward the hut, he cried through the open window: "Hanka, give me something to eat!" and passed in to his own quarters.

The hut was the usual peasants' cabin, divided into two parts by a very wide passageway. The back looked out upon the yard; the four front windows, upon the orchard and the road. Boryna and his daughter, Yuzka, occupied the side next the garden; Antek and his family lived on the other side; while the herdsman and the labourer slept in the stable.

The room was now getting dark, for but little light could filter through its tiny windows, the eaves that overshadowed them, and the trees of the orchard beyond. Only the sheen of the glass that covered the holy images hanging in dark rows from the whitewashed walls, could be seen. The room, though large, looked smaller on account of the low ceiling, with the great beams supporting it, and the amount of furniture which filled the whole place, leaving only a little free space about the big penthouse fire-place that stood close to the passage wall.

Boryna took off his boots there, then entered a dim alcove, and closed the door behind him. He removed a shutter from a small pane of glass, and the sundown at once flooded the closet with blood-red light.

It was a small lumber-room, crowded with household

articles. Poles were fixed across it, from which hung many a striped cloth and *sukmana;*[1] there were piles of grey spinning-yarn, and fleeces rolled into dingy bales, and sacks of feathers. He took a white *sukmana* and a scarlet girdle, and then for a long time fumbled in certain tubs full of grain; also in a corner, underneath a heap of odds and ends—leather and iron fumbled together. But, hearing Hanka in the next room, he quickly replaced the shutter, and again started groping in the tubs of corn.

His supper, an enormous pot of cabbage stewed with fat bacon, was now smoking on a bench just beneath the window. The odour of that mingled in the air with the smell of scrambled eggs in a big dish close by.

"Where did Vitek take the cattle this morning?" he asked, cutting off a mighty piece from a loaf of bread as large as the largest sieve.

"To the manor copse; and the forester drove them out."

"The carrion! It is they who have killed Red-and-White!"

"Yes, she was so tired and overheated with running that something inside her got inflamed."

"Those beggarly dogs! We have a right to graze our cattle there. It is down in black and white, in letters as large as an ox: yet they always drive us away, and say we have no right there."

"They have done the same to others, too. They have beaten up Valek's boy, too, most sorely."

"Ah! I shall go to court, or else to the Commissioner. She was worth three hundred *złoty,* if she was worth a *grosz!*"

"Surely, surely," assented Hanka, greatly relieved to see her father less angry with her.

"Tell Antek that as soon as they have brought the potatoes in, they must see to the cow—skin her and cut her up. I shall lend a hand when I get home from the Voyt's. Hang the quarters from the rafters, out of the reach of dogs and vermin."

[1] *Sukmana*—a long coat worn by Polish peasants.—*Translator's Note.*

Having finished his meal, he got up to dress for the visit, but felt so heavy and drowsy that he flung himself on the bed, just as he was, for just forty winks of sleep.

Hanka cleared the things away, going to the window every now and then to peep at Antek, who was taking his supper under the porch in front of the house. He sat at a civil distance from the platter, taking spoonful after spoonful with a hard but leisurely scrape against the sides of the vessel. At times he would cast a glance over the pond, whose waters gleamed with moving circles of purple and gold, iridescent in the sunset. Amongst these, like white clouds round a rainbow, swam a flock of geese, gabbling and spurting streams of blood-red jewels from their beaks.

The village was seething with life and crowds of people. On the road at either side of the pond, the dust flew and carts rattled; and lowing cattle stood knee-deep in the pond, drinking at leisure and lifting their ponderous heads, while from their jaws streams of water trickled down like strings of opals. Meanwhile, on the farther side, washerwomen were at work, and the bats they wielded clattered loudly on the linen they were beating.

"Antek, please split the firewood for me; I cannot manage it by myself," said his wife timorously, for the man thought nothing of treating her to an oath—nay, even to a blow—on the slightest pretext.

He did not so much as reply, feigning not to have heard her. She dared not repeat her request, but went to hack off such splinters of firewood as she could, while he, moody and spent with a long day's hard work, sat looking over to the other side of the pond, where a large cottage shone with whitewashed walls and window-panes that reflected the sunset glow. A low stone fence, over which some clusters of dahlias nodded their heads, standing out vividly on the white background of cottage wall, ran round the garden; and in front of the house a tall figure was seen to pass from beneath the orchard trees, disappearing in the passage before it could be recognized.

From the porch where he sat, Antek heard his father's

snores and growled fiercely. "The Master sleeps; and *you*, toil on, labourer, toil on!"

He went out into the yard and eyed the cow again.

"She was father's cow, but it is also a loss for us," he remarked to his wife, who had left off hacking wood and gone to the cart which Kuba had now driven home.

"The pits are not yet ready for the potatoes; we must dump them upon the threshing-floor."

"But father said you were to flay the cow and quarter it on the threshing-floor, with Kuba to help you."

"There will be room enough for both cow and potatoes," muttered Kuba, throwing the barn door wide open.

"I," said Antek, "am no slaughter-house workman, that I should flay carcasses!"

No more was said; the potatoes rattled noisily on the barn-floor.

The sun was down, but the dark blood and dead gold of the after-glow were still mistily reflected in the pond; and the quiet waters just trembled, shimmering ruddily with a drowsy murmur.

Presently the village was lost in shadows and plunged in the deep stillness of an autumnal night. The huts seemed smaller, as though sunk into the ground or melted into the trees that hung dreamily above them, or made one with the grey fences surrounding them. Antek and Kuba were carrying the potatoes. Hanka and Yuzka, busy with their household duties, were driving the geese home or feeding the swine that came grunting for food into the passage. Then the cows wanted milking. Vitek had just come home with them from the pasture-lands, and had put a little hay on the racks before them, that they might remain quiet while being milked.

Yuzka had just begun with the first cow, when Vitek asked her in a low trembling voice: "Yuzka, is master very angry?"

"Oh, Lord! that he is! He means to give you a thrashing!" she answered, turning her face to the light and putting out her hand, for the cow, tormented by flies, was whisking her tail, which struck the girl.

"But was it my fault if the forester drove us out? He would have given me a beating, too, but I got away. And she lay down and lowed and moaned, so I came back with her."

He said no more, but she heard him sniffling and weeping quietly.

"Vitek! you are crying like a calf. Don't! Is it the first time father has thrashed you?"

"No, indeed, but I can't bear being thrashed; I am always afraid."

"How silly! A great husky fellow, and afraid? But I'll explain it all to Father."

"Will you really, Yuzka?" he exclaimed joyfully.

"I will, Vitek; only fear no more!"

"If you will,—then here's a bird for you," he whispered, much pleased, and took a marvellous toy out of his bosom. "Just look how it moves, all by itself!"

He placed it on the threshold and wound it up. The bird, lifting up its long legs and shaking its head, began to walk.

"Oh Lord! it's a stork! and it moves as if alive!" she cried out in wonder and, setting her milk pail aside, crouched down and gazed on in rapture.

"Oh, how clever you are to have made it! and it moves by itself, does it?"

"By itself, Yuzka; only I wind it up with this wooden peg. And see! it is strutting about like a gentleman after dinner!" He turned it about. The bird, lifting up its long legs, with comical gravity, strutted on, moving its neck back and forth.

They both started to laugh, heartily amused by these movements; and from time to time Yuzka glanced admiringly at the boy.

Suddenly Boryna raised his voice, calling to Yuzka from outside the cabin.

"Here I am," she answered.

"Come to me."

"I can't; I'm milking."

"Well." he said, "I am off to the Voyt," and added, peeping into the dark shed: "That, that there bastard, isn't he here?"

"Oh, Vitek do you mean? He is gone with Antek," she replied hastily and with uneasiness, for Vitek, terrified, had come to crouch behind her.

"He has run off! . . . A rank beast he is . . . to let such a cow be lost!" he snarled, returning to the hut to put on his new white *sukmana,* and a high-crowned black hat. Then, buckling on a scarlet girdle, he set off in the direction of the mill.

"So much work still to do!" he said to himself as he walked on; "all the winter's firewood to be brought in, some fields not yet sown, and the cabbages still out of doors! The potato-fields, too, must be ploughed; and so must the oat-fields. My God! a man's work is never done; he is like an ox under the yoke. And that law business, besides! . . . A bad one she is, truly: I slept with her indeed! . . . May her tongue rot away, the vile creature!" He spat venomously, filled his pipe, and with some difficulty kindled a damp match by striking it on his trouser-leg.

Then he jogged along slowly, still brooding over his troubles and the death of the cow.

Now he was as lonely as a signpost. There was no one he could complain or tell things to. . . . He had to think of everything, and make up his mind, and care for everything all by himself—a dog's life! . . . Never could he speak to anyone, nor get any advice or assistance . . . and the result was, loss upon loss!

The hamlet was now getting dark. Through the wide-open doors and windows (for the evening was warm) there came from the glowing hearths streaks of light, and the odour of cooked potatoes, and porridge with driblets of fried bacon. Many were supping in the passages, or even outside the cabins, and talking merrily to the clatter of spoons.

Boryna's pace slackened; he was exhausted with the excitement he had gone through, and the thought of the wife he had buried that spring recurred to him and made him gulp down a sob.

"Oh, no! if *she*—how well I recollect her to-night!—if she had been here, Red-and-White would still be alive. Yes, she was a housewife, indeed, a rare housewife. It's true, she had a sharp tongue, and never a good word for anyone: but she was a good wife and manager, for all that." And then he breathed a prayer for her soul, very sore at heart in the remembrance of times gone by.

When he used to come home, all tired and weary, she would give him the best of everything; and time and again would she hand him, on the sly, savoury bits of sausage that she had secreted for him from the children. And, somehow, they throve very well then. Calves and goslings and suckling pigs multiplied; on fair days, there was always plenty to take to town; always cash at hand, and money put by for a rainy day.

And now?

Antek was continually pulling his own way, as was his son-in-law, the blacksmith—always trying to get something out of him. Yuzka?—A frail child, with bran instead of brains in her head; and no wonder, for she was still under ten. And Hanka? She fluttered about like a moth, was for ever ailing, and did nothing but whine like a dog.

So everything was going to rack and ruin. Red-and-White had to be killed that day, a pig died at harvest-time; while the crows had carried off so many goslings that but half of them remained. Such losses! Such disasters! All he had was being frittered away, running out like water through a sieve!

"But I won't give in!" he almost cried aloud: "as long as I can move these limbs of mine, not one acre shall be given up to anyone!"

"Praised be Jesus Christ!" someone greeted him as he passed.

"World without end!" was his instinctive reply as he

turned off from the road into a long-fenced lane at the end of which, some distance back from the highway, stood the Voyt's cottage.

The windows shone brightly. The dogs started to bark, as Boryna walked straight into the best room.

"Is the Voyt at home?" he asked of a stout woman kneeling close to a cradle and suckling a baby.

"No, but he will be presently. Sit down, Matthias; there's someone else waiting for him, besides." And the woman threw her chin forward in the direction of a beggar sitting by the fire—the blind old man we have met before, led by a dog. The chips that were burning on the hearth threw a hard reddish light on his large shaven face, his bald crown, and his wide-open eyes, drawn over with a white film and motionless under grey brows.

"Whence has the Lord led you hither?" asked Boryna, seating himself on the opposite side of the fire.

"From up and down the world, good man; and how were it otherwise with me?" was the answer given in a drawling, plaintive voice, while its owner, who listened attentively to each sound, pulled out a snuff-box.

"Pray take a pinch, good man."

Matthias complied, and such a large pinch did he take that he sneezed three times and the water came to his eyes.

"Awfully strong stuff," he said, and wiped the tears away with his elbow.

"Petersburg snuff, very good for the eyes. May it be so—for yours!"

"Come round to my cabin to-morrow, will you? I have killed a cow."

"God reward you. Boryna, I believe?"

"Ah! you are good at guessing."

"Knew you by your voice and speech."

"Well, coming from up and down the world, what news have you?"

"Ah! what indeed? Some news is good, some bad, and some indifferent. The way of the world. They all complain and lament when it comes to giving a beggar something; and yet they have always money enough for vodka."

"You speak truly; it is just as you say."

"Ho, ho! I have been a wayfarer on this God's earth long enough to know a thing or two."

"What," the Voyt's wife then asked of him, "what has become of the foundling who came with you last year?"

"Ah! the vile creature! he ran away, filching a pretty good sum out of my wallet. Some good people had given me a little money, and I was taking it to Our Lady of Czestochowa to have mass said, when the wretch stole it and made off. . . . Be quiet, Burek! It's the Voyt, I imagine." And at a pull on the string that held it, the dog ceased barking.

He was right. The Voyt came in and, standing on the threshold, threw his whip into a corner and shouted:

"Wife! Supper! I'm starved. How are you, Matthias? And you, old man, what do you need?"

"I have come to ask about the affair I am to appear in to-morrow."

"I can wait your pleasure, sir. Put me in the passage; it shall be well with me; or if, because I am old, you set me by the fire, there I shall sit. Give me to eat of your potatoes or a morsel of bread, and I shall pray for you just as much as if you gave me a kopek or more."

"Sit down. You may sup here and spend the night, too, if you will."

And the Voyt sat down to a steaming dish of newly-mashed potatoes, made savoury with abundant driblets of fried bacon; a platter of sour milk standing close by.

"Take a seat, Matthias, and share what we have," said the Voyt's wife cordially as she laid a third spoon on the table.

"No, thanks. When I got home from the forest I ate a generous supper."

"Take a spoonful at least; the evenings are getting long."

"'Plenty of prayers, plenty of food,
Never does harm, always does good,'"

the beggar put in sententiously.

Boryna stood upon ceremony for a time, but at last the smell of the bacon in his nostrils got the better of him. So he sat down and began to eat, but slowly, daintily, and with great decorum.

The blind man's dog now began to move about uneasily and to whine impatiently for food.

"Be quiet, Burek! The farmer folk are at supper now. You will get your share, don't fear." So spoke the blind man soothingly as he was warming his hands at the fire and inhaling the savoury odour.

When the first pangs of hunger had been appeased, the Voyt, turning to Matthias, said: "Eva has, it appears, lodged a complaint against you."

"She! Oh, well, I declare! Not paid her, indeed? As there is a God, I have—aye, and beyond what she deserved. Yes, and when she had that baby I willingly sent the priest a sack of oats for her at the christening!"

"But she says it was you who——"

"Oh, but that's preposterous! What, is she mad? Is she crazy?"

"Oho! Old as you are, you are still an able craftsman!" And the Voyt and his wife burst out laughing.

"To be old," put in the blind man, "is to know; to know is to be able."

"But she lies like a gipsy! I never touched her, the wench! She was homeless; an outcast who begged and prayed us to take her in—just for the food and a corner to sleep in, because winter was near. I was loath to do it, but my wife that's dead thought we had better. She could do things in the house. Why should we hire a servant when one was ready at hand? I did not like this—another mouth to feed, and in winter, too, when there's always less to be done. But my wife said: 'Don't worry; she knows how to weave cloth and canvas. I'll see to it that she is not idle, and there will always be some work or other for her.' Well, she stayed on with us and got strong; and presently she was with child. But the question is, who was the man?"

"You, according to her."

"I'll kill her for saying so! The miserable liar!"

"Anyway, you will have to appear in court."

"I shall. God reward you for telling me this. I thought it was about her wages: but I have witnesses to prove that I have paid her. A plague on her! A scold, and a beggar into the bargain! Dear me! one trouble after another! I shall never be able to stand all this. And the cow I have had to kill! And the field-work not yet done! And here I am, all alone, with no one in the world to lend a hand!"

"'Who for a wife that's gone must weep is like a wolf-encompassed sheep,'" the old man observed.

"I heard about the cow; they told me in the village."

"As to that, I have a claim against the manor. The forester, I understand, drove the cows away. She was the best of all I have—worth three hundred *zloty*—was with calf—ran so fast and got so blown that I had to kill her. No, I shall not let that pass: I'll bring suit."

The Voyt, however, who was friendly to the manor, strove to calm Boryna: anger was always a bad counsellor, and he should beware of doing anything rash. Then, to change the subject, he said with a wink at his wife:

"Man, you ought to marry, so as to get someone who would take care of the house."

"I say, is this a joke? Why, last Assumption Day I rounded my fifty-eighth year. What are you dreaming of? And she, too, scarcely cold in her grave yet!"

"You just take a wife, one fit for your age, and all will be well with you again, Matthias," said the Voyt's wife, preparing to clear the table.

"'For, sure, a good and kindly wife is the crown of her husband's life,'" added the blind man, groping for the dish which the woman had set before him.

Boryna sat wondering why the thought had not occurred to him before. Certainly some woman or other was to be found, and any one would be better than none.

"Some," continued the old man as he ate, "are silly and speechless, some are quarrelsome, some pull the lads' hair, and others are always dancing or running after music in taverns; but, anyhow, a man is better off with one than without."

"But what would people think of it?" objected Boryna.

"Think? Will they give you back your cow or help you in anything, whatever they think?" the Voyt's wife retorted with much heat.

"Or warm your bed for you?" said the Voyt with a laugh. "There are so many lasses here that, when a man goes about the huts, he is as hot as coal in a fire."

"Ah! the reprobate! look at him! Whom is he hankering after now?"

"Sophie, Gregory's daughter, might do; a slim handsome girl and a good dowry, too."

"What does Matthias, the richest farmer here, want with a dowry?"

" 'Of goods and lands and such, who ever has too much?' " queried the blind man.

"No," the Voyt decided, "Gregory's girl is not for him—too young, too immature."

"Then Andrew's daughter, Catharine," was the next proposal made by the Voyt's wife.

"Already taken. Roch's son, Adam, sent proposers to her yesterday."

"Well, there is Weronka, Stach's daughter."

"A babbler, a gadabout, and with one hip deformed."

"But what about Thomas's widow? She would do very well, I fancy."

"Three children, four acres, two heads of cattle, and an old sheepskin that poor Tom left her."

"Perhaps Ulisia, Adalbert's daughter, who lives by the church?"

"She might do for a single young man. The boy she has is now big enough to tend cattle. But Matthias has his own cowherd, and needs none."

"There are others yet to be married; only I seek someone suitable."

"But, wife, you have overlooked one who would be just the girl for him."

"Who is that?"

"Why, Yagna, daughter of Dominik."

"To be sure; she had escaped my memory."

"A bouncing wench and tall; no fence but would break under her weight."

"Yagna!" repeated Boryna, who had been silently listening to this roll-call; "but they say she runs after men."

"Who has seen her? who knows? Gossips will gossip for gossiping's sake and for envy," cried the Voyt's wife, hot in her defence.

"Oh, I did not say she was that way, but it's common talk. Well, now, I must be off." He adjusted his girdle, put a live coal to his pipe, and pulled at it twice or three times.

"And for what hour is the summons?"

"For nine o'clock; so it stands in black and white in the District Court. You will have to rise early, if you are going there on foot."

"I shall take the filly and drive slowly. God be with you, and thanks for your good cheer and neighbourly advice."

"May God go with you, too. And think over what we have been telling you. Say but the word, and I will go to the old dame with vodka for you; and we shall have a wedding before Yule-tide is out."

Boryna answered not a word, but gave them a parting glance that might mean anything.

"When old with young to wedlock fly, the devil is glad, for he profits thereby," was the blind beggar's reflection as he finished the mashed potatoes. Boryna walked homeward with slow steps, seriously meditating on the advice given him. At the Voyt's he had carefully kept from letting it be known by any sign whatever that the idea was extremely to his liking. How could he? He was not a young whippersnapper, who would at the bare mention of marriage be ready to dance and shout for joy, but a grave, elderly farmer.

Night had already enshrouded the earth. The stars glistened in the sky's sombre depths like silver dew-drops, and all was still, save for an occasional bark of a dog or two. Faintly and far between, a few lights twinkled athwart the orchard trees, and now and then a breath of damp air blew up from the meadows, making the boughs wave slightly and their leaves whisper soft sounds.

Boryna was making for home by another way—direct and leading down over the bridge, under which the waters of the pond, rolling towards the mill, with a hollow bubbling sound, poured into the stream. He then crossed to the other side, skirting the pond, where the waters shone darkly and the trees along its shores cast gloomy shadows over its surface, framing it in ebony; though near the centre, where the shadows were lighter, the twinkling stars were reflected as in a mirror of steel.

Matthias himself could not have said why he did not now go straight home, instead of chosing a roundabout way. Did he want to pass in front of Yagna's house? Possibly he meant only to collect his thoughts and revolve matters within his head.

"Really, it would not be a bad thing. And what they say of her is all very true. Yes, she is a strapping girl!"

A shiver ran through him. It was damp and cold near and about the pond and he came straight from the Voyt's cosy fireside.

"Without a woman at home, I must either be ruined or make over the farm to my children," he thought, and then: "And she's a lusty wench, and as pretty as a picture. My best cow gone to-day! and who knows what else will go to-morrow? Perhaps I ought to look out for a second wife; my first one has left things to wear a plenty. But Dominik's old widow . . . she is a wicked creature!—Three of them, and fifteen acres: about five for Yagna, besides her share of the cabin and the livestock. Five acres of fields—the very ones beyond my own potato-patch. Together with mine, they will make close to thirty-five acres. A nice bit of land!"

He rubbed his hands and set his girdle straight. "The miller would be the only man richer than I. Next year, I would manure and till the whole of my lands for wheat. I would have to purchase another horse. And a cow too, in place of poor Red-and-White.—Oh, but then she would bring a cow of her own. . . ."

So he went on musing, calculating, and dreaming farmers' dreams, till the weight of his thoughts became, he felt, too big for his mind. For he was marshalling every detail, like the intelligent peasant that he was, and considering whether he had not possibly overlooked anything of importance.

"They would raise a hue over it, the rascals!" he said to himself, thinking of his children. But at the thought there rushed over him a wave of indomitable self-confidence, which immediately filled his soul and confirmed him in his purpose, wavering and undecided as he had been hitherto.

"The land is my own. Let anyone else dare claim my property! If they don't like it, they may . . ." Here he broke off, for he was then standing in front of the cabin where Yagna dwelt.

The lamps were not yet out, and a long streak of brightness from the open window, passing through the dahlia bushes and the hedge, illumined the road. Boryna, standing in the shadow, glanced into the room.

A big fire was evidently burning on the hearth, for the crackling of pinewood could be heard; and the great room, though dusky in the corners, was elsewhere filled with a reddish light. The old dame, crouching close to the fire-place, was reading something aloud; and Yagna, dressed only in her smock, her face turned to the window and her sleeves tucked up to the shoulders, was engaged in plucking a live goose.

"A comely wench!" he thought.

She would raise her head now and then, listen to the reading, and heave a deep sigh. Then she would again set to plucking the goose, but so roughly that the bird would gabble audibly with pain, and, escaping from her hands, flap about the room till the feathers were flying everywhere. But she would soon quiet it and hold it fast between her knees, the bird uttering only a few faint cries, to which other cries responded from the passage and the yard.

"A handsome girl, she," he mused and walked away at a rapid pace, for the blood had gone to his head. Raising his hand to his brow, he drew tightened his girdle as he walked.

He was already within his own gates, and had passed the fence, when he looked round at Yagna's dwelling, which stood opposite on the other side of the water. Someone was just then going out, for a quick flash from the opening door lit up the pond. Heavy footsteps were heard tramping along, and the splash of a bucket of water was audible; then at last, amid the darkness and the mists which had come up from the meadows, a voice sang to a slow tune:

"Betwixt us rolls the flood, O grief!
How can I send a kiss from here?
I'll float it down upon a leaf
And waft my love to thee, my dear."

He listened long, but the voice was heard no more; and after a while all the lights were put out.

The moon, now in her full, had risen above the forest-trees, silvering their tops, throwing its radiance through their boughs and upon the pond, and peeping down into the cottage windows. The dogs no longer barked. An unfathomable stillness had settled over the village and over all nature.

Boryna made the round of the yard, took a look at the horses that snorted as they munched their provender, and put his head into the cow-byre, the doors of which stood open because of the heat. The cows were lying and chewing the cud with the low murmurs peculiar to cattle.

He closed the granary doors and, taking off his hat, entered his cabin and said his evening prayers half aloud. All were sleeping. He undressed quietly and went at once to bed.

He could not sleep, however. The coverlet was so hot that he drew it from over his feet. His head, too, was teeming with many a troublesome and worrisome thought. Besides, he was not at his best physically.

"Sour milk," he muttered, "as I always say, is not good to take of an evening."

And then he thought about his children and pondered over what had been said of Yagna, till all this became muddled and confused in his brain. He knew not what to do, and was on the point (as once had been his wont) of calling for advice to the sleeper in the other bed:

"Mary! Am I to marry or not?"

But he remembered in time that his Mary had been lying in the churchyard ever since the spring. Yuzka was there, asleep and breathing heavily. And he was a poor desolate man, with no one on earth to advise him. So he gave a deep sigh, crossed himself, and said a few Ave Marias for the soul of his departed and for the souls of all the faithful in purgatory.

CHAPTER III

WHEN daybreak began to shed its light on the cabin-roofs, and dispel the night, and make the stars to fade, things were already moving about Boryna's hut.

Kuba had left the stable. There was hoar frost on the ground, and it was yet grey dawn; but the East flaunted a tinge of burning red, and the frosty tree-tops likewise. He stretched himself with satisfaction, yawned more than once, and went to the byre to call Vitek; for it was time to rise. But the lad only lifted his drowsy head, and whispering: "Presently, Kuba, presently," laid it down again.

"Well, sleep a little more, poor fellow! sleep yet a little more!" Kuba covered him with a sheepskin coat, and limped away; for he had once received a bullet in the knee, which lamed him for life. He washed at the well, ran his fingers through his scanty hair, that had got matted during the night, and, kneeling down on the stable threshold, proceeded to say his prayers.

The master was still in bed, when the cabin-windows took a purple tint in the ruddy glow of morning. Kuba's rosary glided through his fingers; he prayed for a long time, his eyes wandering nevertheless over the yard, the windows, the orchard with the hoar-frost still not melted on the trunks, and the apple-trees, laden with fruit as large as his fist. Then he threw something at the white head of Lapa, the dog which slept in the kennel close by; but Lapa only growled, curled up, and slept on.

"What, you rascal! would ye sleep till sunrise?" he cried, and threw missile after missile, till the dog came out, with a stretch and a yawn and a wag of its tail, and, approaching him, proceeded to scratch itself and cleanse its shaggy coat with its teeth.

"And unto Thee, and also unto all Thy Saints, do I, O Lord, offer up this my prayer. Amen."

He beat his breast many times, rose from his knees, and called out to Lapa:

"O you dainty dog you, hunting for fleas like a lass going to a wedding!"

Being an industrious fellow, he now set to work, taking the cart out of the shed and greasing the wheels, giving the horses a drink, and filling the racks with hay till they snorted with pleasure and pawed the stable floor. Then he brought from the granary some refuse of corn plentifully seasoned with good oats, which he took to the mare's manger: for she had been given a stall apart.

"Eat, old girl, eat away; you are to have a foal, and you need strength. Eat away!" He stroked her over the nose; and the mare laid her head on his shoulder, and playfully pulled at his shock of hair with her lips.

"Till noon, we shall be bringing in potatoes, and then we shall go to get litter in the evening. Never fear; a cart of litter is no great weight; don't worry."

"But you! for you there's a good flogging in store, you lazy brute!" he said to the gelding that stood close by and was pushing its head forward between the boards that separated it from the mare's manger.

"You hireling, you Jew! Willing enough to devour good oats, you are; but to move one step, save for the whip—not you!"

He passed it by, and looked into the manger that stood next to the wall, from which the filly's head—chestnut-coloured, with a white arrow on the forehead,—had for some time been watching him; and she uttered a gentle neigh.

"Easy, little one, easy! And eat your fill; you will take master to town. . . ." But her flank was soiled, and he wiped it clean with a wisp of hay. Such a full-grown filly, ready for coupling . . . and yet so dirty! Always wallowing in the mire like a sow!"

So he went on, talking continually, and passed round to the sties, to let out the pigs that were squealing for food. Lapa followed him, looking wistfully into his face.

"Want something, eh? Here you are then—a nice bit of bread for you!" He took a piece of bread from his bosom and tossed it into the air. Lapa caught it, and ran away to his kennel, for the pigs would have taken it from him.

"Ha! those swine, they are like some men: all for grabbing what's not theirs."

In the barn he took a long look at the quartered cow that hung from the beams.

"A beast without understanding. Gone in her turn. She will be in the pots by to-morrow. Poor thing! you end by making a Sunday dinner for us."

With a sigh of longing for the feast in store, he went to rouse Vitek. " 'Twill be sunrise directly. Come, drive the cows to grass."

Vitek had no mind; he wrapped his sheepskin round him and grunted; but in the end he got up, and shambled drowsily about the yard.

The master had overslept himself; for the sun was up, up, making the hoar-frost a dust of rubies, and each pane and pool a mirror of fire, and no one had as yet appeared from the cabin.

Vitek sat on the cowbyre threshold, scratching himself and yawning audibly. The sparrows had come down from the roofs to the well, and were now bathing in the troughs. He took a ladder, and went to look at the swallows' nests under the eaves; for it was very still there, and he feared they might have died of cold. Several swallows lay there, benumbed. Taking them out very gently, he placed them within his shirt-bosom.

"See, Kuba, see! they are dead!" And he showed him the bodies, stiff and stark. Kuba took them one by one, laid them to his ear, breathed on their eyes, and gave his opinion.

"They are only numb with last night's cold. Silly things,

not to have left for some warm country yet! Ah, well!" And he went about his work again.

Vitek seated himself in front of the cabin, where the sunbeams poured down upon the whitewashed walls, and flies were already crawling. He took out such swallows as the heat of his body had revived a little; he breathed on them, opened their bills, gave them to drink from his own warm lips, until at length they were restored, opened their eyes, and fluttered to get free. Then, swiftly catching a fly on the wall, he would feed it to a bird and let it go.

"Away to your mother, fly away!" he said, as the young swallows sat on the rafters of the byre, preening themselves and twittering their thanks, as it were.

Lapa, sitting on his hind quarters, looked on with keen interest, whining now and then, running a few paces after each bird to catch it as it fluttered off, and then returning to watch proceedings.

"You might as well try to catch the wind," said Vitek, so absorbed in reviving the swallows, that he took no note of Boryna coming round the hut, until the latter stood in front of him.

"Ha! you filthy knave! Playing with birds, are you?"

The lad jumped up to run for it; but the farmer caught him fast by the coat-collar, while with his other hand he undid the broad thong of tough leather which formed his girdle.

"Oh, but don't beat me, don't beat me, pray!" was all the poor fellow could utter.

"What sort of a cowherd are you, hey?—That's how you tend cattle, hey?—Lost my best cow for me, hey?—You foundling, you!—You Warsaw mooncalf!" And he laid on furiously, wherever he could get a blow home; and the thong whistled in the air, and the lad writhed like an eel and roared for mercy.

"Don't! O Lord! He's killing me! Master! O Jesus, mercy!"

Hanka peered out to see what the matter was; Kuba spat with disgust and withdrew into the stable.

Boryna continued flogging him with might and main, scoring his loss upon the lad's flesh with a vengeance, while Vitek shrieked and yelled at the top of his voice. At last the poor wretch managed to wriggle out of his master's clutch, and holding his posteriors with both hands, ran to the fence, roaring as he ran: "He has killed me! My God! he has killed me!" while the swallows that were still in his bosom, fell out and were scattered along the road.

Boryna, still breathing threats against him, returned to the cottage and looked into Antek's quarters.

"What!" he cried out on seeing him. "Still abed, and the sun up so long?"

"I had to rest. Was tired to death yesterday."

"I am going to the law court. You will bring home the potatoes; and when that work is done, send our people to get litter. You might yourself drive in laths to make the hut a winter coating." [1]

"Do that yourself; there is no wind on our side."

"As you please. I will do my side; and you, Mr. Sluggard, shall freeze."

He slammed the door, and entered his own quarters. The fire was lit and Yuzka was going to milk the cows.

"Give me breakfast instantly: I must be off."

"I can't be in two places, nor do two things at once."

And she went out.

"Not one quiet minute! I am forced to curse and fall foul of everybody," he said to himself, and proceeded to dress in a very vile humour. What everlasting rows with his son, so that at every word each was ready to fly at the other—or worse—to say something that stabbed you like a knife! His ill humour, as he pondered, increased so, that he could not help cursing under his breath, and flinging his boots here and there about the floor.

[1] Polish peasants, in order to keep their huts warmer in winter, put round them a sort of palisade of laths over a yard high, the space between is then stuffed with hay, dry leaves, boughs, etc., often mixed with clay.—*Translator's Note.*

"They ought to obey me, and they don't. For what reason?" he asked himself.

"Because, no doubt, a cudgel, and a good one, is needed to deal with them. I ought long since to have used one. But I did not care to raise a scandal in the village, and could not make up my mind to do that. For I am not a beggarly ploughman; thirty acres are mine. Nor am I of a mean family; Boryna is a well-known name.—But kindness is thrown away upon them!" And then he remembered his son-in-law, the blacksmith, who was setting everyone against him, and continually pressing for a gift of six acres of cornland and one of forest, "willing," he said, "to wait for the rest."

"That is, till I am dead! Oh, yes," he thought bitterly, "you will have to wait, fellow! While I live, you'll not have so much as a smell at my land! You're too clever by half!"

When Yuzka came in from milking, the potatoes were on the boil, and breakfast was soon ready.

"Yuzka, you will sell the meat yourself! To-morrow is Sunday, and people know that we have it, so they will be coming. But no credit, mind! Keep the hind quarters for our own eating. You will call in Ambrose to salt and pickle them."

"But the blacksmith too can do that."

"He'll take his share—the wolf's share of the sheep!"

"But Magda will be hurt. 'Tis our cow; is she to have nothing?"

"Then cut off a piece and send it to Magda: but don't call in the blacksmith."

"Father dear, that's kind of you!"

"All right, little one. Take good care of things here, and I'll bring you a roll or something from town."

He made a pretty good meal, girt himself up, smoothed down his scanty dishevelled hair, took his whip, and looked round the room.

"Is there anything I have forgotten?"

He would have looked into the alcove too, but Yuzka's

eye was upon him: so he merely crossed himself, and went out.

Sitting in the cart, with the reins in his hand, he gave one more order to Yuzka, who stood in the porch.

"When they have done digging the potatoes, send them off to rake up the litter: you'll find the permit stuck behind the picture. . . . And tell them to cut down some young fir or hornbeam: it will come in handy."

The cart had got as far as the fence, when Vitek showed himself among the apple-trees.

"I had forgotten . . . Vitek! Prrru, prrru! Vitek, I say! you will take the kine to the meadow. . . . And tend them well, or you'll get such a flogging as you won't forget."

"Oh, you may kiss—" the lad cried audaciously, and vanished on the other side of the barn.

"None of your impudence! If I get down, you'll see!"

He turned to the right into the road by the church. The sun was by now above the cottages, with ever stronger and stronger rays. From the thatches mists rose up, and water-drops dripped down; but in the shadows of the hedges and ditches, the frost lay white. On the pond, the thin film of morning haze had grown thinner; the waters bubbled and shone in the sunlight.

In the village the round of daily toil was commencing. Folks were livelier and more spirited than usual in this bright cool morning air: some going forth in troops to dig in the fields, carrying hoes and mattocks, and baskets with provisions; some setting out to plough the stubbled fields; some with harrows in carts, and bags full of seed-corn; whilst others wended their way to the wood for litter, and bore rakes on their shoulders. And on either side of the pond the noise increased, when presently the roads became crowded with cattle driven to grass; dogs barked, men shouted, and a heavy dust which the night's dew had but partly laid, rose in the highway.

Boryna carefully threaded his way among the cattle, from time to time cracking his whip at some lamb or calf that would blunder across the filly's path; and at last he got clear of them all, and approached the church, which was screened by a great rampart of limes and plane-trees, with dull yellow foliage. Thence he passed on to a broader road, planted on either side with giant poplars.

The bell had been rung to announce that mass was beginning, and the muffled notes of the organ came from within; he doffed his hat and breathed a devout prayer.

The way was solitary, and strewn with fallen leaves, which covered, as with a carpet of dead gold, all its deep holes and ruts, and the gnarled roots about its surface: a carpet striped by the falling shadows of the poplars, as the sun shone across the way.

"Gee-up! my little one, gee-up!" He cracked his whip, for the road sloped upwards, though slightly, towards the forest, black in the distance.

The silence made Boryna drowsy; he gazed through the colonnade of poplars upon the fields bathed in the rosy radiance, and tried to think of Eva's accusation and of Red-and-White's death; but he could not help feeling slumber coming on. Birds were chirruping in the boughs; through the tree-tops murmured the wind, here and there bringing down a leaflet, like a golden butterfly, that settled with a whirl on the road, or on some dusty clump of thistles, whose fiery eyes opened bravely to the sun. And the poplars talked one with another, and murmured softly with swaying boughs, and then were still.

It was only when he had reached the forest, and the horse stopped, that he woke up completely.

"The corn is coming up nicely here," he mused, gazing sunwards at the grey fields, with their rust-coloured haze of sprouting rye.

"A good bit of land, and next to mine—just as if it had been put there on purpose!—This rye, I think, was not sown long ago." He cast a longing glance at the recently harrowed lands, and then, uttering a sigh, entered the forest.

Here, however, a cold bleak wind, driving in his face, quite dispelled his reverie.

The forest was very old and very great. It stood, compact and thick, in the majesty of age and strength combined. Nearly all the trees were pines; but not unfrequently an ancient spreading oak would appear, or some birches, in their smocks of white bark, let their tangled yellow foliage float in the air. The lower growths—the hazel-nut, the dwarf hornbeam, and the trembling aspen—were crowded around the mighty red pine-trunks, so closely and with branches so intertwined, that the sunbeams could but seldom touch the ground, where they seemed to be crawling, like bright-hued insects, over the mosses and reddish faded ferns.

"All this is mine. Four acres," he reflected, devouring the wood with his eyes, and gloating over the best bits of timber.

"Ah! the Lord will not let us be wronged! Nor will we let people wrong us, either! The manor folk think what we have is too much: we think it too little.—Let me see: my four, and Yagna's one; four and one's . . . Gee-up! foolish beast! Afraid of magpies?" He whipped her up smartly; for, upon the dry Tree, where the crucified Christ was hanging, magpies were quarrelling so violently that the filly had pricked up her ears and stopped short.

"'Magpies' quarrelling, rain will surely bring,'" he muttered, and with a few strokes of the whip mended the filly's pace to a trot.

It was now well past eight, for the people in the fields were sitting down to breakfast, when he came to Timow: a small town whose empty narrow streets were lined with dilapidated houses, like rows of old saleswomen—lining gutters full of rubbish, and dirty Jewish children, and pigs.

He had scarcely entered, when crowds of Jews and Jewesses rushed round him, eager to look into his cart and fumble among the straw it was strewn with,—even under the seat—to find anything he might have to sell.

"Off, ye scurvy louts!" he growled, turning into the market-place, where, in the shadow of a few ancient decayed chestnut-trees slowly dying in the centre of the square, hard on a score of wagons were drawn up, their horses unharnessed.

He drove his own cart in there among them, brushed off

the straw from his coat, and went straight to Mordko the barber's, to get a shave. Presently he issued thence, clean-shaven, and with only one cut on his chin, plastered with a bit of paper, through which the blood oozed.

The court was not yet open; but in front of the building that stood right in the market-place, opposite a very large church, a good many people had already assembled, and were sitting upon the time-worn steps, or lounging outside the windows. Women squatted along the white walls, chatting together, with the red aprons they had worn on their heads as they came, now fallen on to their shoulders.

Boryna perceived Eva holding her boy by the hand, and surrounded by her witnesses. A storm of anger surged within him. He spat contemptuously, and withdrew into the corridor that ran the whole length of the officials' private lodgings. The judgment hall was to the left; the secretary occupied the right side.

Just then the manservant Yacek had passed the threshold of the lodgings with a samovar, and was blowing it so hard that it smoked like a factory chimney. From time to time a shrill angry voice was raised from the extremity of the smoke-darkened corridor.

"Yacek! the young ladies' shoes!"

"Presently, presently."

The samovar was now hissing, and spouting flames, and burning like a volcano.

"Yacek! water for master to wash!"

"Yes, yes, directly, directly!"

Perspiring, distracted, the man ran to and fro about the corridor till it rang again, and returned to blow, and went off anew; for his mistress now screamed:

"Yacek, you rascal, where are my stockings?"

"Confound this devil of a samovar!"

The scene continued for some time yet; but at last the door of the court opened, and in the people rushed, filling the large whitewashed hall.

Yacek was there again, now in his capacity as usher: barefooted, but in a dark-blue jacket and trousers of the same hue, and brass buttons. His red face perspiring freely, he wiped it with his sleeve as he slipped in behind the black grating by which the hall was divided into two parts. Tossing his head like a horse attacked by a gadfly (for his sandy hair fell over his eyes and into them), he sat down for a moment's rest near a huge stove of green delf tiles, after peering cautiously into the adjoining room.

So many people had come in that the place was chock-full. They pressed against the grating till it shook, and after a time began to talk, the murmur of voices soon filling the whole room.

Under the windows outside, Jews were vociferating; within, women clamorously expounded their wrongs, and still more clamorously wept over them; but what those wrongs were, no one could make out. Everybody was cheek by jowl, like a field of red poppies or of rye, waving to and fro in the wind, and rustling and whispering; all clustered together.

It was then that Eva caught sight of Boryna, upright against the grating, and heaped insults upon him, till she cut him to the quick and he answered hotly:

"Silence, you bitch, or I'll give you such a drubbing that your own mother won't know you!"

Eva, in a fury, clawed at him, and tried to reach him through the press; but her kerchief fell off, and her child fell a-screaming. What might have happened, none can say: for just then Yacek started up, opened an inner door, and shouted:

"Hold your peace, yokels! The court is entering."

It was indeed: the stalwart squire of Raciborowice, followed by two assistant magistrates, and the secretary. The latter, sitting down at a side-table, set some papers in order, and eyed the magistrates, as they put their gold chains round their necks, and took their places at a great table, covered with crimson cloth.

At once there fell such a silence that the men chattering outside the windows could be plainly heard; and the session began.

The first complaint was brought by a constable against a petty trader, on account of some nuisance in his yard.—Condemned in default.

Then the case of a boy flogged for having put horses to graze in clover.—A compromise: five roubles for the mother; a new jacket and trousers for the boy.

A complaint of encroachment in ploughing.—No evidence: set aside.

A case of theft of timber in a forest, the judge's property: complainant, the administrator; defendants, the peasants of Rokiciny.—Fined, with alternative of a fortnight's imprisonment. They gave notice of appeal, and made such a noise about the injustice of the sentence, they having the common right to cut firewood in the forest, that the head magistrate made a sign to Yacek, who thundered:

"Silence! silence in the court! This is not a tavern!"

And thus case after case, like furrow following furrow, was dispatched, evenly and quietly enough in general, with a few lamentations and sobs, or even curses at times; but these were promptly suppressed by Yacek.

Some of the people had withdrawn; but so many more came instead, that they all stood like corn-stalks in a sheaf. No one could move, and it grew stiflingly hot, until the magistrate ordered the windows to be opened.

And now came the case of Bartek Koziol, of Lipka, accused of stealing a sow from Martianna Paches, daughter of Anthony. Witnesses, the aforesaid Martianna, her son Simon, Barbara Pyesek, etc.

"Are the witnesses present?" asked one of the assistant magistrates.

"We are here," came the reply in chorus.

Boryna had hitherto stood patiently apart, close to the grating; but he now approached Paches to greet her; for she was no other than Dominik's widow, Yagna's mother.

"Let the defendant come up to the grating."

A low-statured peasant pushed forwards.

"Are you Bartek Koziol?"

The peasant, seemingly bewildered, scratched his thick

hair, of roundhead cut; a silly grin twitched his dry clean-shaven face, and his small red-fringed eyes kept leaping like squirrels from one judge to the other.

As he answered nothing, the judge repeated the question.

"Aye, aye, that he is; he is Bartek Koziol, an't please the most honourable court!" cried an unwieldy woman, forcing her way inside the grating.

"What do you want?"

"An't please you, I am the wife of this poor thing, Bartek Koziol"; and extending her hands, palms downwards to the floor, she bowed till her frilled cap touched the magistrates' table.

"Are you a witness?"

"A witness, did you say? No, but please . . ."

"Usher, outside the grating with her."

"Get out, woman; this is not your place."

He seized her by the shoulders and forced her back.

"An't please this most honourable court," she cried, "my husband is hard of hearing!"

"Out, before I treat you roughly!" Yacek roared, pushing her against the grating till she groaned with pain.

"Go peaceably; we shall speak loud enough for your Koziol to hear."

The examination began.

"What is your name?"

"My name? Surely you know it, since you have called me. Is it my nickname you want?"

"Dolt! give your name," said the inexorable magistrate.

"Bartek Koziol, most honourable court," his wife replied for him.

"How old?"

"How am I to remember? Mother, what age am I?"

"Fifty-two next spring, I think."

"A farmer?"

"Oh, yes: three acres of sandy land and one head of cattle; a fine farmer I am!"

"Ever sentenced?"

"Sentenced?"

"Were you ever put in prison?"

"Is it convicted you mean?—Mother, was I ever in prison?"

"Yes, Bartek, you were—through those rotten manor folks, on account of a dead lamb."

"Ah, so I was.—I found a dead lamb in a pasture-meadow. Well, was it to be eaten by the dogs? So I took it; and they lodged a complaint against me, and swore I had stolen the beast, and the court passed sentence. They put me in prison, and there I had to lie.—But it was unjust—unjust!" he said in a low voice, and casting a side-glance at his wife.

"You are accused of stealing a sow, the property of Martianna Paches: of taking it out of the field, driving it to your hut, and killing and eating it. What defence have you?"

"I never ate it. If I did, may God forsake me at my dying hour! I eat it?—Well, I declare!"

"What defence have you?"

"Oh . . . defence?—Had I aught to say, Mother?—Ah, I remember now.—Yes: not guilty. I did not eat the sow, and this same Martianna Dominik's widow is even as a barking dog!"

"Oh, what liars some men are!" the Dominik woman sighed.

"Explain how Paches' sow got into your hut."

"Into my hut—Paches' sow?—Mother, what did the honourable squire say?"

"Why, Bartek, he asked you about the pig that followed you to our hut."

"Oh, I know . . . I know now. I pray the honourable court to excuse me and listen to what I have said already and repeat now.—It was a pig and not a sow; a white pig, with a black patch about the tail . . . or somewhat lower down."

"Well, but how did it get into your hut?"

"Into my hut? I will tell you all exactly as it took place, and show the right worshipful court and the people here assembled that I am innocent, and that the woman Dominik is a lying gipsy, a cursed and pampered shrew."

"A lying . . . May the Most Holy Mother grant you be struck dead unshriven!" the woman ejaculated, with a deep sigh, and a glance at an image of the Blessed Virgin that hung in a corner. Then she clenched her bony fist, shook it at him, and hissed:

"O you swine-stealer! you villain, you!" and she opened her talons as though about to claw him.

Here Bartek's wife interfered, screaming:

"Would you then? would you hurt him, you jade, you witch, you tyrant of your sons?"

"Be quiet," ordered the judge.

"Hold your tongues when the judge is speaking, or I'll turn you both out of the place!" Yacek chimed in, holding up his trousers; for the braces had given way.

Silence was now restored, and the two old women, who had all but flown at each other's throats, now stood mute, though looking daggers and breathing hate.

"Speak now, Bartek, and tell us the whole truth."

"Yes, the truth, the truth itself, as clear as crystal. As if I were at confession.—It was in this wise. . . ."

"Look well into your head," his wife Magda put in, "lest you should forget anything."

"I will do so, Magda.—It was in this wise. I was walking along (it was in spring, and I was close to Boryna's clover-field, just beyond the Wolf-Hole). . . . So I walked along, saying my prayers, for night was coming on.—Now, on my way, I heard . . . was it a voice, or not? I wondered. Did it grunt, or not? . . . Behind me I looked, but saw nothing: all was still. Was it the devil after me? . . . I went on my way, shuddering with fear, and said a Hail Mary. . . . Again—a grunt! So I said to myself it was only a sow, or it might be a pig. . . . But I walked a few steps aside into the clover; and what did I see? Something following me. I stopped, it stopped. A long white thing, low on its legs; its eyes blazed like a wildcat's or a devil's. . . . I crossed myself; and having goose-flesh, mended my pace. For I knew not what thing it could be, prowling thus by night. Also, as all men know, the Wolf's Hole is a haunted place."

"Yes, that's a truth," his wife observed; "last year Sikora was passing there at night, and something took him by the throat, threw him down, and beat him so, that he kept his bed for a fortnight."

"Hold your peace, Madga.—So on, on, on I went, with the thing still running after me—and grunting! Just then the moon shone out clear, and I saw.—Lo, it was a pig, and no devil at all! . . . I was angered; for what did the foolish thing mean by frightening me thus? So, throwing a stick at it, I make for my home, along the path between Michael's beetroots and Boryna's wheat, and then between Thomas' sown corn and Yashek's oats (him they took to the army last year, and whose wife had a baby yesterday). . . . And the pig still ran after me as a dog would run, and then going on one side, and into Dominik's potato-patch, grunted all the way. I turned off, and followed a slanting pathway across the fields: and it followed still.—I felt hot all over. My God! a strange sow!—Perhaps it was no sow! I went round nigh the crucifix, and the pig after me. . . . I leapt the ditch: it leaped too! Then I went to the mounds beyond the crucifix. . . . After me still! Then I ran by the pear-trees, and it came between my legs, and tripped me up. . . . I wondered whether it was a possessed pig! I had scarce got up, when it began to run on before me, with its tail in the air. 'Away with you, then, you pest of a beast!' I said. But it did not go from me: straight to my hut, to my very hut, did it go! It passed the fence, most honourable court! by the fence into the passage, and into the room through the open door. So help me God! Amen!"

"And so you killed and ate it, did you?" the magistrate asked, with a smile.

"Killed? Ate?—Well, what was to be done? One day went by: the pig would not go. A week passed, and there was no getting rid of it: it always returned, squealing. My wife gave it all she could to eat. Were we to let it starve?

it was as much God's creature as we were. . . . But let the most honourable court, in its wisdom, take this into account: what was I, a poor orphan, to do with it? Nobody came for the beast, we were needy people; and it ate, and ate . . . as much at least as two other pigs would have done. What then? In a month, we should have been eaten out of house and home, aye, and out of our skins too. . . . What, then, could we do? It was a case of eat or be eaten.—So we did; but only a little of it; for they heard of it in the village, and the Dominik woman complained to the Soltys,[1] and came with him, and took everything away."

"Everything, indeed!" interrupted the Dominik woman, angrily. "And what became of the hind quarters?"

"Ask that of Kruchek and the other dogs. We had put it into the barn for the night. Now, the dogs were on the watch, and there was a hole in the door; so they got in, and had a good feast on . . . what I am accused of stealing."

"So the sow went after you by herself, did it? Tell that story to an idiot, not to this court! You thieving blackguard! Who was it took the miller's ram? who stole his Reverence's geese? Say who?"

"Have you seen who? have you seen?" shrieked Koziol's wife, rushing forwards to use her nails. But the other continued mercilessly:

"Who plundered the organist's potato-pit? Who is it that snaps up everything missing in the village—be it gosling, or chicken, or rake or hoe?"

"You carrion, you! All you did when a lass—what your Yagna is doing now with the farm-lads—oh, no one reminds you of that now, vile trollop that you have been!"

This stung Dominikova to the very quick. "You dare to name my Yagna!" she roared furiously. "You dare! I'll knock your teeth down your throat!"

"Silence, hussies! or I shall have to drive you out!" said Yacek, to quiet them, holding his trousers up with one hand.

The witnesses were then heard.

[1] *Soltys*—the village headman.—*Translator's Note.*

Dominikova, the plaintiff, spoke first. She had taken a subdued and pious tone of voice, every now and then calling Our Lady of Chenstohova to witness. She averred that the sow was hers, that Koziol had stolen it from the meadow where it fed. She did not ask the most honourable court to punish him for that—may our Lord give him a longer time in purgatory instead!—but (and here she raised her voice to its loudest tones) for having heaped such foul outrages, and so publicly, upon Yagna and herself.

Simon, Dominikova's son, with clasped hands held under his cap, as one saying prayers in church, and with his eyes always fixed upon the judge, bore witness afterwards, in a dull plaintive voice, saying that the sow was his mother's, that it was white all over, with a black patch about the tail, and one ear torn by Lapa, Boryna's dog, which had attacked her last spring, and she had squealed so that he could hear her from the barn.

Then came the other witnesses, who all confirmed what he said, while Magda poured denials and curses through the grating, and Dominikova kept her eyes fixed on the holy image, or on Koziol, who listened attentively, with glances darted now at the witnesses, now at his wife.

The audience gave ear with intense interest, sometimes uttering a murmur, or an ironical comment, or a peal of laughter, severely suppressed by Yacek.

The case was gone into thoroughly, and only settled after the adjournment of the court to discuss the matter; during which time the people dispersed into the passages and outside the building, to get a breath of air, take refreshments, speak to the witnesses, or hold forth about their wrongs: others again, to complain of injustice with fierce invectives, as is usual on such occasions.

The adjournment over and sentence given, Boryna's case came on. Eva stood up in court, dandling her baby. With floods of tears, she related how she had come to serve at his house and worked herself off her legs, and never got a kind word, nor a corner to sleep in, no, nor enough to eat, so that she had to beg food from the neighbours, and he had not paid her, but driven her away, and his own child too, on to the high roads.—Here she burst into bitter tears, and fell at the feet of the magistrates, screaming.

"Such, most honourable court, is the wrong done me: and this is his child!"

Boryna muttered indignantly: "She lies, like the wretch that she is."

"Lie? Why, the whole village of Lipka knows . . ."

"That you are a wanton and a drab!"

"O most honourable court! and he used to call me Yevka and names more tender still; and would bring me beads, and often and often rolls, when he came from town; and would say: 'Here you are, Yevka, here you are, my dearest! And now . . . O Jesus! O Jesus!"

At that, she bellowed aloud.

"You gipsy trull! Why not say I brought you a featherbed too, and cried: 'Sleep under it, Yevka, sleep!' "

There was a roar of laughter.

"What, did you not? Was there anything you did not promise me?"

"Good God!" exclaimed Boryna, in fierce bewilderment. "It's monstrous! And yet the lightning has not struck her!"

"Honourable court, it is known to the world that this thing has been: all Lipka can testify that I speak the truth. Let the witnesses speak and bear testimony!" she cried out, with a tempest of tears and ejaculations.

As a matter of fact, however, all they had to say amounted only to bits of gossip and malicious talk: so she set herself again to bring forward what proofs she had. As a last resource, she displayed her baby and exposed it to the eyes of the judges, while it kicked up its naked legs and roared lustily.

"The honourable court," she cried out, "will see with their own eyes whose it is: whose is this potato nose, whose are these grey-brown blear eyes? Boryna and he are as like as two drops of water."

But this was too much for the court's gravity; and the

audience was also convulsed with uproarious merriment, when they compared the child with Boryna. Witticisms came forth in plenty.

"There's a handsome lass for you. For all the world like a skinned dog!"

"Let the widower Boryna marry her: the boy will do for a swineherd."

"Why, she is getting as bald as a cow in spring."

"A comely girl she is! Put her as a scarecrow in a millet-field; all the birds will take fright."

"Her face is smeared all over with grease and grime."

"Because she's a thrifty soul: washes once a year to save soap!"

"No wonder; she is so busy, having to light the Jews' stoves."[1]

They were growing more and more caustic and biting every moment, and Eva stood dumbstruck, with the vacant look of a hunted dog in her eyes as she gazed round upon the crowd, hazily revolving something or other in her mind, when Dominikova called out aloud: "Be silent! It is a sin to revile an unfortunate like her!" Whereupon there was a sudden hush, and more than one man showed evident signs of shame.

But the accusation failed completely.

Boryna felt exceedingly relieved. Innocent as he was, he would have felt keenly both the scandal of a condemnation and the burden of an order to pay for the boy; and, as he thought, the law would often enough punish the innocent instead of the guilty: you never could tell. He knew many such cases.

He left the place directly, and, waiting till Dominikova joined him, began to consider the whole business again. He could not make out Eva's motive in thus accusing him.

"No, it is not her doing; she has not the headpiece for

[1] Orthodox Jews are forbidden to light fires on the Sabbath, even in winter. They therefore engage some poor woman to go round and light their stoves for them on that day.—*Translator's Note.*

that. Someone else has been egging her on.—Who can it be?"

He went with Dominikova and Simon to have a drink and a morsel to eat in a tavern; for it was past noon. Dominikova hinted that the whole business was the blacksmith his son-in-law's work; but this he could not believe.

"What would he get by that?"

"The pleasure of worrying and mortifying you, and making you a laughing-stock. That fellow would like to flay a man alive, just for the delight of the thing!"

"This spite of Eva's—I cannot understand it. I never harmed her in any way; nay, I gave his Reverence a sack of oats at her bastard's christening!"

"Why, she serves the miller; the miller is hand in glove with the blacksmith.—Don't you see?"

"I see, but cannot account for it.—Have another drink?"

"Yes, please; but you first, Matthias."

They had another drink, then a third, and finished off another pound of sausages, and half a loaf of bread; and Boryna bought a lot of rolls for Yuzka and prepared to depart.

"Come with me, Dominikova; we shall have a talk. It is tedious to be by oneself."

"All right; but I must go to church first, and say some prayers."

She was soon back, and off they started.

The sun was drawing westward by the time they reached the forest.

Now and then they said a few words to each other, but only out of courtesy: it would never do for them to sit moping together. But they only talked just enough not to doze, and to "keep their tongues wet," as the saying goes.

Boryna whipped up the filly, which now, all in a lather, and tired and overheated, was going too slowly. He would whistle now and then, and again relapse into silence, ruminating and pondering over something in his mind, and calculating things: not infrequently stealing a look at the old woman, with that dried hard face, set and furrowed, and in hue like bleached wax. Her toothless jaws moved a little, as if she were praying silently. Sometimes she would draw the red apron she had tied round her neck, further over her brow; for the sun shone right into her face. She sat motionless, save for the gleaming of her grey-brown eyes.

"Have you dug all your potatoes?" he asked at length.

"We have. And a pretty good crop it is."

"All the easier for you to keep a pig."

"I am fattening one; it will come in handy during the carnival."

"Surely, surely.—They say that Valek, Rafal's son, has sent messengers to you with vodka."

"Yes, and others have done the same; but they have lost their money. No, my Yagna is not for the likes of them."

Raising her head, she looked him straight in the eyes, like a hawk. But Boryna, a man of mature years, was not confused as a youth might have been. He met her glance with calm and unfathomable serenity. For a considerable time neither spoke; each seemed vying in taciturnity with the other.

It was not fitting for Boryna to make the first advances. How could he—he, already past middle age, one of the first men in Lipka—blurt out to her that he had taken a fancy to her Yagna? Nevertheless, being of a hot temperament, he felt his choler rise within him, thus forced to parley and beat about the bush.

Dominikova saw he was annoyed, and knew why; but she would not help him out by so much as one word, and continued to eye him in silence. At last, however, in order to say something, she remarked:

"You look as hot as though it were harvest-time."

"Because I am."

And indeed it was very hot. The forest was all round them; its mighty barrier let no breath of air pass, and the sun burned so fiercely that the tree-tops, scorched with its rays, were drooping over the road, while a faint fungus-like odour, pungent in the nostrils, came up from the drying pools and the dry oak-leaves on the ground.

"Do you know," said the old woman, "I, and others too, have often wondered why such a man as you, a man of such high repute amongst us, so wealthy and so much more able than most men—has no ambition to occupy some official position?"

"You are right to say I am without ambition. What would such a post profit me? I was Soltys here for three years: it cost me a pretty sum. I lost so much by it that my wife was angry with me."

"She was quite right. To be an official always ought to mean both honour and profit."

"Thank you! A great honour it is, surely, to have to bow to the constables, and lout low to every clerk and every underling at court. . . . And if taxes are unpaid, or a bridge is out of order, or if a dog hit by a cart-shaft goes mad, who is to blame? Why, the Soltys always! And the profit! How many a fowl and goose and score of eggs have I not had to send to the clerks and the district officials!"

"You say true; but then Peter the Voyt here has no grounds of complaint. He has purchased some land, and built a barn too."

"Yes; but when he is Voyt no longer, what will he do?"

"Then you think that . . ."

"Oh, I have my eyes open, and can see a thing or two."

"He is most conceited, and at sixes and sevens with the priest."

"And if he gets on at all, it is his wife's doing: she is the real Voyt, and holds all the cards in her hands."

There was silence again for the space of a long pater noster.

"Tell me," she said at last, very deliberately, "are you not going to send anyone messengers with vodka?"

"Ah, the desire of women is no longer with me: I am an old man."

"Do not speak vain words. A man is old when he can

go about no more, nor lift a spoon to his mouth by himself, nor sit elsewhere but by the stove. Why, I have seen you shouldering a sackful of rye!"

"Granted that I am yet hale: but who would care to have me?"

"That you cannot know until you have tried."

"Besides, my children are grown up, and I cannot take the first lass that comes."

"Make a deed of gift, and the very best of them will not hold back."

"A deed of gift! To get an acre of land, a girl would take a beggar from the church porch."

"What of men? They wouldn't take a girl with a dowry, would they?"

He made no reply, but whipped the filly to a gallop.

Another silence ensued, broken only when they were out of the forest and upon the poplar-lined road; when Boryna suddenly exclaimed:

"To the devil with the world as it goes on now! For everything, nay, even for a good word, you must pay! It is so bad that worse cannot be. Even children rise up against their parents; there is nowhere any obedience, and everyone would devour everyone else! The dogs!"

"They are fools, not remembering that we shall all lie one day together in consecrated ground."

"One has scarce begun to be a man, when he flies in his father's face, loudly demanding a portion of his land; and the young only scoff at the old. Scoundrels, for whom their own village is a hole, who despise all ancient rules, and who —some of them—are even ashamed of their peasant's dress!"

"All because they have not the fear of God."

"Because or not because of that, things are wrong."

"And will surely not mend."

"They must! But who can compel men to do right?"

"God's judgments! For behold, That Day will come, and He will punish them!"

"Yes, but before That Day, how many shall be lost!"

"Times are so bad, that a plague were better."

"Times are bad, but men are so, too. What of the blacksmith? And of the Voyt? They quarrel with our priest, they make people rebel; they seduce them and are believed by the purblind. That blacksmith, though my son-in-law, is yet as poison to me."

They continued to complain in chorus of the world's wickedness, as they looked through the poplars towards the village they were nearing.

In the distance, there could be seen, outside the churchyard, a row of women bending down, indistinctly visible through a thin haze round them, and the dull monotonous thudding sound of cluttering swingles came to them, borne on the breeze from the low-lying meadows.

"Just the weather for scutching flax. I shall get down to speak to them, for Yagna is there too."

"I'll drive you to her; it will make no difference to me."

"How very kind you are to-day, Matthias!" she said with a sly smile.

They turned off from the poplar road to the by-way that led over the fields to the churchyard. There, outside the low wall of grey stone which surrounded it, in the shadow of some birches and maples, and of a few crosses, too, which leaned over the wall, hard on twenty women were very busily scutching and beating the dry flax: a mist of threads hung over them in the air, and a few filaments had caught on to the yellow birch-leaves, or hung suspended from the dark-hued arms of the crosses. Further down, fires had been kindled in pits, over and across which poles were laid, and upon them damp flax was drying.

The swingles were hard at work, and all the womenfolk bent and rose with quick short jerks up and down: now and then one or another stood up, beat a wisp of flax free from remnants of woody matter, and, rolling it up, tossed it on to a piece of linen spread out in front of her.

The sun, being at present over the forest, shone directly in their faces, but they did not mind: work and laughter and merry talk never ceased for an instant.

"God bless your work!" cried Boryna to Yagna, who was

swingling the flax with all her might. She had nothing on but her white smock, a red petticoat, and an apron tied over her head against the dust.

"Bless you for the wish!" she returned blithely, raising her dark-blue eyes to his, while a smile lit up her handsome sunburnt face.

"Is it quite dry, dear?" her mother asked, fingering the scutched flax.

"Dry as a peppercorn; quite brittle."

And again she eyed the old man with a smile that made him tingle all over. He smacked his whip and drove away, looking back at her again and again, though she was not to be seen any more; for his mind's eye saw her still.

"A girl as graceful as a hind!" he muttered. "Aye, even so!"

CHAPTER IV

SUNDAY had come round: a bright September Sunday, with plenty of gossamers and sunshine in the air.

All Boryna's livestock was feeding in the stubble beyond the barn; and Kuba, watching heedfully over them in the shadow of a tall and dome-like cornstack, was at the same time teaching Vitek his prayers.

"Now attend to what I am telling you," he said solemnly; "these are holy words."

"I'm attending, Kuba, I'm attending."

"Then why are you looking at those orchards?"

"I see the Klembas have got some apples on their trees still."

"Oh! and you'd like to eat them? Did you plant them?—Come, say the Creed again."

"You did not hatch the partridges, either; yet you have taken the whole brood."

"Silly lad! the apples are Klemba's, but partridges belong to our Lord. Do you see?"

"But the field where you took them belongs to the Squire."

"And the field, too, is the Lord's. You're too clever by half.—Now say the Creed."

He did so, but in haste, for it hurt him to stay on his knees so long.

"I think that filly is going into Michael's clover!" he exclaimed, preparing to run after her.

"Don't trouble about her, but say your prayers."

He went through them at last, but had to rest on his heels, and turned and twisted in every direction. A band of sparrows having settled on a tree close by, he shied a clod of earth at them, and at once beat his breast in contrition.

"Ah, what about the Offering at the end? Swallowed like an overripe pear, I suppose?"

He said the Offering, and immediately started up to wake Lapa and play with it.

"The calf-like witling! Always scampering about!"

Are you going to take the birds to his Reverence?"

"Yes, I am."

"They would be nice, if roasted here. . . ."

"You have potatoes to roast. What would you more?"

"See, they are going to church already!" cried Vitek, glancing through the hedge and the orchard-trees at the red aprons that went twinkling along the road.

It was pretty warm, and all the doors and windows of the huts had been thrown wide open. Here and there, in front of the huts, some were still washing their faces, or combing or plaiting their hair, or beating their Sunday garments, which had suffered from a week's stay in the trunks; but others had already started, in raiment of the hues of vermilion poppies, or saffron-tinted dahlias, or nasturtium flowers. Women and girls, in bright array, farm-hands, little children, grave husbandmen, in long white capotes that reminded you of huge sheaves of rye, were all slowly wending their way to church along the roads that led to the pond, which reflected the sunbeams like a golden trencher.

And joyfully the big bells boomed, and told of Sunday, and rest, and prayer.

Kuba had meant to wait till they rang no longer, but his patience gave way, so, putting the partridges under his capote, he said:

"Vitek! as soon as they have done ringing, drive the cattle to the byre, and then come to church."

He then started off—as fast as he could, for he was very lame—along the road, bordered with orchards, and so strewn with yellow linden leaves, that he seemed to be walking over a carpet of motley fallow hue.

The priest's dwelling stood over against the church, at the bottom of a large garden, in which there were trees still laden with green pears or ruddy apples. All over the porch there grew a wild vine, the leaves of which were now of a rich crimson. Kuba stopped outside, embarrassed, and looking timidly in at the window and the passage. He durst not go in, and stayed by a large flower-bed, gay with roses, gilly-flowers, and asters, whose fragrance was very sweet. From the roof, green with moss, a flock of white doves flew down to settle on the porch.

The priest was walking in his garden, saying his Office; but time and again he would shake an apple or a pear-tree. The fruit fell in a sounding shower, and he gathered them up in the skirts of his soutane.

Kuba came up to him, and humbly embraced his knees.

"What is it you say?—Ah, Kuba, Boryna's man."

"Yes. I have brought your Reverence a few partridges."

"Thanks for your gift. Come this way."

Kuba accordingly entered the passage, but stopped at the threshold of the room. He feared to go in, and would only look through the open door at the various pictures that hung against the walls. He crossed himself, and breathed a devout sigh, so dazzled by the splendour he saw, that the tears started to his eyes, and he felt like saying prayers. Only he was afraid to kneel down upon the polished slippery floor, lest he should soil it.

Presently the priest came out of the room, saying, as he handed him a *zloty:*

"God reward you, Kuba; you are a good man and a godly one, who never miss church on Sundays."

Kuba again embraced the priest's knees, so overwhelmed with bliss that he never knew how he got out and on to the road.

"What, so much money for so few birds! How I love his Reverence!" he whispered, looking over the coins given him. He had more than once brought him birds, or a leveret, or mushrooms; but never had he received so much: at most, ten kopeks and a kind word. And now! O sweet Lord! a whole *zloty!*—And he had called Kuba into his room besides, and said such gentle words! Lord, Lord!

"None but the priest has regard for poor people, no one

else!—May God and the Blessed Virgin of Chenstohova grant him health!—Yes, a good man you are, and a kind one!—All the village, farm-hands and owners, only give me nicknames—call me Cripple, Good-for-Nothing, and Hanger-on. No one else speaks to me with the least kindness or compassion . . . no one cares for me, but the horses and the dogs. And yet I am of an honest family: no foundling, but a farmer's son."

He raised his head higher at the thought, straightened himself, and looked almost defiantly on those about him going to the churchyard, and on the horses which stood harnessed to the carts outside the enclosure. He donned his cap, and covered his head of tangled hair, and slowly, with dignified mien, made for the church; thrusting his hands into his girdle, as a farmer would have done, though the dust flew up as he dragged his lame leg after him.

No. This day he would not, as his wont was, stay in the entrance. He pushed boldly through the crowd, even close to the High Altar railings, where only the husbandmen used to stand, where his master was standing, and the Voyt himself, and the men who carried the canopy over his Reverence in the procession, and those who, taper in hand, surrounded the altar at the Elevation!

They regarded him with amazement and indignation. More than once he heard taunts and words of upbraiding, and was scowled at, as one scowls at a dog that goes where it is not wanted. But to-day he did not mind. The money was tight in his clenched fist; his mind, full of sweet and gentle feelings. He had a sensation as if he had but now been shriven; nay, he felt even better.

Divine Service began. He knelt down close to the Communion Table, and sang along with the others, his eyes piously fixed upon the altar, whereon was seen the image of God the Father: a hoary magnate, stern-looking—just like the Squire of Djasgova Vola. In the centre, Our Lady of Chenstohova, in gilt raiment, looked down upon him.

On every side, gold shone bright, tapers gleamed, and nosegays of red flowers were flaming. From the walls, from the stained-glass windows, austere saintly visages, surrounded with aureoles, bent above him; streams of gold, purple, and violet came down, flooding his face and head with rainbow tints, and he felt as when he plunged into the pond at sundown, when its waters reflected the sky. Dissolved into ecstasies with the joy of the beauty before him, he was too much awed to move, and knelt motionless, gazing at the sweet dark maternal face of the Virgin of Chenstohova, and with parched lips said prayer after prayer, and sang with such force and fervour, welling up from the inmost depths of his enraptured heart, that his husky tuneless voice was heard high above the others.

"Kuba! you are bleating like the Jew's goat!" someone whispered at his elbow.

"For the Lord Jesus and His Virgin Mother!" he replied.

The priest had now gone up to the pulpit. All present lifted their heads to gaze on that white-surpliced figure, which, bending forward over the people, read the Gospel of that Sunday to them. This ended, the sermon began: long, but so powerful that many wept tears, and many heads were bowed down in remorse. Kuba's looks were fixed on him, as on some holy image: he marvelled at the thought that this was the very man who had just talked with him, and given him a *zloty*. For now he was transfigured into an archangel in a chariot of fiery light. His face turned pale and his eyes flashed, as he raised his voice to denounce the sins of his people: greed and drunkenness, lust and spite, disrespect for the aged, and ungodly behaviour. And his voice resounded, calling upon them, and entreating and beseeching them to repent; until Kuba, dismayed at the thought of all these sins, and the pity and the sorrow of them, wept aloud, and all the congregation after him—not women only, but burly husbandmen as well—and the whole place was filled with the sounds of sobs. Then, when the priest, concluding with an Act of Contrition, turned towards the altar, and went down on his knees, a cry ran through the building; all the people fell prostrate on the pavement, like a forest blown down by a whirlwind; and a cloud of dust rose over the multitude that lay thus, tearful and lamenting, heart-broken and contrite, imploring the mercy of God.

Then silence again prevailed—the silence of prayer and of heartfelt communing with God: for now High Mass had begun. The organ poured forth low muffled sounds of awe and adoration; and Kuba's soul was full, even to bursting, of love and ecstatic bliss.

Suddenly the accents of the priest were audible from the altar, floating above the bowed heads of the multitude—strange thrilling sounds, and holy, holy words; and then the bells thundered in a rapid volley, and the incense rose in odoriferous pillars, wrapping the worshippers in a sweet-smelling mist. Oh, then Kuba was seized with such blissful rapture that he could only sigh, and stretch his arms wide, and beat his breast, swooning almost with the joy of his own nothingness!

"O Jesus! Jesus whom I love!" he murmured, in dazed annihilation. But he held the *zloty* tight in his clenched fist: for now the Elevation was over, and Ambrose was now coming round with the plate, clinking the coins thereon to tell of the collection for the church tapers. Kuba rose, threw his *zloty* on to the plate, and slowly took back from it a few kopeks—just as he had seen the farmers doing many a time. And with infinite delight, he heard Ambrose say:

"May God reward you!"

Presently they brought the tapers round, for the Blessed Sacrament was exposed, and there was to be a procession round the church afterwards. Kuba put forth his hand, having a great mind for a larger one: but his eye met the cold reproving glance of Dominikova, who was standing near him, along with Yagna: so he chose a small taper. This he lit immediately; for the priest was holding the Monstrance in his hands, and turning towards the people. Intoning the hymn, the Celebrant slowly descended the altar-steps and into the lane at once formed for him—a lane of singers, of flickering lights, and gaudy colours, and droning voices. The procession began to move, the organ thundered mightily, the bells joined in with clamorous uproar, and the congregation took up the chant with voices raised in the grand unison of faith. In front of the crowd, and of the twinkling sinuous lines of tapers moving on, there gleamed a silver crucifix; following this came the holy images, dimly seen through a haze of cambric, and surrounded with flowers and lace and ornaments of tinsel. The procession arrived at the great church door, through which the sun irradiated the clouds of incense that it pierced; and as the banners stooped to pass, the breezes made them float and flutter and flap, like the wings of some great green and purple birds.

Round the church the procession went, Kuba sheltering his taper well with one hand, as he doggedly limped on, close to the priest, over whom Boryna, the blacksmith, the Voyt, and Thomas Klemba bore a red canopy. Under this, the golden-rayed Monstrance shot forth its beams, and was so directly turned to the sun that you could see it shine through the semi-transparency of the Sacred Host at the centre.

He was so absorbed that he more than once stumbled or trod upon someone's foot.

"Clumsy one, take heed!"

"You lame scarecrow, you!"

But he did not hear these invectives. Grandly the chants resounded, rising like billows of melody that dashed and broke around that pale white sun within the Monstrance. The throats of bronze overhead unceasingly rolled out their sonorous notes into the air, till the maples and the linden-trees shook their boughs, and now and then some reddish leaf flew down from their tops, like a frightened bird. And high, very high above them, over the church steeple and the drooping trees, a flock of startled doves was wheeling.

. . . .

The service was over, and they all poured into the cemetery round the church, Kuba amongst the rest.

Though he knew there would be a feast that day at the

farm-house, he was in no hurry, but stayed to talk with his acquaintances, and gradually drew near his masters, where Antek and his wife were standing in conversation with others, as is the custom after High Mass.

Another group, that had met in the road outside the lich-gate, had for leader the blacksmith: a stalwart fellow, dressed town-fashion from head to foot, in a black capote (spotted with drops of wax on the back!), and a dark-blue cap; he wore his trousers over his boots, and a silver chain adorned his waistcoat. His face was ruddy, his hair curly, his moustache red, his talk loud. And his laugh too: his was the smartest wit in all the village, and when he made a butt of anyone—well, that man's lot was not happy. Boryna watched him and listened. He could make out that the blacksmith spared not even his own people. Was he, then, likely to spare a father-in-law, with whom he was at odds for his wife's dowry? But Boryna could not hear much: Dominikova, just leaving church with Yagna, now passed in front of him. They did not get on fast, for they stopped in the churchyard to greet or converse with many people. He heard a few words about the priest, said by Dominikova in low and pious tones; meanwhile Yagna looked about her at the people. Having the advantage of a stature as tall as the tallest there, she was also looked at by many a farm-hand, who smoked cigarettes and grinned at her from outside the lichgate. She was indeed a fine woman, and well dressed, and with such a bearing that many a country gentleman's daughter could scarce vie with her.

The girls and married women who passed by all gazed on her, either in envy or simply with the desire of feasting their eyes on her striped skirt of rich stuff and ever-changing rainbow tints; her black highlows, laced up with red shoe-strings to where the dainty white stockings appeared; her corset of cherry-coloured velvet, gold-embroidered, flaming, dazzling; and the strings of amber and coral beads she wore round her full white throat, whence a bunch of particoloured ribbons streamed down her back.

But Yagna took no note of envious looks. Her deep-blue eyes strayed to and fro, till they met Antek's, fixed upon her; then she flushed crimson, and plucked at her mother's sleeve to go home.

"Wait a little, Yagna!" the latter called after her, greeting Boryna.

She could hardly get away, for the farm-hands were now crowding about her, with salutations and jests—the latter addressed to Kuba, and not without a sharp tang. For Kuba was following her, and staring as at some fair picture. With a gesture of contempt, he turned to limp home; his masters were going that way, and he had to see to the horses.

"Yes, she's a picture!" he blurted out, when he had seated himself in the porch.

Yuzka was just then bringing the dinner in. "Who's a picture?" she asked.

He cast his eyes down, abashed and afraid lest he should have betrayed himself. But the dinner was long and abundant; so he soon forgot all about that.

They all ate leisurely, with grave miens and in silence, until the edge of their appetite was blunted, and they could now talk and enjoy their meal with more dainty zest.

Yuzka was that day on duty as housewife, and saw to it that the platters should be always properly supplied, ever and anon bringing more food, lest the bottom of any dish perchance be seen.

The porch where they were dining was obviously the best place in such pleasant weather. Lapa ran to and fro, whining for food, and even rising up to look into the dishes, till someone threw him a bone. He carried it off, and barked for joy when his masters called him by name, and jumped at the sparrows, perched upon the hedge in expectation of crumbs to eat.

Passers-by merrily wished them joy: to which good wishes they all would answer with thanks in chorus.

"I hear you have been taking some birds to his Reverence," Boryna said.

"Yes, I have." And, setting down his spoon, Kuba told how the priest had invited him into the room, and what a number of big books he had seen there.

"When has he time to read them all?" Yuzka wondered.

"When? Why, of an evening. He walks about the room, and drinks tea, and is continually reading."

"Books of piety they must all be," Kuba added.

"What else should they be? Not spelling-books, surely!"

"He reads the paper the village factor brings him daily," Hanka added. And her husband remarked:

"Yes, for by the papers we know what's done all the world over."

"The smith takes a paper in, and the miller too."

"A paper fit for the smith, no doubt," remarked Boryna, with a sneer.

"As it happens, the same paper that his Reverence takes in," was Antek's hot retort.

"You know, then? Have you read it?"

"Yes, I have . . . more than once."

"You'll get none the wiser for his counsels."

"And whom do you hold wise? One with seventeen acres, or eight head of cattle, perhaps?"

"Hold your tongue before I lose my temper! Always picking quarrels with me!—You're too full of bread—*my* bread!"

"Aye, so full that like a fishbone it sticks in my throat!"

"Then seek better bread. Hanka's three acres will give you rolls!"

"Potatoes only; but these none will grudge me."

"I grudge you nothing."

"No? I work like an ox, nor ever get a kind word."

"Elsewhere life is easier, and food given free!"

"Elsewhere it is better, surely."

"Then go and try it!"

"What, empty-handed? Not I!"

"I'll give you a staff, to keep the dogs away."

"Father!" Antek shouted, starting to his feet, but falling back at once, for Hanka caught him round the waist. The old man glared at him fiercely: then, crossing himself as if dinner were over, he went out and into his room, saying in a hard voice:

"D'ye think I'll let myself be pensioned off by you? Never!"

All rose at once and left the porch, except Antek, who stayed alone there, pondering. Kuba took the horses to the clover beyond the barn, and lay down to sleep beside a cornstack. But he could not; the full meal lay heavy on his chest. Moreover, it now occurred to him that if he had a gun he could kill birds enough—and, it might be, a leveret or two into the bargain—to offer every Sunday to his Reverence.

The smith could forge him a gun. He had made one for the keeper; and this, when let off in the woods, was plainly heard in the village!

"A first-rate workman!—But then he wants five roubles to make one!" He fell into a brown study.

"Where am I to get them from? Winter is at hand: I must buy me a sheepskin coat. My boots, too, will not last beyond Yuletide.—Well, there are due me ten roubles, and two bits of clothing—trousers and a shirt. A sheepskin coat, short though it may be, will come to five roubles. Boots, three more. I must get a cap; and a rouble will have to go besides, for his Reverence to say a mass for my departed. So then nothing at all will be left!"—He was disappointed, fumbled in his pockets for a little tobacco that might be left, and so came upon the ready money he had previously forgotten.

"Ah! here I have some cash!"—He no longer cared to sleep. From the tavern there came a far-off sound of music, an echo of shouts, softened by the distance.

"There they are—dancing, and drinking vodka, and smoking too!" he sighed; and, lying down again on his stomach, he glanced over at the hobbled horses, that had gathered together and were nibbling at each other's necks. Then he decided that in the evening he too would go to the tavern, purchase some tobacco, and just have a look at the dancers.

From time to time, he would glance at his money, then at the sun, which was that day going down with exceeding sluggishness, as if it also needed its Sunday rest. His longing for the tavern was now so great that he could hardly bear it; but he refrained from going just then, and only turned over on his side, and groaned within himself. Antek and Hanka had come out from behind the barn, and were walking along the dividing pathway between the fields.

Antek went foremost; Hanka, leading her little boy by the hand, came after. At times, as they walked on slowly, they spoke a few words. Then Antek would bend down, and stroke the blades that were sprouting forth.

"It is growing up.—As thick as the bristles of a brush," he muttered, casting his eyes over those acres, sown by himself and for himself: the wages of work done for his father.

"Thick, yes: but Father's corn is better still. It grows up like a forest," Hanka said, casting a look on the neighbouring cornfields.

"The land might be better manured, had we but three cows."

"And a horse of our own. . . ."

"Aye, then we might raise some fowls or things for market. As it is, what can we do? Father counts every husk of chaff, and thinks a lot of a potato-peeling."

"And taunts us with every morsel he gives!"

They could speak no more. Their hearts were too full of gall and bitterness, and the angry gnawing pain of revolt.

After a time: "Eight acres or thereabouts would be our share, if . . ." he observed, absently.

"No more. There's Yuzka, and the smith's wife, and Gregory and ourselves," she counted.

"If we paid money down to the smith, and kept the hut, and sixteen acres with it?"

"But have you the money to pay?" she cried, overwhelmed with a sense of helplessness; and the tears started to her eyes, as she gazed at her father-in-law's fields—that land, precious as pure gold, whereon, aye, on every inch of it, wheat and rye and barley and beets might be grown.

"Don't cry, you silly thing; at any rate, we shall have eight acres of our own one day."

"Oh, if we had but half as many, with the hut and the cabbagepatch!" She pointed to the long stretch of ground, bluish-green with heads of cabbages; and they both bent their steps that way. At its edge they sat down under a bush; Hanka suckled the child, which had begun to cry for food, while Antek rolled a cigarette, lit it, puffed, and scowled.

He said not a word to his wife of the pain that was devouring him, and burned within his heart like coals of fire. For neither could he have told her, nor she have understood him: as is usual with women, who have no sort of initiative, who neither reflect nor catch the sense of things, but who live—so to say—only as the shadows which men throw.

"But," Hanka went on to say, "Father has ready money by him, has he not?"

"That he has!"

"Why, he brought Yuzka a coral necklace worth as much as a cow; and he is always sending money to Gregory through the Voyt."

Antek assented, but his mind was wandering elsewhere.

"It is wronging us all!—And the clothes your mother left! he has them locked up, nor so much as lets them see the light: skirts and kerchiefs, caps and beads. . . ." She went on thus a long time, telling of all these things, and of wrongs done, and grievances, and hopes: but Antek remained obstinately silent. At last, out of patience, she shook him by the shoulder:

"Are you awake?"

"Aye, and listening. Talk away, it will do you good. And when you have done, say so."

Hanka, who was naturally inclined to weep, and had many a cause for sadness besides, here burst into tears;

he spoke to her, she cried, as to a girl he scorned: he cared neither for her nor for her child.

At this, Antek rose to his feet, and replied contemptuously:

"Lift up your voice: these"—with a toss of his head towards some crows flying past them—"these will hear and take pity on you!" and, settling his cap on his head, he made for the village with great strides.

"Antek! Antek!" she called after him, in sorrow; but he did not even turn his head.

With a very heavy heart, she wrapped up the baby, and made for home.—So he would not let her talk to him about things, or complain of anything. Oh, he was very friendly, Antek, he was indeed! It was always, Work, work, work; and, See to this, and to that, and to the other thing; and, Stay at home! Nothing else! No consideration, no compassion, no fellowship at all!—Other women enjoyed themselves in the tavern, or went to a wedding.—But Antek! She knew not what to make of him. Sometimes he was so gentle, that gentler could not be; but again, and for weeks together, he would scarce utter a word to her, or give her a glance: it was think, think, think—all the time. True, he had cause enough. . . . Why should not his father make over the land to him now? . . . It was high time for the old man to retire and let them keep him. . . . If he did, she would take as much care of him as she would of her own father. . . .

She would willingly have talked to Kuba; but he leaned back against the cornstack, pretending to sleep, though the sun was shining straight into his eyes. And no sooner had she disappeared round the corner of the barn than he got up, brushed the straw from his clothes, and slowly took his way by the orchards to the tavern.

The tavern stood at the farther end of the village, beyond the priest's house, at the beginning of the poplar road.

There were not many people there yet. The music was heard at intervals, but no one had begun to dance. The lads and lasses preferred to romp in the orchard, or to stand about the house, or close to the walls, where plenty of women and girls were sitting on piles of deal logs, still fresh and yellow from the forest. The biggest room, with its dingy smoke-tinged rafters, was all but empty; the tiny window-panes, grey with dust, let so little pass of the red glow of the approaching sundown, that scarcely any got through to fall on the worn uneven floor; and in the nooks and corners the dusk was very deep.

Only Ambrose was there, with a member of the village Confraternity; they stood, bottle in hand, chatting together close to the window, and frequently drinking to each other's health.

Yagustynka was at the tavern, too, making herself unpleasant to everyone, and uncompromisingly angry with the whole world, because her children had treated her ill, and she had in her old age to seek work away from them. No one, however, answered her invectives; so she made for the small dark chamber, where the smith was sitting together with Antek and several other younger men.

A lamp swung from the murky beams, shedding a dim yellowish light on heads shaggy with luxuriant blond hair. The men sat in a circle, with their elbows on the table. All eyes were fixed on the blacksmith, who, flushed and bending forward, now stretched out his arms, now banged the table with his fists; but he spoke, nevertheless, in subdued tones.

Outside, the bass-viols were grumbling, like the humming flight of a bumble-bee that has got into a room. The violin would suddenly shed forth strong loud notes, as of a bird calling its mate; or the cymbal set up a drumming quavering din: and then all would again be quiet.

Kuba had made straight for the bar, behind which Yankel, the Jewish tavern-keeper, was sitting, in his skull-cap and shirt-sleeves (for the weather was warm), stroking his grey beard, swaying to and fro, and reading out of a book he held close to his eyes.

Kuba, taking thought, came forward step by step, counted his money over, scratched his head, and then stood still,

till Yankel noticed him, and without interruption in his prayers and swaying motions, jingled the glasses once or twice.

"One-eighth of a litre—but no water in it!" was his order at last.

Yankel silently held his left hand out for the money, and throwing the verdigris-eaten coins into a tray, inquired:

"In a glass?"

"Not in a boot, I suppose!" Kuba returned. Withdrawing to the very end of the bar, he drank off the first glass, spat on the ground, and looked round the room; the second dispatched, he held the flask up to the light, saw it empty, and pounded on the bar with it.

"Another!—And a packet of tobacco!" he ordered; more boldly now, for the vodka was filling him with pleasant warmth, and a peculiar sense of confidence.

"Got your wages to-day, Kuba?"

"Not likely. Is it New Year's Day?"

"Have a little rum?"

"No. I don't care." He counted his money, and sorrowfully glanced at the rum-bottle.

"But I'll trust you; don't I know Kuba?"

"I dare not.—'Who purchases on trust will soon not have a crust,'" he answered, dryly.

Nevertheless, Yankel left the rum-bottle close at his elbow. He wanted not to take it, and meant to go out; but the rum had such a scent that he at last gave way, and took a long draught on the impulse of the moment.

"This money, did you earn it in the forest?" Yankel inquired, with patient importunity.

"Caught birds in a net; gave six to his Reverence. He gave me a *zloty*."

"A *zloty* for six, did he? Why, I would have given you five kopeks for each of them.

"But—but——" cried Kuba, astounded, "are partridges kosher?"

"Never mind about that; only bring me lots of them, and

for every one you bring, you will get five kopeks of ready money. And the rum you have drunk will be thrown into the bargain. Is it well?"

"What, Yankel! Five kopeks for each?"

"My word is no idle wind. For those six partridges, Kuba, you would have got, not two-eighths of a litre of vodka, but four! together with rum, and a herring, and a roll, and a packet of tobacco. Do you understand?"

"I do. Half a litre, and a herring, and . . . I am not a fool, I can make it all out.—Quite true.—Half a litre, and rum, and tobacco, and rolls, and one entire herring. . . ." He was by this time somewhat fuddled by the fumes of the vodka.

"Will you bring the birds to me, Kuba?"

"Half a litre, and a herring, and . . . Yes, I will.—You see, had I but a gun," he continued, his brain now a little clearer; but then he fell to counting again. "A sheepskin, now, will come to five roubles . . . and boots, too, I need . . . three roubles. No, I can't manage it: the smith wants five for a gun—as much from me as from Rafal.—No!" He was thinking out loud.

Yankel make a swift calculation with a bit of chalk, and then whispered low in his ear:

"Could you shoot a doe?"

"With my fists—how? With a gun I could."

"Can you shoot then—properly?"

"You're a Jew, Yankel, so you don't know this: but everybody here knows I went along with the masters in the last insurrection; that's how I got shot in the leg. Oh, yes, yes, I can shoot!"

"I'll get you a gun and powder, and whatever you may want. Only, what you shoot you are to bring to me, Kuba! For a doe, you shall have a whole rouble. You hear me? a whole rouble! For the powder, you will pay fifteen kopeks, that I shall deduct for every doe shot. Then, for the wear and tear of the gun, I shall want half a bushel of oats."

"A rouble for a doe? and fifteen kopeks for the powder? . . . A whole rouble? How do you make that out?"

Yankel again went over every particular. Kuba only understood one point.

"Take oats out of the horses' mouths?" he said. "That I'm not going to do."

"Why should you? Boryna has oats . . . not only in the mangers."

"But—but that would be like . . ." He stared at Yankel, and tried to make things out.

"They all do that! Did you never wonder where the farm-hands got all their money from? How else are they to have their tobacco, and their nip of vodka, and their dance of Sundays?"

"How? what? you scurvy fellow! Am I a thief, say?" he suddenly thundered out, striking on the table with his fist, so that the glasses rang.

"Ah! Kuba, you'll fly out at me, will you? Then pay your score and go to the devil!"

But he neither paid nor left. He was penniless, and in debt to the Jews besides. So he only drooped heavily over the bar, in an attempt to make out the reckoning. And Yankel, growing kind, poured him out some more rum—pure this time—and said not a word.

More and more people had by now thronged into the tavern, for the twilight had deepened, and the lamps were lit. The music sounded to a quicker measure; the noise waxed loud; the folk formed groups around the bar, or along the walls, or in the centre of the room. They talked, gossiped, grumbled; and some drank one to another. But as a rule this was at rare intervals. For how could they do otherwise? They had not come to carouse, but only—well, so: to meet in a neighbourly way, and confabulate, and learn what there was to be learned. It was Sunday, and there was surely no sin in indulging one's curiosity a little, and drinking a few glasses here and there with one's acquaintances: provided always it was done seemingly, without offending God. His Reverence himself did not forbid that. Why, even beasts of burden, for example, were glad and required to rest after labour! So the elderly husbandmen sat at the table, and certain of the women, too, in red petticoats and red kerchiefs, each looking like a hollyhock in bloom. And as all talked at once, the murmur of voices filled the whole place, like the rustling of a great wood; and the trampling of feet was as the strokes of flails beating the wheat upon the threshing-floor: while the fiddle sang out with a merry tune:

"Who will—who will after me?" they cried, and the bass-viols growled the reply:

"All must follow—follow thee!" Meanwhile the cymbal, fluttering about with a sound as of laughter, made a joyful noise with its jingling little bells.

There were not many dancers; but these stamped with such lusty goodwill that the floor creaked, the table rocked, the bottles clinked one against the other now and then, or even a glass would be knocked over.

But it was no grand affair after all: the day was one of no special solemnity, such as a wedding or a betrothal in church. They merely danced to have a little fun and make their backs and their legs straighter from the week's work. Only, there were the lads who were to be taken into the army towards the end of autumn: those drank deep for very grief. And no wonder, having so soon to go amongst strangers, and into a foreign land.

Of these, the Voyt's young brother was the noisiest; and after him, Martin Byalek, Thomas Sikora, Paul Boryna (a first cousin of Antek who had also come at twilight to the tavern: only that day he did not dance, but sat in the smaller room with the smith and his companions), and lastly Franek from the mill, a short, thick-set, curly-headed young man: the greatest talker of them all, a rakish youngster much given to joking, and so excessively fond of girls that his face was seldom without a bruise or a scratch. This evening he was quite tipsy to start with, and stood near the bar now, along with fat Magda (from the organist's house), who was six months gone with child.

The priest had given him public reproof from the pulpit, and urged him to marry her. But Franek would not obey, because he had to go to the army in autumn, and what should he do with a wife there?

Magda now drew him into a corner, and was saying something in a tearful voice; but he answered as ever:

"You're a fool. Did I entice you, say? I'll pay for the christening, and give you a rouble or so—as much as I choose to give." He was stupefied with drink, and pushed her away so roughly that she sank down on the ground near Kuba, who was sleeping close to the stove, his head in the ashes. Then Kranek went off to drink again with Ambrose and the farmers, who were all willing to pay for him, to get their corn ground sooner.

"Have a drink, Franek, and pray get my stuff ground quick: my wife is worrying me—says she hasn't enough flour to make any more dumplings."

"Ah! and mine is continually grumbling, because we have no groats."

"And mine must have oatmeal for the pig we are fattening."

Franek drank, promised everything, and bragged very loud about what he could do. It was by his orders, he said, that everything was done at the mill. The miller had to do his will . . . and if not! well, he, Franek, knew of means to cause vermin to breed in the flour-bins—to make the stream run dry—to kill the fishes till the pond should stink—and rot the flour, so that it would be good for nothing in the world. . . .

"And I, if you did that to me, would pluck the wool off your curly ram's head!" cried a voice: it was Yagustynka's. She was always present where she found most company, being there most likely to find also some gossip or kinsman to offer her a drop of vodka, fearing her acrimonious tongue. Franek too, drunk as he was, felt apprehensive, and answered her not a word. She knew, indeed, too much about him and his management of the mill. Triumphant, and also rather flustered with drink, she set her arms akimbo, and danced and stamped and shouted in time with the music.

"What I say is true," the smith in the adjoining room remarked; "for there it stands, in print in the papers—letters as big as an ox. There is no nation on earth that lives as we do. Not one!—Why, every big landowner domineers over us; so does every priest; so does every official. And all we have to do is work, and starve, and bow low to all men, lest they strike us in the face!—We have so little land of our own, that—for many of us—there presently will not be the least little patch left. . . . Meanwhile, the Squire has more land to himself than two villages put together!—Yesterday they were saying in court that there is to be a redistribution of land."

"Whose land?"

"The gentlemen's, of course."

Yagustynka, who had come in, leaned over the table and laughed.

"Did you give it them, that you take it away! You are marvellous free with other people's property!"

"Folk have self-government there," the smith continued, without heeding the old woman's interruption. "There, everybody goes to school; they all live in gentlemen's houses, and are gentlemen."

"Where may that be?" Yagustynka asked of Antek, who sat at the farther end of the table.

"In warm countries."

"Then," she screamed out angrily, "why does the smith not go there himself? The dirty dog! he is throwing dust in your eyes, lying to you . . . and you blockheads believe him!"

"Yagustynka, pray be so good as to go peacefully whence you came."

"No, I will not! The tavern is for us all; and I, poor as I am, have as much right here as you. You play the teacher here! you, who serve the Jews, who cringe to the officials, who pull off your cap to the Squire from a mile away! You loud-mouthed ranter, you! Oh, I know of . . ." She said no more. The smith had taken her under the ribs, pushed the door open with his foot, and pitched her into the big room, where she lay sprawling on the floor.

Without a word of reviling, she picked herself up, and called out cheerily:

"As strong as a horse, you are! I'd fain have such a husband!"

The folk burst into a guffaw, and she went out to curse in silence and alone.

By this time the tavern had begun to empty; the music had ceased, and the people were going home. The night was warm and the moon shone bright: no one stayed but the recruits, who shouted and drank their fill, and Ambrose, who, being exceeding mellow, had rushed into the middle of the road, singing and reeling, from one side to the other.

The knot of men who had the blacksmith for leader had also left the place.

The recruits too, a little later, when Yankel was putting out the lights, staggered forth, all arm in arm, and went down the road, bawling songs and howling and bellowing so that the dogs bayed at them.

Kuba alone remained, so fast asleep in the ashes, that Yankel had to awaken him. He would not rise, though, but kicked out, and aimed blows in the air.

"Off, Jew!" he stammered. "I will sleep as I choose. A tiller of the land am I; and you—you are a scurvy rascal and a villain!"

A pail of water sobered him so much that he rose, and with astonishment and dismay, learned that, having drunk a whole rouble's worth, he was in Yankel's debt for that amount.

"What! a quarter of a litre, rum, one herring, tobacco, and another quarter besides: can they make up a rouble? How's that?" His brain was swimming.

Yankel, however, at last convinced him, and they came to an understanding about the gun which the Jew was to supply; although Kuba was firm in refusing to give him the oats demanded.

"My father was not a thief; neither am I."

"Now go away, Kuba; it is time, and I have still some prayers to say."

"Hear the old hypocrite! Asking a man to steal, and saying his prayers on the top of that!" he muttered, as he walked homewards, trying to remember things and sift them clear: for somehow he could not believe he had drunk a whole rouble's worth. But he was not yet sober, and the cold night air made him dizzy; so he reeled and staggered along, now falling against the hedges, now against the logs of timber piled up outside the huts. He swore.

"May the devil wring your necks for cumbering the road so, rascals! You must have been tipsy when you did it. Yes, drunken wretches! and his Reverence's warnings have been all for naught. . . . His Reverence . . ." Here reflection came to him; he realized the condition he was in, and felt overwhelmed with contrition. He stopped short, looking about him for some hard thing that might be handy. Then he forgot about that, and clutched at his shaggy mane, and beat his face with his fists.

"You drunken wretch, you plague-stricken swine! I will drag you before his Reverence, and he will rebuke you in presence of the whole congregation, and say you are a dog, and a miserable drunkard; you have drunk half a litre of vodka—a whole rouble's worth—and are a beast, worse than a beast!"—A sudden wave of self-compassion then came over him; he sat down in the road and burst into tears.

The moon, large and splendid, was floating through the dark space; like silver nails in the firmament, a few stars shone, sparsely scattered about; a thin grey tissue of mist hung over the pond like a veil, and waved its folds above the village. The world had entered into that unfathomable quiet of the autumn night, save that the few who were going home sang as they went, and dogs were heard to bark now and then.

Also, upon the road in front of the tavern, Ambrose, still reeling from one side to the other, quavered forth his song:

> "Tell, Marysia mine,
> Tell, O best and truest,
> Tell whose ale thou brewest,
> Tell, Marysia mine!"

which he repeated with interminable reiteration, until such time as the effects of his potations should cease.

CHAPTER V

AUTUMN was growing ever more and more autumnal. The pale days passed, dragging themselves over the empty soundless fields, and died away beyond the forest, always stiller, always paler, like the Sacred Host in the glimmer of a taper that is going out.

And every dawn the morning came more and more sluggishly, benumbed, as it were, by the cold of the hoarfrosts, and the sorrowful stillness and the life ebbing out of the land. The sun, dim, shorn of its beams, came blossoming forth from the depths; and crows and daws that had started up from somewhere in the East flew circling round its disk: they skimmed over the fields in long low flight, and croaked with dull mournful voices. Following them, the wind swept along, bitter and bleak, ruffling the stirred waters, burning up all that was left of greenery, and tearing away the last dead leaves from the poplars on the roads: these fell slowly, like trickling tears—tears of blood, shed by the summer as it lay dying.

And every dawn, the villages woke up somewhat later, the cattle went to graze with more slothful steps, the barn-doors swung open with less stridulous creaking; men's voices seemed muffled as they sounded in the deathly void of the fields, and their very life beat now with fainter pulsations. From time to time, they appeared outside their cabins or out in the country, and, suddenly stopping, peered for a long time into the livid murky distance. Or mighty hornèd heads would be sometimes raised from the grass of the yellow pastures; and as they slowly chewed the cud, their eyes would likewise go staring far, far away, while at intervals a hollow lowing would resound through the desolate waste.

And every dawn, it grew colder, darker; the smoke floated lower above the bare orchard trees, and more birds came swarming into the village to take shelter near the granaries. Crows perched on the ridges of the roofs or on the bare boughs, or flitted along close to the ground, croaking hoarsely—singing, as it were, the dismal song of approaching winter.

Noontide was sunny as a rule: but so silent! The murmuring of the woods was heard afar as a faint whisper, and the rippling of the river sounded like sobs of pain. The stillness of that noontide had something of death in it; and on the unfrequented ways and in the leafless orchards there lurked a profound sadness, mingled with a sense of shrinking from what was to come.

The ploughing was nearly over, and some finished their work, ending the last furrow when it was already dark, and looking back at the fields as they went home, wishing and longing for next spring to arrive soon.

Often, before evening set in, chilly rains would fall; and these, as time went on, continued even till twilight—that long autumn twilight when the cabin windows would shine flaming like golden blossoms, and the pools in the deserted roads glistened as glass—and even till the cold wet wind of the night flung its drops against the panes and moaned among the orchard trees.

One broken-winged stork that had remained perforce, and was often seen stalking about the meadows, now began to draw near to Boryna's cornstacks, and Vitek took delight in attracting it by giving it food.

Dziads,[1] too, now passed through the village more and more frequently; not only those of the usual kind, who went from house to house with their cavernous wallets and their lengthy prayers, and at whose approach the house-dogs always fell a-baying; but also certain others of a very different sort. These had travelled much and far, to many holy

[1] *Dziad* signifies in Polish a grandfather, an old man, or an ancestor, but is now mostly used to mean a beggar of a special type. —*Translator's Note.*

places; they knew Chenstohova, and Ostrobrama, and Kalvarya well, and in the long evenings they would willingly entertain the village folk by tales of what was going on in the world, and the strange things done in foreign parts. And there were even some who told of the Holy Land, and related such marvels about the vast seas they had crossed, and the adventures which had befallen them, that the people listened in pious amazement, and more than one could scarcely believe that such things could be.

Ah, it was autumn, late autumn now!

Neither rollicking songs, nor merry shouts, nor even the chirruping of little birds, could be heard in the village any more: only the blast howling over the thatched roofs, the icy rain pouring glass-like films down the rattling panes. and the quick dull thudding of the flails on the threshing-floors, which grew daily louder and louder.

It was indeed Autumn, the mother of Winter.

One comfort there was. Hitherto the weather had not been really bad, and the roads had not yet softened into bogs; so possibly it might hold until the fair, to which, as to a village fête, all Lipka was presently going.

It was to take place on St. Cordula's day and, it being the last fair previous to Yuletide, everybody had made preparations.

Many days before, the great question, What ought to be sold? had been debated: whether cattle, or corn, or some livestock of the smaller kind. It would also be needful, since winter was coming on, to make purchases; and those to no small amount. Thence arose not a few bickerings and tiffs and jars in the families: all knew that no one had much money to spare, and cash was harder to get every day.

Besides, it was just then that the taxes had to be paid, and the communal rates too, and various sums to be laid out, borrowed money to be returned in many cases, and not infrequently, the servants' wages were due. So that more than one owner (even of seventeen acres!) was sometimes in straits to know what he had better do.

And so, some took a cow out of the byre, cleansed her

dung-plastered sides with straw, gave her plenty of clover for the night, or a mess of barley boiled with potatoes, and did all they could to fatten her up a little; while others experimented with some blind old jade, completely worthless, endeavouring to make it look at least something like a horse.

And others in order to have their corn ready in time, were busily threshing it all day long.

At Boryna's, too, all were working amain. Aided by Kuba, the old man threshed out all his wheat, while Yuzka and Hanka employed every leisure moment in fattening the sow, or such of the geese as they had selected for sale. And, as rain was expected at any moment, Antek went time and again to the wood with Vitek, to get dry boughs and brushwood for fuel and litter: of this, some went to the cow-house, and the rest to make a warm outer coating for the hut.

This forced spell of work was kept up till late the last evening before the fair; and it was not until the wheat, all in sacks upon the cart, had been wheeled into the barn, and everything was quite ready for the morrow, that they all sat down together to supper in Boryna's cabin.

The fire was leaping merrily up the chimney, and by its light they ate with leisurely decorum and in silence; but when the meal was over, and the womenfolk had cleared away pots and pans, Boryna drew a little closer to the fire and said:

"We shall have to start ere day breaks."

"Certainly, not a whit later," Antek replied, and set to greasing the harness, while Kuba was engaged in whittling a swipple for his flail; and Vitek, occupied in peeling potatoes for next morning's meal, nevertheless found means to play with Lapa, who lay close by and searched for fleas.

Nothing was heard for some time but the crackling of the logs, the shrill cry of crickets beside the hearth, the splashing of water outside the room, and the clinking of pots and dishes.

"Kuba, do you intend to remain in my service next year?"

He let his knife drop, and gazed so long and steadily into

the fire that Boryna asked him whether he had heard the question.

"Heard it? I have: but I was thinking.—Truly, you have not treated me ill in any wise. . . . Only——" Here he broke off in some confusion.

"Yuzka! Bring vodka and a bit of something.—Are we like Jews, to be dry when we do business?"

Thus he gave his order, and drew a bench closer to the fire. Yuzka presently brought in a bottle and a loaf and a string of sausages, and set them on the bench.

"Drink, Kuba, drink, and say your say."

"Thanks, master.—Well, I'd like to stay, but . . . but . . ."

"Some increase of wages, perhaps?"

"It were good. For see, my sheepskin coat is all in rags. So are my boots; and I need a capote besides. If I go to church as I am, I must stay in the porch. How can I stand before the altar in such a dress?"

"Yes," Boryna sternly put in, "the other Sunday you did not care: you pushed and thrust yourself to where the foremost were standing!"

"It is true. . . . Yes, but . . ." he stammered, greatly abashed and flushing crimson.

"And his Reverence himself teaches us that the elders ought to be respected.—Now, Kuba, drink to a good understanding between us, and hearken to what I say. You know very well that a farm-hand is not a farmer. Everyone has his place, given to him by our Lord. To you also hath the Lord Jesus given yours. Keep it therefore, do not push forward, nor set yourself above other folk, for this were a grievous sin. His Reverence will tell you the very same thing. It must be so, else there would be no order in the world.—Do you follow me?"

"I am not a brute beast, and know what words mean."

"Well, then, see to it that you do not set yourself above anyone."

"But my only desire was to be nearer God's altar!"

"In whatsoever nook you are, God will hear you: fear

nothing. Also, why should you thrust yourself amongst the foremost, since all here know you?"

"You are right, very right. If I were a farmer, I should bear the canopy and support his Reverence, and sit on a bench, and sing aloud out of a book. But," he concluded, with a sigh, "being only a labourer—though a husbandman's son, mind you!—it behoves me to stand in the vestibule, or outside in the porch, like a dog."

"So is it ordained throughout the world, and you will not change it by taking thought."

"Without doubt I shall not."

"Take another drop, Kuba, and say what increase of wages you would have."

Kuba took the vodka. Now, as he was already somewhat flustered, he presently felt as in the tavern, with Michael (from the organist's) or any other boon companion at his side, whom he could talk with freely and joyously, as an equal. So he undid a button or two of his capote, stretched out his legs, struck the bench with his fist, and cried out:

"Four paper roubles more, with a silver one besides, and I'll stay with you!"

"You're drunk or mad, I fancy," was Boryna's protest; but Kuba, now fairly started in pursuit of what he wished and dreamed for, never heard his master's words. His imagination was no longer under control, his mind began to take wings, his self-assurance to grow great, and he felt himself as high and mighty as any farmer might feel.

"Yes. Four paper roubles more, and one other as earnest money, and I'll stay. If not, then, curse it! I'll go to the fair. There I shall find service, were it only as a coachman at some manor. They know me—know I am honest, and able to do any farm work, afield or in the house; many a farmer might learn a good deal of me, how I tend the cattle. —Or else . . . I know how to shoot, and can get birds for his Reverence, or for Yankel. . . . Or else . . ."

"See him!" the old man roared; "behold how grandly this lame one is prancing!"

The insult effectually sobered Kuba, and roused him from

his dreamings. He said no more of what he could do; but held doggedly none the less to what he had said. Boryna had to give way by half a rouble or one *zloty* at a time, and ended by agreeing to give him three roubles more, and a couple of shirts in lieu of earnest money.

"Ho! Ho! what a fellow you are!" he said, as he drank with him to clinch the agreement, though he was angry at having to spend so much. All the same he thought Kuba was worth it, and more. A man as good as two for hard work; scrupulously honest besides, and more heedful of the beasts he tended than of himself; one, moreover, so well acquainted with husbandry that he could be relied on both to do his duty, and to see that the others did theirs.

After settling two or three minor points, Kuba was about to leave. At the door, however, he turned round, and spoke in faltering tones:

"The agreement is made, then: three roubles and a couple of shirts. But . . . but . . . I beseech you, don't sell the filly. I saw her into the world, and spread my sheepskin over her, lest she should die of cold. . . . I could never bear to see her ill-used, perhaps by a Jew! . . . A horse is so docile, a man is nothing beside it. . . . Please don't sell her!"

"I never thought of doing such a thing."

"Folk talked of it in the tavern, and I heard."

"Meddlesome dogs and busybodies! They always know best what is to be done."

Kuba was so delighted that, had he dared, he would have embraced his master's knees. He made the best of his way to bed, for it was late, and there was the fair on the morrow.

. . . .

Next day, before the cock had crowed twice, every highway and by-way towards Tymov was thronged with people wending their way thither.

There had been a heavy rain ere morning. In the East it had cleared up a little, but the sky was threatening, with many a dun-coloured cloud. Over the low-lying fields crept fogs, dripping wet and grey as coarse canvas; and the pathways glistened with many a pool.

They had set out from Lipka at early dawn.

All along the poplar-planted road beyond the church and as far as the forest stretched a chain of slowly-rolling wagons, one close after another; and either side of the highway was variegated by a line of red petticoats and white capotes.

The multitude was so great that all the village seemed to be there.

The poorer husbandmen went on foot; so did the women and the farm-hands and the lasses. So, too, did some common labourers and inferior workers, this being the fair at which service was taken or changed.

Some went to buy, and some to sell, and some just to enjoy the fair.

One man led a cow or a big calf by a rope; one drove a flock of shorn sheep in front of him; another walked behind a sow with her little ones, or a lot of white geese, with their wings tied; another trotted by, riding a sorry nag; while from under many an apron the red comb of a cock peered forth.—The wagons and carts, too, were well laden. Often, from the basketwork and straw within one of them, a hog's snout would appear, squealing clamorously, till the geese gaggled in consternation, and the dogs that ran to market by their masters' sides, barked in chorus.

But Boryna only left his cabin when the day had fully risen, and the sky had quite cleared. Hanka and Yuzka had started before him at the very break of day, with the sow and the fatted pig; and Antek had taken ten sacks of wheat and fifty pounds of red clover-seed in the cart. Kuba alone had remained at home, with Vitek, and old Yagustynka, hired to cook the dinner and milk the cows.

Vitek, who wanted to go to the fair, was blubbering noisily outside the cow-house.

"What is the matter with the fool?" Boryna grunted; and making the sign of the Cross, he started off on foot, expecting that someone would give him a lift by the way.

Which also came to pass; for just beyond the tavern the organist, who was driving in a britzka with a couple of lusty horses, caught up with him.

"What, Matthias, are you on foot?"

"Aye, stretching my legs.—Praised be Jesus Christ!"

"For ever!" the organist's wife answered. "Jump up; there is room for you."

"Many thanks. I should have walked, but, as the saying is: 'They that ride in a cart are ay joyful at heart' "—and he sat down on the front seat, with his back to the horses.

"And so young Yanek is not at school now? How's that?" he inquired of a lad who was driving, and sitting in front with a farm-hand.

"Oh, I'm only just here for the fair!" he sang out in reply. He was the organist's son. His father said, tapping a box which he held out to Boryna: "French snuff: take a pinch." They both did so, and both sneezed solemnly.

"Well, how goes it with you? Selling anything to-day?"

"Nothing much. Wheat sent earlier, and a pig, taken by the girls."

"Not bad, not bad at all!" the organist's wife exclaimed. "Yanek, put this comforter on: it is chilly."

"Oh, I am all right," he answered; but she insisted on his putting it on.

"But," Boryna pointed out, "think of my expenses; I can scarce pay my way."

"Matthias, do not complain; you have no reason to. Thank God that you have enough."

Boryna, not liking to be thus reproved in the presence of a hired man, leaned forward hastily, and whispered:

"Is Yanek to remain at school much longer?"

"Only till Easter."

"And after? Is he to stay at home, or become an official?"

"My good man, what should he be doing at home? We have lots of children, and only fifteen acres. And times are hard—hard as stones!—There are christenings in plenty indeed; but what do we get from them?"

"On the other hand," Boryna satirically remarked, "there is no lack of funerals."

"And what do funerals bring us? Nobody dies but poor people. A farmer's burial, really worth something to us, comes only once or twice a year."

"And votive masses," she added, "are ever more seldom, and people bargain for them like Jews!"

"That," Boryna explained, "is on account of present hard times, and poverty."

"Also because men now think less of their salvation, and of the duty to help poor souls in purgatory!"

The organist here added: "And we get less from the manors as well. Formerly, when on our rounds at harvest-time, or offering wafers, or at Yuletide, or with our lists of parishioners newly made up, we used to go straight to the manor, where they grudged us neither corn, nor money, nor flour for pastry. And now, good heavens! all have grown so stingy that, if one offers us a little sheaf of rye, it must have been gnawed by mice; and if a bushel of oats, it will be chaff for the greater part. Had we not a bit of land, we should have to beg our bread," he concluded, holding out his snuffbox to Boryna.

"True, true," the latter replied, though under no delusion. He well knew the organist had money, some in the bank, some out at interest, and profitably lent to farm-hands. So he only smiled to hear his lamentations, and once more asked about Yanek.

"Are you going to make a Government clerk of him?"

"Of him? My Yanek—a Government official? I have not denied myself bread for him that the poor boy should have to finish his classes. No, no; he shall be a priest."

"What, a priest?"

"Aye, why not? Shall he lose aught thereby? Whom does it hurt to become a priest?"

"No one. No one, certainly," he answered with deliberation, looking respectfully over his shoulder at the young fellow. "It is an honour. And also, as the saying is: 'A priest's kith and kin will never grow thin.' "

"They said that Staho, the miller's son, was to enter the seminary; but I hear he is now at a college, studying medicine."

"Ah! such an evil-liver, a priest! Why, my servant Magda is six months with child—and by him!"

"By the miller's man, they say."

"No. His mother says so, but it is only to screen him. Oh, such a profligate! . . . God forbid! . . . As a physician, he'll do very well."

Boryna said: "Yes, yes, a priest's vocation is by far the best," and continued to humour her, tactfully listening to her gossip, while the organist would many a time lift his cap, answering "For ever!" to the greetings of those he passed by. They went at a good trot; Yanek drove splendidly, threading his way among the wagons and people and livestock upon the road, till they got to the forest, where the crush was not so great, and the road wider.

There they came up with Dominikova, who was going with Yagna and Simon, and a cow tied by the horns to the cart, from which, hissing like so many adders, the white necks of some ganders protruded.

They greeted each other, and Boryna went so far, when the wagons were abreast, as to lean forwards, and say: "You will be late!"

"Oh, we've time in plenty!" Yagna laughed in reply.

When they had been passed, the organist's son looked round at her several times, and asked at last:

"Is that Dominikova's Yagna?"

"The same, yes," Boryna returned, with his eyes upon her, a good way behind already.

"I was not sure: it is a good couple of years since I last saw her."

"Ah, she was then tending kine. She's very young still; but she has grown as stout as a clover-fed heifer."

"Aye, aye; comely she is; so well-favoured that every week messengers are sent to her with vodka—and a proposal."

"But she'll none of them. The old woman thinks," the

organist's wife whispered spitefully, "that a steward may come for her, and drive all the peasants away."

"Well, she would do, even for the wife of a thirty-five acres' farmer."

"O Matthias, if you think so much of the lass, send proposers to her yourself," she said with a laugh. Thenceforward Boryna spoke not one word.

"You town-bred riff-raff, here become a big personage—who look under the tail of every peasant's hen to see if there are eggs for you—who seek for money in every peasant's fist—will you make a mock of me, a husbandman born! You leave Yagna alone!" So he thought, and looked straight in front of him, in a very ill humour indeed, at Dominikova's cart, bright with the gleams of aprons thrown over kerchiefs, and now rapidly dropping astern; for Yanek was flogging the horses vigorously, and their hoofs made great holes in the mud.

The good woman went on talking, but to no purpose. Boryna only nodded, or mumbled indistinctly, and stubbornly refrained from any utterance whatever.

And no sooner had they reached the unspeakable pavement of the little town, than he got down, with thanks for the lift.

"We shall be returning about nightfall," she said, and asked whether he would care to go back with them.

"Very much obliged to you," he replied, "but I have horses of my own. People would jest—say I was applying for the post of organ-blower or assistant; and I can't sing a note or learn how to use an extinguisher!"

They went down a by-street, and he walked with swift steps up a main one, till he got to the market-place. It was a first-class fair, and the streets were already pretty well crowded. All the thoroughfares, squares, lanes and courtyards were full of people and vehicles and all sorts of country produce, like a flood into which human rivers were constantly flowing, with dense waves rolling through the narrow alleys and seeming about to bring the houses down, until it poured into the great square near the monastery. On the way townwards, there had been relatively little mud; but here, trodden and trampled by thousands of feet, it was ankle-deep, splashing in every direction from under the wheels of the carts.

Every instant, the din grew louder. Nothing could be heard distinctly save a cow bellowing now and then, a barrel-organ accompanying the merry-go-round, the obstreperous wailing of *Dziads,* or the ear-splitting whistles of basket-makers.

Truly, it was a very big fair, so crowded that one could scarce make one's way forwards; and by the time that Boryna had reached the main square, he had to push and elbow a passage by main force amongst the stalls.

And the things that were there! They could not be told or even conceived. How, then, is it possible to describe them?

And, first, those lofty canvas booths, which stood in front of the convent in two rows, all of them devoted to articles for women's use: pieces of linen cloth, and kerchiefs, suspended from poles, and all of them as scarlet as scarlet poppies, making the eyes ache; and then, close by, another booth hung with the same wares, but all of the purest yellow; and another, again, of the deep crimson of the beetroot. . . . But who could remember all these things?

Lasses and women stood there in such serried crowds that there was not room, as they say, to thrust a stick in amongst them—some bargaining and choosing; and some only looking on, gloating over those things of beauty!

Farther, there were stalls that positively blazed with beads, looking-glasses, tinsel ornaments, and ribbons and flowers—green and golden and many-coloured—and caps too . . . and the Lord knows what besides!

Elsewhere, the sellers of holy images had set them forth in glazed and gilded frames, so gloriously brilliant that (although they only stood ranged along the walls, or even lay along the ground) more than one peasant would take his hat off and make the sign of the Holy Cross.

Boryna bought Yuzka the kerchief he had promised

her in spring, and withdrew, pushing his way onwards to the swine-market beyond the monastery. He made but slow progress, owing both to the terrible crush and to the many interesting objects which he saw.

The capmakers, for instance, had put up wide ladders in front of their shops, and embellished these with caps from top to bottom.

The bootmakers had formed a real lane with trestles and horses, from which endless rows of boots dangled, suspended by the lugs: some of the common sort—tawny and only requiring to be greased lest the water should get in; some, lustrous with blacking like varnish; some, women's boots, high-heeled, red-laced, and beautifully polished.

Farther were the saddlers' stalls, superb with horse-collars and harnesses hanging in festoon from many a peg.

Then came the booths of the rope-makers, of them that sold nets, and of the itinerant sieve-venders; of those whose trade was to go from fair to fair with groats for sale; and of the wheelwrights and of the tanners.

Elsewhere, tailors and furriers had set forth their respective goods, the latter pungent in the nostrils with the spices used to preserve them; and they, since winter was coming on, had customers not a few.

After these came rows of tables sheltered under canvas roofs, displaying enormous coils of russet-hued sausages, as thick as a ship's mooring-rope; and piles of yellow fat and grease, brown flitches of smoked bacon, whole sides of fat salt pork, and hams by scores, rose in multitudinous tiers: while at other stalls, entire carcasses of hogs were hooked up, wide-opened, gaping, and so dripping with blood that the dogs gathered round, and had to be driven away.

Close by the butchers were their brethren of the baking-oven; and on thick layers of straw, on wagons, upon tables and in baskets, and wheresoever they could be placed, lay monstrous piles of loaves, each as large as a small cart-wheel. Cakes, too, were there, glazed over with yellow egg-yolks; and little rolls, and great ones as well.

Nor were stalls for playthings wanting. Some were made of gingerbread, in the shape of many a kind of beast, of soldiers, and hearts—and strange forms, whose meaning no one could make out. At other stalls you could have seen almanacs, prayer-books, tales about robbers and fierce *Magielons;*[1] at others, cheap whistles, mouth-organs, singing-birds of baked clay, and similar musical instruments were to be bought, on which those "Jew rascals" who sold them made such a row as was hardly to be borne; for the birds chirped, the trumpets blew, the whistles squeaked with long-drawn shrillness, and the little kettledrums at times joined in, beating a tattoo: and the uproar was enough to split any man's head.

But in the centre of the market-place, under the trees, coopers, tinmen and earthenware dealers had made up a group apart. There were so many pots, pans, pipkins and porringers that it was no easy thing to get past. Beyond these were stationed the joiners, with a show of painted bedsteads and chests, wardrobes, and tiers of shelves, and tables.

Now, in every place—upon the carts, along the walls, in the gutters, and, in short, wherever they found room—saleswomen were sitting: with onions in strings, or in baskets; with cloth fabrics and petticoats of their own making; with eggs, cheeses, mushrooms, pats of butter of oblong shape and wrapped in a linen cloth. Some had potatoes to sell, some a couple of geese, or a fowl already plucked and drawn; others, flax fibres finely combed out, or skeins of spun flaxen thread. Each of them sat by her wares and chatted pleasantly with her neighbour, as folk are wont to do at the fair. And when a purchaser appeared, they dealt with him quietly, gravely, leisurely, as decent peasant people: not like those Jews, who quarrel and scream and push one another, as though they were out of their minds.

Amid carts and booths, smoke was seen here and there

[1] *Magielon,* probably from "Magellan," means a wild adventurer, the hero of some tale of derring-do.—*Translator's Note.*

curling up from sheet-iron stoves. Here they sold hot tea. At others, there were eatables: fried sausages, cabbage, *barszcz*[1] and boiled potatoes.

Everywhere, *Dziads* were about in vast swarms: the blind, the halt, the dumb; cripples with never an arm, cripples with never a leg: just as at a local village fête. They played hymn tunes on tiny kits they held, or sang godly songs, clinking money in their wooden bowls. From the house-walls, from among the wagons, from the mud-deluged street, they all came to beg timidly, and implore a trifle in money or in kind.

On all this did Boryna gaze, not infrequently with admiration, as he exchanged a few words with acquaintances whom he met. At last he got to the swine-market, which was beyond the monastery: a very large space of sandy ground, with a few houses sprinkled here and there. Close to the monastery garden wall, and shaded by many a huge oak-tree that stretched out its branches over the wall, still covered with withered leaves, were grouped a good many people and carts, together with a large number of swine brought to the fair for sale.

He soon saw Hanka and Yuzka, who stood at the outside of the group.

"Have you sold, hey?"

"Oh, the butchers have been here already to bargain for the sow; but they offer too little."

"Are swine dear?"

"Dear? Not at all. So many have come, and the buyers are too few."

"Anybody from Lipka?"

"The Klembas have brought some small pigs; and Simon, Dominikova's son, has one too."

"Well, be as quick as you can, that you may enjoy the fair."

"We have enough of waiting already."

"How much will they give for the sow?"

[1] *Barszcz*—pronounced "barshch"—a soup made of sour beetroots. —*Translator's Note.*

"Thirty paper roubles. They say she is not well fed; big bones, but no fat on them."

"That's the biggest of lies! She has four fingers' thickness of fat!" he cried, feeling the sow's back and sides. "The young pig is not fat on the sides, but then its hams are well clad," he added, driving it out of the wet sand where it was wallowing and half buried.

"Sell at thirty-five. I shall just see Antek, and come back to you directly.—Haven't you a mind to eat?"

"Our bread is eaten already."

"I'll buy you a bit of sausage besides. Only get a good price for the pigs."

"Father, won't you think of buying me the kerchief you promised last spring?"

Boryna put his hand to his bosom, but stopped, as though struck with some idea, took out his hand again, and waved it, saying merely:

"You shall have it, Yuzka."

Instantly he moved off, for he had descried Yagna's face amongst the wagons; but before he got to her, she had disappeared, and was nowhere to be seen. So he went in search of Antek: no easy task, for the street from the swine-market to the great square was so thronged with carts, one after another and several abreast, that one could drive past only with the greatest care and difficulty.

However, he happened upon him at once, sitting on the sacks of wheat, and flicking with his whip at the Jews' poultry, which came running about near the bags out of which the horses were eating, while he made surly replies to the bargainers.

"I said seven, and seven it shall be."

"I give six and a half: the wheat is damaged."

"You scurvy dog! let me but fetch a blow at your ugly face, and it will be damaged enough: but my wheat is as good as good can be."

"Perhaps; but it's damp. . . . I'll take it by measure, and at six roubles five *zloty*."

"No. By weight, and at seven.—I have said."

"But, my good farmer, why so angry? Buying or not buying, one may always try to bargain."

"Then bargain away, if it amuses you." And he paid no more heed to the Jews, who came opening the sacks one after another, to examine the wheat.

"Antek, I am just going to the scrivener's. I shall be back in the twinkling of an eye."

"What? With your complaint against the manor-folk?"

"Think you I'll not resent the wrong done me?"

"Just get hold of the keeper, fasten him to a pine-trunk, and cudgel him till his ribs clatter: then you'll have justice done!"

"Aye, and serve him right too; but the manor-folk must come in for their share," he answered in a hard voice.

"Hand me over a *zloty*."

"What for?"

"To drink a drop and eat a bit."

"Always looking into your father's purse! Have you no money of your own?"

Antek, furious, turned his back on his father, whistling derisively; and the old man, though very unwillingly, pulled out a *zloty* and gave it to him.

"Yes; coin your blood to money, and give it away to all!" he thought, as he pushed his way towards a large tavern at the corner, where many guests had come to eat. The scrivener lived in a tiny room in the courtyard. Clad only in his shirt, unwashed, unkempt, but with a cigar in his mouth, he was then sitting at a table near the window.—On a mattress in the corner a woman lay, with a greatcoat over her.

"Sit down, my good man!" He tossed some garments on to the floor off a chair which he offered to Boryna, who presently explained the whole business to him in detail.

"As sure as a Pater ends with Amen, you'll get a verdict in your favour! What! A cow dead, and the boy frightened into an illness! We are bound to win!" He rubbed his hands, and looked about the table for some paper.

"But the boy is quite well."

"All the same, he might have fallen ill: the keeper gave him a beating."

"Not him, but a neighbour's cowherd."

"A pity; that would have been still better. But we shall word it so that it may seem both that the cow died, and that the boy had an illness. Let the manor-folk pay!"

"Surely. I want nothing but justice."

"I'll draw up your complaint instantly.—Franka, you sluggard!" he cried, kicking the woman on the mattress so hard that she lifted up her tousled head. "Fetch us vodka and something to eat!"

"I have not one kopek, Gutek; and they'll give us nothing on trust, you know," she grumbled, and, rising from her disorderly couch, yawned and stretched herself. She was a big woman, with a drunkard's face, bruised and bloated, but the thin reedy voice of a baby.

The scrivener set to work, with noisy pen scratching the paper. He puffed at his cigar, blowing the smoke into Boryna's face, as the latter was looking on. Now and then he paused to rub his freckled hands and turn his haggard pimply face towards Franka. He wore a great black moustache; his front teeth were broken, his lips livid.

The complaint was soon made out. It cost a rouble, and another for the stamp; and he agreed to present it at the court for three more.

Boryna willingly allowed the expenses incurred, feeling sure that the manor would have to pay them, with heavy damages besides.

"There must be justice in the world!" he cried, on departing.

"If we don't win in the Communal Court, we shall try the Assembly; if not there, why then, the District Court, and then the Judgment Chamber: I won't give in."

"Why should I abandon what is mine?" he said, with fierce obstinacy. "And to whom? To those manor-folk, owners of forests and of fields without end? No!"

Such thoughts were filling his mind, as he went forth into

the market-place: but just as he passed the capmakers' stalls, he met with Yagna.

There she stood, with one dark-blue cap on her head, cheapening another.

"See here, Matthias! this 'yellow one'[1] would have me believe this is a good cap: but no doubt he is lying."

"A very nice cap. Is't for Andrew?"

"It is: Simon's is already bought."

"Will it not be too small for him?"

"His head is just the size of mine."

"What a well-favoured stable-boy you would make!"

"Ah! shouldn't I?" she exclaimed, with a jaunty air, and cocking her cap on one side.

"I'd take you to my service directly!"

"Only my terms might prove much too high." She laughed.

"For some, perhaps; not for me."

"But I'd do no work in the fields."

"Oh, I would do the work for you, Yagna!" he whispered, and the look he darted at her was so passionate that she shrank back in confusion, and paid for the cap without bargaining.

"Have you sold your cow?" he asked her, after a time, when he had become more master of himself, and overcome the sensation which had so suddenly gone to his head, like strong vodka.

"Yes, they bought her for the priest in Yerzov. Mother has gone with the organist, who wants to engage a farm-labourer."

"Well then, let's just go and take a drop of sweetened vodka together."

"What's that you say?"

"You are cold, Yagna; it will warm you somewhat."

"Go with you for a drink? . . . Where could I go?"

"Then, Yagna, I'll bring some, and we'll drink it here together."

[1] *Yellow one.*—A nickname sometimes given to Jews by peasants. —*Translator's Note.*

"God reward your kindness, but I must look for Mother."

"Yagna, I'll help you to find her," he whispered very low, and going foremost, elbowed a way for her so powerfully that she was easily able to get through the crowd. But when they stood before the booths of linen goods, the girl walked more slowly, and presently stopped, her eyes beaming with joy at the various objects before her.

"Oh, what splendid things! Lord, dear Lord!" she murmured, stopping in front of the ribbons which, hanging above her, waved in the air, like a mobile and flaming rainbow.

"Choose the one you like best, Yagna!"

"Why, that yellow one embroidered with flowers must cost a rouble, or perhaps even ten *zloty!*"

"Let not that trouble you, but take it."

Yagna, however—regretfully indeed and with a great effort—let the ribbon go, and passed on to the next booth: Boryna remaining a little behind for a few instants.

Now her gaze again fell on kerchiefs, and stuffs for bodices, and jackets.

"O Lord, O Lord! what beautiful things!" she murmured low, rapt with the glamour of it all; and more than once she would plunge her quivering hands into those folds of green or red satin, till her eyes grew dim and her heart went pit-a-pat with delight.

And what head-dresses those kerchiefs made! Scarlet silk, embroidered all round with green flowers; or all of a golden hue; or a deep blue, like the sky after rain! And those—the finest of them all—of changeful shimmering colours, pure as water shining in the evening sunlight, and no heavier than floating gossamer! . . . No, she could not help it: she must try that kerchief on her head, and see herself in the looking-glass the Jewess of the booth was holding out to her.

Yes, it suited her to perfection; it was like a glorious aureole over her light flaxen tresses, and made the deep azure of her eyes shine so intensely with the joy of it that they glowed violet amid the splendour of her face. And people turned to gaze at her, so handsome she appeared, surrounded with so bright an emanation of youth and health!

"Is not this the daughter of some Squire, disguising herself?" they whispered among themselves.

For a long time she contemplated the kerchief, and then, with a deep sigh, took it off, and set to bargaining: not meaning to buy it—this was impossible—but only for the pleasure of enjoying its beauty a little longer.

Presently, however, her ardour cooled. The Jewess had put the price at five roubles!—Even Boryna at once dissuaded her.

Again they came to a stop before the stalls of beads. How many strings there were! And how they looked! As if the whole stall were oversprinkled with precious gems: so brilliant, so resplendent! Hard, indeed, it was to take one's eyes away from them—from those amber globules of pellucid gold, looking for all the world as if made of sweet-scented resin; and the coral drops, like threaded beads of blood; and the white pearls, as big as hazel-nuts; and those other drops of silver and of gold!

Yagna tried on more than one, and made her choice of the most beautiful. At last she caught sight of one very lovely string of coral beads, passed it four times round her neck, and, turning to the old man, said:

"Does it suit me? Tell me true."

"Splendidly, Yagna!—But coral beads are no strange thing to me. In a chest at my home there lies a necklace of eight rows. 'Twas my wife's. Every bead is as big as the biggest pea. "This he said to her with studied indifference.

"And what's that to me, if it is not mine?" She flung the beads back and hastened away, moody and repining.

"Yagna, let's sit down awhile."

"I must go to mother."

"No fear of her leaving you behind."

They sat down together on the shaft of a wagon.

"It's a big fair," remarked Boryna, looking round the market-place.

"It's not small," she returned, casting a sorrowful glance at the stalls they had left behind them, and heaving a deep sigh. A pause ensued; then, trying to shake off her sadness, she spoke:

"Ah, well it is for anyone who is a Squire! Once I saw the daughter of the Squire of Vola, with other ladies, buying, as they did at every fair, such quantities of things that they were carried by a manservant!"

" 'Who goes oft to the fair shall lose all he has there.' " Boryna remarked.

"The proverb is not for them."

"Not so long as they can borrow from Jews," he answered, with such bitterness that Yagna stared at him, knowing not what to reply. Looking away from her, he asked, in a low voice:

"They have been to you with a proposal from Michael, Voytek's son, have they not?"

"They went away as they came. Such a dolt, to send a proposal to me!"

Boryna then rose hurriedly, taking out of his bosom a kerchief, and something else wrapped up in paper.

"Keep this, Yagna; I must go to Antek."

Her eyes sparkled at the name. "Is he at the fair?"

"Yes; down that lane, selling the corn.—Take this, Yagna, it is for you," he added, seeing her gaze at the kerchief with bewildered eyes.

"Do you give it me? Me—really? Oh, how pretty it is!" She unwrapped the paper. There lay the very same ribbon that had pleased her so vastly just before. "Can you be in earnest?" she exclaimed. "Why do you give me all this? It is very costly, and the kerchief is of pure silk."

"Take it, Yagna, take it, it is all bought for you. And when some peasant shall come to drink to you, do not drink back to him. Why hurry?—Now, I must go."

"Are these things my own? Say you true?"

"And wherefore should I lie to you?"

"I can scarce believe it," she said, unwrapping the kerchief, and then the ribbon again.

"God be with you, Yagna!"

"How I thank you, Matthias!"

He left her. Yagna once more unwrapped the things, and gloated over them. Then she wrapped them up both together, with a mind to run after him and give them back: for how could she accept such gifts from a stranger? But he was no longer in sight. So she walked along slowly, to seek her mother, secretly and fingering with intense pleasure the parcel hidden in her bosom. She was full of joy; her cheeks glowed red, and her white teeth flashed as she smiled.

"Yagna! Pray give some aid to a poor creature. Your people are good, true Christians! I'll say a Hail Mary for your departed. . . . O Yagna!"

Yagna, thus recalled to herself, looked to see who it was that spoke, and saw Agatha, who was sitting close to the monastery wall, upon a bundle of straw: for the mud was there more than ankle-deep.

Coming to a standstill, she fumbled in her dress for some coppers; and Agatha, overjoyed to have met someone of her village, began to ask her what was going on at Lipka.

"Are all the potatoes in?"

"To the very last."

"Anything new at the Klembas'?"

"What, they have sent you away to beg . . . and you still care about them?"

"Sent me away? That they did not; I went by myself, for it was needful. And I care about them, because they are my kinsfolk."

"And what are you doing now?"

"Going from church to church, from hamlet to hamlet, from fair to fair; and, as guerdon for my prayers, the good people give me, here a corner to sleep in, there a morsel to feed me, and at times a copper or two. The people are good; they will not let a poor creature starve, not they!" She broke off, and asked, with some hesitation: "Do you know if all the Klembas are in good health?"

"They are; and how are you?"

"Oh, my health is nothing to boast of. Always a pain in my chest; and when I take cold, I spit hot blood. I shall not last long, no!—If I can but hold out till spring, I will go back to the village to die among my own people. I ask naught else of our Lord . . . Naught else."

Say a prayer for Father's soul?" Yagna whispered, slipping some coins into her hand.

"That will be for all the holy souls in purgatory; for as it is, I always pray for all those I know, living and dead.—But . . . Yagna! . . . Have they sent no one to you with vodka?"

"Yes."

"And you would drink back to none?"

"To none," she replied briefly. "God be with you, and come next spring to see us." And she went to rejoin her mother, whom she perceived at some distance with the organist.

Boryna was returning to Antek, but slowly, both on account of the crowds, and because the thought of Yagna was haunting him. Before he saw his son, however, the blacksmith met him. They greeted one another, and walked on side by side without speaking. At last:

"Are you going to settle with me, or not?" the smith began, in no friendly voice. Boryna was up in arms at once.

"Settle what? Lipka was the place to speak with me."

"These three years I have been waiting. People advise me to bring an action at law . . . but . . ."

"Do so. I'll introduce you to a scrivener; yes, and pay him a rouble to draw up a complaint for you!"

". . . But I think," the smith went on, with crafty moderation, "it were best to have a friendly understanding."

"Right. 'By a neighbourly course get what's not got by force!' "

"You say wisely."

"You will get it neither in one way nor in the other."

"I have always told my wife that you, Father, loved justice."

"Everyone wants justice . . . on his side. I am indifferent, for I owe nothing." At those stern words, the blacksmith saw he would get nothing by his former tactics, so he changed them. As if there had been no dispute, he very quietly uttered the request:

"Will you stand me a drink? I should like one."

"Certainly, dearest son-in-law: yes, even should you ask for a litre." The tones were rather sneering; but they entered the corner tavern together. Here they found Ambrose, not drinking, but seated in a corner, sulky and sad.

"I feel my bones ache; we shall have nasty weather," Ambrose predicted.

They drank once and again, but saying not a word, each angry with the other.

"You take your vodka as they do at a funeral," Ambrose said; he felt sore at not being invited, for he had scarcely taken anything that morning.

"How can we talk? Father-in-law is selling so much today that he must think to whom he had best lend his cash out at interest."

"Matthias, Matthias!" cried Ambrose; I say to you that our Lord . . ."

"Matthias I am—for some, not for you, you saucy fellow!—Look at him! 'Fain would the swine say to the swineherd, Brother!' "

The smith had already taken a couple of stiff drams, and felt inclined to argue. He lowered his tone, to say:

"Father-in-law, tell me once for all: will you, or will you not, give what I ask?"

"You have heard my answer. I cannot take my land to the grave with me; but, while I am living, not one acre will I give up. I will not be fed at your expense, and mean to enjoy a year or two in this world still."

"Then pay me off!"

"I have spoken: have you heard?"

"He is looking out," Ambrose whispered, "for a third wife. What are his children to him?"

"That's likely, indeed!"

"Marry I shall, if I choose," put in Boryna. "Do you object?"

"Object? No; but . . ."

"If I choose, I shall send a proposal—yes, and no later than to-morrow!"

"Do so. What have I against it? Only let me have Red-and-White's calf, and I'll even help you all I can. You, a reasonable man, must know what is best for you. I have said so many a time to my wife: you want a woman in the house to keep it in order."

"Michael! You said that?"

"May I die unshriven if I did not! Yes, I did say so. I, who advise the whole village, each man as he requires, should I not know what is good for you?"

"You rogue, you are lying like a gipsy!—But come to-morrow, and you shall have the calf. . . . What I am asked for, I may give; but claim it as a right, and you'll get only a broken cudgel—or worse."

They continued their potations, the smith now treating Boryna, and inviting Ambrose to join them. This he did very willingly, and told many a merry tale and jest, so that they presently roared with laughter.

The two separated on good terms. But neither trusted the other a jot.—Each was transparent to each as a pane of glass, each as easy to know as a horse with a star on the forehead.

Ambrose remained, expecting gossips and acquaintances willing to offer him the least little drop. For "a hungry dog will try even to catch a fly."

The fair was drawing to its close.

For a moment the sun had shone out at noon, flashing on the world like the glint of a brandished mirror; then it plunged anew behind the clouds. Before evening had come, everything was in profound gloom; heavy masses of vapour rolled down, almost touching the house-roofs, and a fine rain drizzled as though sifted through a sieve. . . . The folk therefore hastened to drive away, anxious to get home before nightfall and a heavy downpour.

Twilight fell, swift, louring, and dank: the town was once more empty and silent.

Only along a wall here and there, some *Dziads* were moaning, and the voices of revelling and quarrelling were loud in the taverns.

Evening was well advanced when Boryna drove away with his people. They had sold all they brought, purchased various articles, and enjoyed the fair to the full. Antek flogged the horses with all his might, and the cart hurtled athwart the depths of the mud; for he felt cold, and they had all drunk plentifully. The old man, stingy though he was, and ready to make a fuss for a *grosz*[1] had that day treated them so well with things to eat and drink, and friendly words, that they were all amazed at him.

When they reached the forest, it was black night—so dark that nothing could be seen. The rain was falling, ever in larger drops. Along the road a clatter of wagon-wheels, the brawling howl of a drunken song, or the sucking steps of someone plodding in the mire, were to be heard.

But, in the middle of the poplar-road, whose trees murmured and muttered as though shivering with cold, Ambrose, now quite drunk, staggered along from one side to the other, now stumbling against a tree, now falling into the mud; but he would quickly rise and go on, singing, as was his wont, with noisy vociferation.

[1] *Grosz*—the smallest Polish coin—about one-fourth of an American cent.—*Translator's Note.*

CHAPTER VI

THE rain had now begun to come down in earnest.

Ever since the fair, all things had been drowned in a grey turbid shimmer, through which only the dim outlines of the forest or the hamlet loomed, embroidered, as it were, on a ground of wet canvas.

The autumn downpours swooped down, icily cold, piercingly sharp, and never-ending.

The rain, like scourges of ashen-grey hue, unceasingly beat upon the earth, soaking every tree to its very centre, and making every blade of grass quiver, as in dire pain.

From underneath those thick clouds and that ghastly grey rain there would appear, now and again, strips of fields, blackened, flat, and sodden; or there would gleam forth streaks of foam-flecked water, flowing down the furrows; or the trees along the pathways would stand forth, dark and stark, as their dripping branches, wet to the inmost pith, shaking off the last rags of leaves, seemed struggling desperately, like hounds straining at a leash.

The deserted roads were now transformed into interminable quagmires of filth.

The short, sad, sunless days crawled by; bleak and dull, with ceaseless sounds of monotonous plashing, fell the nights.

Mute were the fields, dumb the hamlets, silent the woods. The houses dusky and colourless, seemed melting into and making one with the earth, the fences, and the stripped orchards, tossing their boughs with feeble moans.

A livid whirling downpour had covered the land, taken all colour out of it, quenched its tints, and plunged the world into twilight. All seemed confused, and as in a dream. A sadness rose up from the mouldering fields, from the palsy-stricken woods, from the dead wilderness; thence it floated like a heavy cloud, lingering about the melancholy cross-ways, under the crucifixes which stretched forth their mournful arms and on the waste roads, where the trees would suddenly quake as with dread, and sob as if in anguish; it looked with vacant stare into each deserted nest, and on each fallen cabin; it crept about the burial-places around the graves of the forgotten dead, and the decaying crosses; it spread over all the country.

And the drizzle was never-ceasing: but when the heavy rain swooped down, it wrapped all Lipka in its folds, so that the dark thatches, the dank stones of the enclosures, the dingy tangles of smoke which twirled above the chimneys and wandered over the orchards, were visible only at rare intervals.

The village was noiseless, except for some barns, where men were threshing. But these were few: the people were all out in the cabbage plantations. The miry roads lay waste; and waste, too, were the cabin-surroundings. If now and then anyone appeared, a ghost in the fog, he vanished at once, and only the sound of his wooden clogs was audible, as he trudged through the mud. Or from time to time a cart laden with cabbages would roll slowly away from the peat bogs, and scatter the geese wading about to snap up such leaves as it let fall.

The pond struggled within the narrow shores which confined it. It was continually rising; and ere it flooded the lower parts of the road on Boryna's side, it came up to the enclosures, and splashed and foamed before the very cabin-walls.

But the whole village was out, busy cutting the cabbages, and conveying them home. They were housed everywhere, on threshing-floors, in passages, in dwelling-rooms, and in some cases, even under the eaves—bluish-green cabbage-heads were to be seen by hundreds.

They made haste, for it was continually raining, and the ways were all fast becoming sloughs of mire, and impassable.

That day, they were cutting Dominikova's plantation.

Yagna, along with Simon, had been there since morning, for Andrew had stayed at home to mend the roof.

Evening was at hand, and the old housewife again and again came out, looking towards the mill, and listening for the sound of their coming.

But the work was still going on busily in the low-lying plantation beyond the mill. Over the meadows stretched a dense fog; only in places, wide ditches gleamed, full of grey turbid water; and long bands on the higher ground where the cabbages grew, here of a pallid green, there of a rusty red. About these flitted dimly the crimson petticoats of women, piling up heaps of newly cut cabbages.

In the misty distance, close to the river that ran frothing among thickets of brushwood, there rose many a heap of dull brown peat. Here the carts were stationed; they could come no nearer, because of the quaggy nature of the soil, and every sheetful of cabbages had to be taken to them as a bundle carried on the back.

In some fields cutting was over already, and the people were going home; from patch to patch, ever louder and louder, their voices sounded through the fog.

Yagna had only just got through with the work. She was tired out, very sharp-set, and completely drenched to boot. Even her clogs were streaming with wet, for they sank more than ankle-deep into the dun-coloured peaty soil, and she often had to take them off and pour the water out.

"Simon! be quick now! I can feel my limbs no more!" she called out wearily; but, seeing that the young man was unable to lift his burden, she impatiently seized the great bundle, raised it on to her back, and carried it off to the wagon.

"A big fellow like you—yet with the loins of a woman after childbed!" She spoke scornfully, as she poured the cabbages out into the straw at the bottom of the cart.

Simon, much abashed, muttered, growled, scratched his head, and put the horse to.

"Hurry now, Simon!" she cried, swiftly bearing one huge bundle after another to the cart.

But night fell, the shades grew blacker, the rain fell heavier, pouring upon the pulpy ground and into the ditches with a sound as of dropping corn.

"Yuzka! have you done for to-day?" she cried to Boryna's daughter, who had been cutting along with Hanka and Kuba.

"Yes, we have. Time to go home: the weather is frightful, and I am wet through. Are you going too?"

"Aye. It would soon be so dark that we could not find our way. The rest must stand over till to-morrow.—Oh, your cabbages are splendid!" she exclaimed, leaning over towards them, and getting a glimpse of the heaps that loomed through the mist.

"Yours are very good too, and your turnips far larger than ours."

"Ah, they were planted from a new kind of seed, brought from Warsaw by his Reverence."

"Yagna!"—it was Yuzka's voice, calling again to her out of the fog—"do you know, Valek, Joseph's son, is sending people to-morrow to propose to Mary Pociotek?"

"What, that little girl? Is she not too young? Only last year she was herding kine, I think."

"Yes, she is old enough. Besides, she has so many acres that the lads are in haste to marry her."

"You, too, Yuzka, they will be in haste to marry by and by."

"Unless your father takes another wife," shouted Yagustynka from the third field.

"What do you mean?" said Hanka, in a tone of alarm. "He buried her mother only last spring."

"What does that matter to a man? Every one is even as a swine; however full, always ready to thrust his snout into a fresh trough. Ho, ho! one is not quite cold, nay, not yet dead, and the goodman is after another.—They are dogs, all of them. What about Sikora? He took a second wife only three weeks after burying his first."

"True: but then he was left with five little ones."

"As you say. But only a fool can believe he married for

their sake. For his own!—He was fain to share his blanket with someone."

"But," put in Yuzka, with great energy, "that we would not let Father do. Never!"

"Silly baby that you are! The land is your father's own; and so is his will."

"Yet his children too ought to be considered; they have their rights," Hanka rejoined.

"Better to leap into the deep than cumber another man's wagon," Yagustynka muttered.

Yagna, who had taken no part in this talk, smiled to herself as she carried the cabbages. She was reminded of what had happened at the fair.

As soon as the wagon was full, Simon made for the road.

"May God be with you!" Yagna then cried to her neighbours.

"And with you! We are coming directly. . . . Yagna, you'll come to us to pluck off the leaves, won't you?"

"Tell me when, and I'll be there."

"The boys have arranged for music at the Klembas' next Sunday: do you know?"

"I know, Yuzka, I know."

"If you meet Antek," Hanka asked, "pray tell him to hurry. We are waiting."

"All right."

She ran fast to catch the cart, for Simon had started, and could be heard swearing at the horse. The cart had stuck in the mire of the soft peaty ground, and was over the axles in mud; so they both had to work and help the horse past the worst sloughs.

Neither spoke to the other. Simon led the horse, taking care not to let the cart upset, for the way was everywhere full of deep holes. Yagna put her shoulder to the cart behind, considering all the while how she should dress when she went for the leaf-plucking to the Borynas.

It was so dark that the horse was all but invisible. The rain had abated a little, but the fog hung heavy and damp, and the wind blew and whistled above them, lashing the trees on the embankment which they were now going up.

It was a hard ascent, the ground being both steep and slippery.

"The cart is too full for one horse!" exclaimed a voice on the embankment.

"Is that you, Antek?"

"Surely."

"Then be quick; Hanka is expecting you.—But give us a helping hand now."

"Wait awhile: I must get down first.—It is so dark that you can't see anything."

They were up the embankment in no time, for the helping hand had pushed so powerfully that the horse scrambled up at once, and only came to a halt at the top.

"Thanks most heartily," she said; "but, good God! you *are* strong!"

And she stretched out her hand to shake his.

They were mute. The cart went on before them, while they walked on, side by side, unable to find words, and both of them strangely agitated.

"Are you going back?" she asked in a low whisper.

"I shall only go with you as far as the mill, Yagna; the water has made a nasty hole there."

"Very dark, isn't it?" she said.

"Are you afraid, Yagna?" he murmured, drawing closer.

"Why should I be?"

They were mute again, walking on shoulder to shoulder, side touching side.

"How bright your eyes shine! . . . Like a wolf's."

"Will you come to the Klembas' on Sunday for the music?"

"Will Mother allow me?"

"Do come, Yagna, do come!" he entreated her, in a strangled husky voice.

"Is it your wish?" she asked him softly, looking into his eyes.

"Why, Lord! 'twas I ordered the fiddler from Vola, only for you; and only for you did I beg Klemba to let us have his cabin." He spoke in a low tone; his face was so close to hers, and his breath came so quick, that she drew back a little, quivering all over with emotion.

"Go now—they are waiting for you—someone may see us.—Go!"

"Will you come?"

"I will—I will," she repeated, turning to look at him as he went away: but the fog had swallowed him up, and she only heard his feet, as they squashed away through the thick slush.

Then an irrepressible shiver seized her; and yet it was a fiery blast that went through her heart and brain. She knew not what it was that had come upon her: her eyes were full of flames; her breath failed her; she could not still the passionate throbbing of her heart. Instinctively she stretched forth her arms as for an embrace: then stiffened herself, taken with so wild a fit of sudden shuddering that she could have cried out aloud. But she reached the wagon and, catching hold, gave it a forward push with great though needless violence. The cart creaked and lurched over, so that several cabbages fell out into the mud. But still she saw before her that face, and ah! those eyes, so bright, so full of ardent craving!

"He is not a man, he's a whirlwind," she mused blankly. "Can there be such another in the whole world?"

She came back to her senses with the noise of the mill they were passing, and with the roar of the water pouring over the wheel and under the sluices; for those, owing to the high level of the water, had been thrown open; with a noisy rush the stream rolled down, breaking up into volumes of yeast-like foam that formed long white streaks on the broad expanse of the river.

At the miller's house, just by the roadside, a lamp had been lit and placed on a table, whence it could be seen through the curtained windows.

"They really have a lamp, just as at his Reverence's or at some manor-house!"

"For are they not rich folk?" said Simon. "They have

more land than Boryna himself; they put their money out at interest; and how they cheat us when they grind our wheat!"

"They live like big landowners. . . . It is well for such as they. . . . They strut about the rooms, they loll upon the sofas, and eat dainty food, and make others work for them." So thought his sister, but without envious feelings, nor paying any heed to what Simon went on saying; who, usually taciturn, now held forth on this subject at interminable length.

At last they arrived. In their bright warm cabin, a fire was blazing merrily on the hearth. Andrew was peeling potatoes, and their mother preparing supper.

Close to the fire sat a hoary-headed old man.

"Is all the work over, Yagna?"

"Only about three sheets full are still to be cut."

She went into the inner room to change, and was back again at once, getting things ready for the meal, all the time keenly and curiously observant of the old man, who sat profoundly silent, looking into the fire, while his lips moved and his rosary passed through his fingers, bead by bead. When they sat down to the meal, the old dame placed a spoon for him, and asked him to eat with them.

"Remain ye with God: I go," he answered. "But I shall look in here again, and perchance make a longer stay at Lipka."

Kneeling down in the centre of the room, he bent before the holy images, crossed himself, and walked out.

"Who is that?" Yagna asked.

"A saintly pilgrim. He comes from the Sepulchre of Jesus. This many a year have I known him. He has been here more than once, and brought me holy things from afar. . . . About three years since . . ."

She was interrupted by the entrance of Ambrose, who, after the usual greetings, took a seat by the fire.

"It is so cold and wet that even my wooden leg feels numb!"

"Why wander so, in such weather, and in the night too?"

Dominikova grumbled. "You had far better have stayed at home and said your prayers."

"At home I was a-weary; so, coming out to see a girl or two, I came first of all to you, Yagna!"

"Death is the name of the only girl for you."

"Oh, *she!* she has forgotten me quite; she prefers dancing with the young."

"What do you mean?" Dominikova asked.

"That his Reverence has just carried the Holy Viaticum to Bartek over the water."

"Why, he was quite well when I saw him but now at the fair!"

"He has been so savagely cudgelled by his son-in-law that his liver was ruptured."

"When? and on what account?"

"On account of the land, of course. They have been at odds these six months, and to-day at noon they settled the matter."

"Why," Yagna cried, "is there no judgment of the Lord upon such murderers?"

"It will come," her mother replied sternly, raising her eyes to the holy images.

"Yes, but it will not bring the dead to life," Ambrose muttered.

"Sit down, and share our board."

"I have naught against that. I still can get through a dish—if only large enough."

"You think of nothing but jesting and drollery."

"I have nought else in the wide world: why should I care!"

They seated themselves round the bench on which the two dishes—potatoes and sour milk—had been put, and set to eating with the usual deliberation and taciturnity, while Andrew saw to the pots' being abundantly supplied. Only Ambrose now and again said something funny, at which he himself was the first to laugh.

"Is his Reverence at home?" Dominikova asked towards the end of the meal.

"Where else, in such weather? Yes, at home, poring over books like a Jew."

"A learned, a most learned man!"

"And so good! The best man in the world," Yagna chimed in.

"Ah, yes. No harm in him. . . . Takes care of himself, and hurts nobody."

"That's not the way to speak, Ambrose!"

They had done. Yagna had gone with her mother to where the distaffs were fixed in front of the fire-place, while her brothers, as was their custom, cleared away and washed and set things in order. Dominikova had always ruled her sons with iron sway, and brought them up to do the duties of girls, that Yagna's beautiful hands might not grow coarse.

Ambrose lit his pipe, puffed up the chimney, and poked the embers, while adding some faggots, with furtive glances at the womanfolk. He was pondering over something and settling how to begin.

"I fancy you must have had a proposal or two."

"More."

"Naturally. Yagna is as pretty as a picture. His Reverence says there is none so pretty in the whole village."

"Yagna blushed scarlet with delight.

"Did he say so?" quoth the old dame. "May the Lord grant him health! I have long, long been getting money together for a votive mass: I will have one sung directly."

"There's somebody that would like to send you a proposal; but he is somewhat shy."

"A farm-hand?" Dominikova inquired, turning the spindle swiftly, till it fluttered about the floor.

"A man with a household under him. Comes of a good stock, but is a widower."

"What, nurse another's children? Not I."

"Fear nothing, Yagna; they are all well out of leading-strings."

"Young as she is, why should she accept an old man? Let her wait for a young one, if any such should come."

"Oh, there are plenty. No lack of young men, no! Lads as straight as arrows, smoking cigarettes, dancing in the tavern, swallowing drams of vodka, and with a keen eye for any girl that has a few acres and a bit of money. Wretched husbandmen, though, who rise at noonday, and in the afternoon carry dung in a wheelbarrow, and till the land with a hoe!"

"I will not let my Yagna stoop to any such!"

"They say you are the wisest of us all; and they say true."

"On the other hand—small delight can an old man give a young girl."

"She may find young ones to delight her—not a few."

She eyed him severely. "So reverend in years, yet so careless in talk!"

A pause ensued.

"He's an honourable elder, and not greedy of other folk's money."

"No, no! naught but sin can come of it!"

"Well, but he might make a marriage settlement," he continued, now quite serious, and knocking the ashes out of his pipe.

The reply, when it came, was given with hesitation.

"Yagna has enough of her own."

"He would give more than what he received; certainly more."

"What's that you say?"

"What I know. Neither the wind nor my fancy has taught it me: I come here in another's name."

Silence again. The old housewife took a long time to straighten the tangled flax on the distaff; then, wetting her left thumb and finger, she drew out the long fibres, while her right set the spindle whirling, flapping and whirring along the floor like a top.

"Well then, shall he send her his friends with vodka?"

"He? Who?"

"Know you not? He that dwells over there!" And Ambrose pointed to the lights in Boryna's hut, twinkling across the pond.

"His family are grown up: they will oppose it. Besides, they have a right to their portions."

"But he can always make a settlement with what is his own! He is a good man, and no indifferent farmer; religious into the bargain. And hale! Lord, I have seen the man heave more than two bushels of rye in a sack on to his shoulders. Let your Yagna wish for anything in the world except pigeon's milk, and she will get it. And then, the lad Andrew is next year to be a conscript. Now, Boryna knows all about official matters, and whom to apply to, and may be of great use."

"But how do you, Yagna, look upon this?"

"Indifferently.—If you say: 'Marry him' I will. It is for you, not for me, to decide." She spoke very low, her forehead touching her distaff, while, looking vacantly into the fire, she listened as the faggots crackled merrily.

"Well?" Ambrose queried, rising from his seat.

"Let his friends come"; the words dropped one by one from the old dame's lips. "A betrothal is not a wedding yet."

Ambrose crossed himself and went out, making straight for Boryna's cabin.

Yagna was sitting dumb and motionless.

"Yagna dearest, what do you say to this?"

"Naught whatever; it is all the same to me. If you like, I marry Boryna; if not, I stay with you. . . . By your side, I am very well off."

Her mother spoke in subdued tones as she went on spinning:

"I would fain do all for the best, my dear. True, he is old, but strong and hearty still. And, besides, he will treat you courteously, not as other peasants might do. You will be the mistress and the head of his house. Also, when he makes the settlement, I shall arrange matters so that the land he will leave to us will touch ours. . . . And then, were the amount only six acres—think of it, Yagna! six acres more!—And then remember: you must marry, you *must!* Why should the tongues of all the village gossips wag to defame you? . . . We should have to kill the pig . . ." Here she broke off, and went on to settle other matters within herself; for Yagna was spinning mechanically, as if she had heard nothing said.

Was she, she mused, unhappy at her mother's? She did what she liked; no one ever said a cross word to her. Acres, settlement, possessions, nay, even a husband—what did she care for them all? Were the lads who sought her few in number? Had she a mind, she could bring them all to propose to her the same evening. . . . Her mind was little by little being made up, as was the flaxen thread she span; and as that thread turned in one direction only, so she determined on one thing—to marry Boryna, if her mother cared for the marriage.—Yes; she liked him better than the rest: had he not bought her a ribbon and a kerchief?—True; yet Antek, and others as well, if they owned Boryna's money, would do as much for her.—No, no: let her mother choose, whose head was good at such things: her own was not.

She looked towards the window, where the withered and blackened dahlia bushes were tapping, lashed by the gale. By and by she forgot them, forgot everything, forgot her very self, and fell into a state of beatific inertness like that which now held the earth around her in those deathly quiet nights of autumn. For Yagna's soul was even as that earth; as that earth, it had its abysses, dreamy, chaotic, known to none. Vast it was, but unconscious of its own vastness; mighty, yet without either will or desire or longing—inanimate, yet immortal; like that earth, too, swept by every blast that took hold of her, and seized upon her, and did with her whatsoever it listed. . . . And likewise, in the springtime, the warm sun would awake her, and flood her with life, and fill her with the quivering flame of desire and love; and like the earth, her soul would conceive—it could do naught else; would live and sing, rule, create, and annihilate its creations—it could do naught else; it would exist —it could not but exist! Such was that hallowed earth; such was the soul of Yagna, like unto that same earth.

Long did she sit thus, mute: only those eyes of hers were glittering as still waters at noon in spring, or as gleam the stars.

Suddenly she awoke from her reverie: someone had opened the front door. It was Yuzka, who rushed breathless into the room.

Shaking the water out of her clogs, she said: "Yagna, we have the leaf-plucking to-morrow: will you come?"

"Of course."

"We shall do the work in the big room. Ambrose is sitting there now with father, so I made shift to slip out and let you know. There will be Ulisia, and Mary, and Vitka, and all the other Pociotek girls. Lads will be there too. Peter has promised to come and bring his fiddle."

"Peter? Who is that?"

"The son of Michael who dwells beyond the Voyt's house. He that returned from the army when potato-digging began, and talks so queerly now, one can scarce understand what he says." [1]

After chattering on in this way, she ran off home.

Again the room was plunged in silence.

The raindrops pattered on the window-panes, like handfuls of sand thrown upon them. The wind roared and played about the garden, or blew down the chimney, till the brands on the hearthstone were scattered about, and whiffs of smoke came into the room. But the spindles never ceased from whirring about the floor.

Thus the long evening dragged on tediously, until Yagna's mother began to sing in a faint, quavering voice:

> "May all that we this day have done . . . ";

Yagna and her brothers taking up the hymn in so high-pitched a key that the fowls roosting in the passage clucked and cackled in chorus.

[1] Four years in the Russian army, often in the very depths of Russia, were wont to make havoc with a Polish peasant's mother-tongue.—*Translator's Note.*

CHAPTER VII

THE next day was as rainy and dreary as the one before.

Every now and then, someone would come out of a hut to peer anxiously into a mist-blurred world, and see if it was clearing up a little. And nothing met the eye but the slate-coloured clouds, so low that they touched the very tree-tops. And the rain rained on.

The folk were cooped up in the cabins, and getting out of sorts. One or two went out through the mud and rain to a neighbour's, lamenting that So-and-so had left his cattle-litter in the forest, not having been able to remove it; that another had not yet brought in his firewood; that many, almost all, had cabbages in the ground still, and could not now go to cut them, because the pond had risen so much during the night that the sluices had been perforce opened, and the water let out into the river; which consequently had swollen very greatly and the meadows were flooded, and all the cabbage plantations like sombre islands amid the drab and foaming swirl.

Nor had Dominikova been able to get home the cabbages she had afield.

Ever since morning, Yagna was feeling greatly upset, heaving sighs of vexation as she went from corner to corner, and looked out of the window at the dahlia bushes, now beaten to the ground by the flood, and at the whole dripping landscape.

"Good Lord, how weary I am!" she said, impatiently awaiting the close of day and the start for Boryna's cabin. The hours crawled by, like an old man trudging in the mud—so sluggishly, so wearily, so drearily, that it became intolerable. She grew very restless, and was continually scolding her brothers, and flinging about such articles as she happened to find at hand. Withal, her head began to ache, and she had to put a warm oatmeal poultice, sprinkled with vinegar, on the top of her head, before it passed off. But, though now better, she felt completely out of gear; her work fell from her hands, and she many a time cast her eyes upon that surging pond which, like some huge bird, spread out ponderous wings, and flapped them, and struggled up, foaming, till the water rose and splashed all over the road—and all but soared into the air.

Dominikova had been out since the morning, called away to attend a woman in child-bed at the farther end of the village; for she knew a good deal about medicine, and how to heal various ailments.

So then Yagna was feeling very ill at ease. She longed to go out of doors and see someone; but whenever she tied her apron over her head and peered out beyond the threshold at the mire and the downpour, her desire vanished away. At last, knowing not what to do with herself, she opened her chest and took out all her holiday apparel, which she spread upon the beds, till the room glowed crimson with striped skirts and jackets and aprons. But that day she cared nothing for any of them. At all those her possessions she gazed with tired indifferent eyes; nevertheless, she drew Boryna's gifts—the kerchief and the ribbon—from the bottom of the chest, and adorning herself with them, took a look at the glass.

"They will do. I shall put them on this evening," she decided; but took them off again hurriedly, for someone was coming to the hut, creeping along by the fence.

This was no other than Matthew. Yagna cried out in astonishment as he came in: the very man on whose account the village folk had talked most against her as having met him by night in the orchard and elsewhere many a time. He was a man rather beyond the prime of life, being well over thirty; still a bachelor, for he did not care to marry, having sisters at home (or rather, according to Yagustynka's malicious tongue, because lasses and neighbours' wives were very much to his liking); a tall fellow, strong as an oak, very sure of himself, and consequently so proud and headstrong that he was feared by almost everyone. And he could—what could he not do?—play the flute, construct a wagon, build a hut, arrange a stove; and whatever he did, he did so well that his hands were always full of work. Never of money, though: however much he earned, he would get rid of it directly, drinking, standing drinks, and lending to his friends. He was called "Dove," though in his eyes and his fiery nature he had much more of the hawk.

"Matthew!"

"Yes, 'tis I, Yagna!"

He seized both her hands, and riveted his eyes on hers with a glance of such passionate eagerness that she turned red, and looked uneasily towards the door.

"You have been away these six months," she stammered.

"Six, and twenty-three days besides, is the true reckoning." He did not drop her hand.

"I shall get a light!" she cried; for it was really getting dark, and she wanted to free her hands.

"Give me a greeting, Yagna!" he begged, in a whisper, and tried to put his arm round her waist. She slipped away, and ran to the fire-place to kindle a light, fearing lest her mother should find her in the dark with Matthew. He, however, was too quick, caught her, squeezed her close, and set to kissing her with wild impetuosity.

She struggled like a snared bird, but could not free herself from the ravenous creature that hugged her till her ribs cracked and showered upon her such mad kisses that she grew faint; a veil dimmed her eyes, and she could not breathe.

"Matthew, good Matthew, please let me go!"

"Yet awhile, Yagna, yet again . . . for I am frantic!" And he kissed till the girl drooped and sank limp in his arms, weak as water. But at that moment he heard steps in the passage; so he let her go, lit a hand-lamp at the fire-place, and rolled a cigarette, looking the while at Yagna with eyes that sparkled with delight.

Andrew came in, blew the fire on the hearth into a blaze, and pottered about the room; so they said but little, those two, whilst exchanging hot glances of hungry, starving desire all the time.

A few minutes later, Dominikova came in. She must have been vexed at something or other, for she began by rating Simon soundly in the passage. Seeing Matthew, she darted a fierce look at him, paid no heed to his greeting, and went into the bedroom to change her dress.

"Go away," Yagna begged, "or mother will curse you when she comes."

But he only implored her to come out and meet him.

Dominikova entered. "You . . . you! Back again?" she asked, as if she had not seen him before.

"Yes, back again, Mother," he answered gently, trying to kiss her hand.

"Am I a cur, that you call me mother?" she snarled, snatching her hand away angrily. "Why do you come? Once for all, I have said you are not wanted here."

"I come, not for you, but for Yagna," he answered, with a defiant air: he was losing his temper.

"You're to drop Yagna for good, I say! Drop her! Folks shall not again defame her on your account! . . . Off, and out of my sight, you . . . !"

"Why croak so loud? All the village will hear!"

"Let them hear! Let them come! Let them know that you are sticking to Yagna as a burr sticks to a dog's tail—that we need an ovenrake to drive you from us!"

"Oh, that you were a man! How you would smart for this!"

"Try then, hound that you are! Just try, you ruffian, you bully!" And with those words she grasped the poker.

This brought the scene to an end. Matthew spat furiously on the ground and went out instantly, slamming the door. For how could he make a laughing-stock of himself by coming to blows with a woman?

Thereupon the beldame turned to Yagna, to vent her fury on her. With what upbraidings did she fall upon the girl, and discharge her soul of the gall she was bursting with! At first Yagna sat dumbstruck and petrified with dismay; but soon her mother's bitter words stung her to the quick. She hid her face in the bed she was sitting by, and burst into tears and lamentations. She was cut to the heart. . . . What wrong had she done? . . . She had not even asked him in: he had come by himself. . . . Mother had reminded her of last spring. . . . Well . . . he had met her at the stile. . . . How could she get away from so impetuous a fire-drake, when a fit of faintness came over her so? . . . And after that . . . how could she keep him off? Impossible! . . . It was always the case with her: when a man looked deep into her eyes, or embraced her with a powerful hug . . . then all within her trembled, and her strength forsook her, and her inwards swooned away, and she knew nothing more. Was she in any wise to blame for this?

These complaints she uttered in a choking voice, between bursts of tears; and at last her mother, softening towards her, wiped her face and eyes with tender care, and stroked her tresses, and soothed her.

"Come, come, Yagna; be calm: do not weep. Why, your eyes will look like a rabbit's: and how will you be able to go to Boryna's then?"

"Is't time to go now?" she asked after a while, a little comforted.

"It is.—Now dress and array yourself.—There will be many there, and even Boryna will notice you."

Yagna instantly rose and prepared to deck herself out.

"Shall I boil some milk for you?"

"I have no mind at all to eat, Mother dear."

"Simon! you hulking oaf! Warming yourself at the fire, indeed—and the kine gnawing at the empty mangers!" she cried, exhaling the last of her anger on the lad, who fled in bodily fear.

"'Tis my mind," she remarked, helping Yagna dress, "that the blacksmith has been reconciled with Boryna: I met him leading a calf home from the old man's farm.—A pity! 'twas worth fifteen roubles at least. And yet it may be as well that they agree together; for the smith has a dangerous tongue, and knows the law besides. . . ." She stepped back, and looked lovingly at her daughter. "Alas! they have let that thief Koziol out of jail already; and now we shall have to watch, and lock every door well."

Yagna set off; but for some distance on her way she heard her mother inveighing against Andrew for leaving the swine out of their sties, and letting the fowls roost in the trees.

Many people were already at Boryna's when she arrived.

The fire was leaping up the chimney, lighting the big room, making the glazed picture-frames glisten, and giving a semblance of motion to the many globes made of coloured wafers that dangled from the grimy, smoke-blackened rafters. In the middle there lay a heap of cabbages, round which, in a wide semicircle, with faces turned towards the hearth, a good many girls and some women of maturer age sat side by side, stripping the cabbages of their outer and withered leaves, and throwing them on to a great sheet that was spread out under the window.

Having warmed her hands at the fire, Yagna took her clogs off, and at once sat down to work at the end of the row, next to old Yagustynka.

The room soon grew noisier, more men and women coming in: some of the former, together with Kuba, helping to bring the cabbages in from the barn, but for the most part only smoking cigarettes and grinning at the lasses, or cracking jokes together.

Yuzka, though hardly in her teens as yet, presided over the work and the fun; for old Boryna had not come home, and Hanka was as usual flitting about everywhere like a moth.

"Why, the room glows like a field of red poppies!" exclaimed Antek, who, having rolled several barrels into the passage, had now set the cabbage-cutter by the fire, but a little on one side.

"Bah! they are dressed up as though for a wedding!" remarked an elderly woman.

tongues waxed bold, and the work went on swifter and swifter. The knives rattled upon the stalks, the cabbages fell into the sheet like a running fire of cannon-balls: every moment the heap rose higher. Antek was using the cabbage-cutter over a big barrel rolled close to the fire—undressed, save for his shirt and the striped drawers that he wore, flushed, dishevelled, streaming with perspiration, and yet so handsome that Yagna feasted her eyes on his picturesque form. From time to time he paused to take breath; and then he would look at her, and she would cast her eyes down and blush. This, however, was noticed by none save Yagustynka, who pretended to have seen nothing, whilst taking thought how best to spread the news about the village.

"They say Martianna is confined," Klembova said.

"That's no news, but a yearly thing."

"The woman's an aurochs! But for the babies she has, she would certainly get a stroke!" Yagustynka grumbled, and would have gone on, had not the others rebuked her for talking of such things in the presence of girls.

"Fear not for them," she replied. "They know a good deal more than that already. In these days, you cannot speak to a goose-boy about the stork, but he will laugh in your face. No, no, it was otherwise of old times."

"Well, you at any rate knew everything when you were a cow-herd," said Vavrek's old wife, very gravely. "Have I forgotten all you did when tending cattle?"

"If you have not, then keep it to yourself!" cried Yagustynka, with wrathful asperity.

"I was then already married. Let me see: with Matthew? No, with Michael; Vavrek was my third," she muttered, not quite clear as to the date of the old hag's youthful frailties.

Here Nastusia, Matthew's sister, burst breathless into the room, crying out: "What, are you all sitting here, and know ye not what has befallen?"

Questioned on every side, and with every eye fixed on

her: "Why," she said, "the miller's horses have been stolen!"

"When?"

"But two minutes ago. Our Matthew has just heard of it from Yankel."

"Yankel always knows of this sort of things from the first—and perhaps a little before, too."

"They were taken out of the stables. The farm-servant went to the mill to get provender; and when he came back, the stable was bare, both of horses and harness! And the dog was found poisoned in its kennel."

"Winter is coming on, and strange things happen in winter."

"Because there is really no punishment at all for thieves. Why, what do they get? A warm prison cell, food in plenty, and so much to learn from their fellow-thieves that, when they get out, they know twice as much, and are twice as bad."

"Oh, but if anyone should steal my horses, and I got hold of him, I would kill him on the spot like a mad dog!" cried one of the farm-hands.

"Only fools look for justice in this world. Anyone who can, may right his own wrongs."

"Should such a one be caught by a great number of men and killed, these surely could not be punished: impossible to punish all of them!"

"I remember," said Vavrek's wife, "something in that way, done here amongst us. . . . I had then my second husband —no, let me see; Matthew was yet living then . . ."

Her reminiscences were cut short by the entrance of Boryna.

"Oh," he cried in a merry mood, "the noise of your chattering can be heard across the water!" and taking off his cap, he greeted each guest, one after another. Possibly he was already slightly elevated, being as red as a beetroot; and contrary to his custom, he unbuttoned his capote, and talked loud and long. He greatly wished to come over and sit by stretched fields and pine-forests and hamlets. One must go a hundred leagues, or perhaps a thousand, she thought. She was strangely drawn to put some questions to the man; but how could she? The folk would only laugh at her.

Rafal's son, who had just come back from the army, had brought his fiddle; and now, having tuned it, began to play one tune after another. Silence came over the room; only the rain was heard, pattering upon the panes, and the voices of the dogs whining outside.

He played and played on, ever some new tune, drawing his bow across the strings, and the melody seemed to come forth by itself at its caressing touch. First he played religious tunes, as though in honour of the pilgrim, who never took his eyes off the young man. Then came other and quite worldly airs; for instance, the one about "Johnny has gone to the wars," which the girls were used to sing in the fields so often; and he drew the notes out with such infinite sadness that an icy shudder ran down one's spine; and Yagna, who was sensitive to music as are but few, felt tears, one after another, trickling down her cheeks.

"Oh, do leave off!" Nastka called out. "You are making Yagna cry."

"No, no; I always feel tearful when there is music," Yagna whispered, covering her face with her apron.

But she could not help the tears that flowed against her will, called forth by the strange yearning which she felt within her—and for what? She knew not.

The young fellow went on playing; only the fiddle now poured out riotous Mazurs and such lively Obertas that the girls could scarce remain seated, but must perforce squeeze their restless quivering knees together to do so, while the boys stamped merrily and hummed the tunes, and the whole room was in a tumult of noise and laughter, and the very window-panes were shaking.

On a sudden, a dog in the passage set up a lamentable howl, a howl so piercing that on the spot the room became as still as death.

"What is that?"

Roch had dashed out so suddenly that he had narrowly missed falling over the cabbage-cutter.

"No great thing," Antek cried, after a look into the passage; "some lad has been squeezing a dog's tail in the doorway."

"Vitek's work, I make no doubt," Boryna said.

Yuzka defended the boy most earnestly: "What, Vitek cruel to a dog? Never!"

Roch now returned, very greatly agitated. He had probably let the dog loose, for it was heard outside, whining close to the fence.

"A dog, too, is God's creature," he said excitedly, "and it suffers when ill-treated, as does any man. Our Lord also had a dog of His own, and suffered no one to use it ill."

"What? The Lord Jesus had a dog, just as men have?" queried Yagustynka the doubter.

"I tell you that He had; and Burek was its name."

The statement was received with a chorus of exclamations: "Well-a-day!—How now? Can this be!" and so on.

Roch was silent for a while; then, raising his hoary head, covered with long hair save in front, where it was cut straight and short over the forehead, and fixing upon the fire those eyes out of which the colour seemed to have been washed by many a tear, he began to speak slowly, his beads slipping meanwhile through his fingers.

"In those far-off bygone times, when Jesus our Lord yet walked upon this earth, and ruled over the nations in His own Person, the thing of which I shall tell you came to pass.

"Now, Jesus was going to the local feast in the parish of Mstov. And there was no road thither, but the way was through desolate burning sands only; and the sun beat hot upon them, and the air was even as when a storm is nigh at hand.

"Nor was there any shade or shelter anywhere.

"Our Lord walked on patiently; but though He was not yet near the forest, His holy feet were quite numb with weary travel, and He felt exceeding great thirst. Therefore did he again and again stop to rest on some hillock upon the way: albeit the heat there was still greater, and there was not enough shadow from the few dry stalks of mullein for even a fowl of the air to find shelter.

"But when He had seated Himself, it was hard for Him, without air to breathe; for lo, immediately the Evil One—as a foul goshawk swooping down on some weary little bird—would swoop down, beating up the sand with his hoofs, and wallowing therein as would some unclean beast; and a cloud of sand arose, hiding all things from sight in darkness.

"Now Our Lord, although He neither could well breathe, nor indeed move (so dark it was), rose up and walked on, only laughing to scorn the foolish one, the fiend who would make Him lose His way, so that He might not be there at the local feast to save the sinful people.

"And Jesus walked and walked, until He came to the forest.

"There, in the shadow, He rested somewhat, and refreshed Himself with water, and with that which was in His scrip. . . . Then, breaking off a bough for a staff, He crossed Himself, and entered the forest.

"Now, that forest was most ancient and thick, with great fastnesses of deep mire, and matted tangles of undergrowth and dense brushwood, almost impervious even for a bird, wherein the Evil One himself surely did dwell. Yet Jesus entered thither.

"Whereupon, what did the fiend not do? He shook the forest, and howled, and broke in twain the great branches with the help of the blast, as his wicked attendant aiding him all it could; blowing the oak-trees down, tearing the branches off, and roaring through the forest like one mad!

"Moreover, it grew dark, blindingly dark, and on this side there was a hubbub, and on that side a din, and on the other a whirlwind. And round about Jesus there ran hellish imps, leaping, showing their long teeth, glaring and snarling, and all but clutching at Him with their claws. Only that they durst not do, for the awe they had of Christ's most sacred Person.

"But when our Lord grew weary of all those foolish hobgoblins, being in haste to arrive at the local feast, He made the sign of the Cross over them—and behold, all the evil spirits with their impish helpers straightway disappeared in the brushwood.

"And lo, there remained only one wild dog; for in those days the dog had not yet become the friend of man.

"This dog therefore fled not, but, running after our Lord, barked at Him; and following after, it tore at His capote, and snapped at His scrip, and would fain have seized the meat which was therein. . . . But our Lord, being merciful, and unwilling to harm any of His creatures, said unto it:

" 'Silly one, hungry one, behold! here is meat for thee!' And He threw it some, which He took from out of His scrip.

"But the dog waxed still more angry, and in its fury it bared its teeth and, snarling, attacked our Lord, and tore the hose which He was wearing.

" 'I gave bread unto thee; I harmed thee not: and yet thou tearest My garments, and barkest to no avail? Thou art foolish, thou little dog of mine, that thou knowest not thy Master! Because thou hast done this, shalt thou be the servant of man, and helpless without him evermore.'

"When our Lord had said this, speaking in a loud voice, the dog sat down on its hind quarters; and then, stupefied, with its tail between its legs, it went away into the wide world.

"Now, at the local feast, there were many, many people, thick as the blades of grass on the meadows.

"Only the church was empty. They were carousing in the taverns, and had set up a great fair in the church cloisters, with drinking and lechery, and sins against God, such as do happen even in our days.

"Our Lord arrived when High Mass was over. He saw the people agitated like the corn in the breeze, and running to and fro, some striking with whips, some pulling stakes out of the fences, and others seeking for stones; and the women were screaming and rushing to scramble over the hedges, or into their carts; and the children wept.

"They all were shouting aloud: 'Lo, a mad dog! a mad dog!'

"And through the waves of the people the dog sped on, for all made way for it to pass: so, with tongue lolling out, it darted straight towards the Lord Jesus.

"Our Lord feared it not, and He knew that it was the dog from the forest; and He doffed His capote, speaking unto the dog; and it straightway went no further.

" 'Come hither, Burek,' He said; 'here, by My side, thou shalt be safer than ever thou wast in the forest.'

"He covered it with His capote, and spread His hands out over it, and said:

" 'Kill it not, O men: for behold, it is a creature of God, wretched and hungry, hunted and without a master.'

"Howbeit the peasants began to cry aloud, murmuring, and striking with their staves upon the earth.

" 'It was a wild and savage beast; it had carried away many geese and lambs of theirs, and never ceased from doing evil. Nor did it reverence man at all, but snapped at him with its fangs, so that none could go abroad, unless he bore a stick. Wherefore it must needs be slain.'

"But Jesus waxed wroth, and cried:

" 'Let no one stir!—O ye drunkards, ye fear a dog, and ye fear not the Lord your God?'

"They then shrank back, for He had spoken with a mighty voice. And then He said further that they were evil-doers, who had come to gain the indulgence, and did but drink in the taverns, and offend God, and repented them not; men accursed, ungodly, thieves and torturers one of another; but they should not escape the judgments of God!

"And having ended these words, the Lord Jesus took up His staff, and made as if to depart.

"But the people now knew who He was, and knelt down before Him, and cried out and wept with great lamentations, saying: 'Abide with us, abide, O Lord Jesus! and we will be faithful unto Thee, we drunkards, we ungodly ones, we evil-doers—only abide with us! Punish us, smite us, but forsake us not, helpless orphans, a masterless people!'

And they wept so sore, and begged so earnestly, kissing His sacred hands and feet, that His heart softened towards them, and He remained the space of a few prayers, teaching and shriving and blessing them all.

"And when He departed from among them, He said: 'Hath the dog done any harm to you? Lo, it will henceforward be your servant, and watch over the geese and drive your sheep: and if one or another of you shall sleep, having drunk over much, it shall be the guardian of your little holdings, and your friend.

" 'Only do ye treat it with kindness, nor do it any wrong.'

"So Jesus went forth, and left them. And looking round, He saw Burek, sitting where He had stood by its side to defend it.

" 'Wilt thou come with Me, Burek, or abide here in thy foolishness?'

"And thereupon the dog rose up; and thenceforth it always followed Jesus, as quiet, as faithful, as watchful as the best of servants could be.

"And from that time forth, they were always together.

"And if at any time a famine came over the land, the dog would catch a small bird, or a gosling, or a lambkin; so that they both had wherewithal to live.

"Ofttimes also, when Jesus was tired, and rested Himself, Burek would drive away wicked men and evil beasts, and not let them hurt Jesus.

"But when it came to pass that the vile Jews and their cruel Pharisees seized our Lord to put Him to death, then Burek flew at them all, poor loving creature! and defended Him, using its teeth as it could.

"But Jesus, stooping beneath the Tree which He was bearing for His sacred Passion, said unto Burek:

" 'Thou canst do no good: and behold, their consciences will bite them deeper than thy teeth!'

"And when they hanged Him on the bitter Cross, Burek sat beside it, and did howl.

"Now, the next day, when all men had departed, and neither His blessed Mother, nor His holy Apostles were there, Burek alone abode by His side, and licked again and again the sacred dying feet of our Lord, pierced through with nails; and it howled, and howled, and howled.

"And when the third day rose, Jesus awoke from His swoon, and looked; and no one was nigh Him beside the Cross, save only Burek, whining pitifully, and fawning at His feet.

"Then did Christ Jesus, our most Holy Lord, look mercifully upon it in that hour, and say with His last dying breath:

" 'Come with me, Burek!

. . . .

"And the dog at that very instant did breathe its last, and follow its Lord!

"Amen.

"All this came to pass as I have said, O dearly beloved," Roch concluded, pleasantly; and, making the sign of the cross, he passed over to the other lodgings, where Hanka had prepared him a corner to sleep in; for he was very tired.

There was dead silence through the room for a time. All were pondering over that strange fantastic story. Some of the girls—Yagna, Yuzka, and Nastka amongst them—stealthily brushed their tears away; for their emotions had been strongly excited, both by the doom of Christ, and by the part played in it by the dog Burek. Also, the very fact that there had been a dog upon earth better and more faithful to our Lord than men were, gave them all much matter for reflection. Slowly, and at first under their breath, they began to make various comments upon so wonderful a Divine ordinance; when Yagustynka, who all the time had listened with great attention, lifted up her head, and said with a sneer:

"Fiddle-de-dee, fiddle-de-dee!—One fable and two make three! I'll tell you a far better tale: how a man made an ox.

"'Of old the steer,
Not the ox, was made;
But a man took a blade—
Lo, the ox is here!'

"My tale is at least as true as Roch's," she said, with a burst of laughter. Those about her laughed likewise, and presently the room was full of jokes, and funny sayings and tales of all sorts.

"Ah, there's nothing that Yagustynka does not know!"

"She has learned, she has learned; has she not buried three husbands?"

"Oh, yes: the first taught her in the morning with a whip; the second at noon with a strap; and the third in the evening with a cudgel!" Rafal cried.

"And a fourth would I take, but not you: too stupid a hobbledehoy for me!"

Here one of the young men observed: "As our Lord's dog could not do without men, so women cannot do without beating: the want of that is what makes Yagustynka so spiteful."

"You're a fool," she retorted, with a fierce snarl. "Just you take heed no one sees you, when you steal your father's corn for Yankel; let widows alone, they are beyond your understanding!" Everyone was silent, fearing lest she might, in a fit of anger, tell all she possibly might know. Indeed, she was a most stiff-necked woman, who held her own opinion on every matter, and would often utter such words as made men's flesh creep, and their hair stand on end. She had respect for no one, not even for the priest and the Church. His Reverence had more than once admonished her, but without effect: nay, she even talked about his rebukes in the village.

"Oh, without any priest we can all manage with God, if we are but honest folk!—Let him rather take more heed of his housekeeper: she is with child for the third time, and will soon be dropping it somewhere, as she did before."

Such was her character.

When they were about to separate, the Voyt came in with the Soltys, giving orders that the peasants should go next day to work at repairing the road by the mill: it had been damaged by the rains. No sooner had the Voyt come in than he exclaimed, stretching out both arms:

"Why, the old boy has invited all the prettiest girls in the village!"

And so he had: all were of the best stock, and robust and blooming,

The Voyt had a private talk with old Boryna, but no one could catch what they said. He withdrew, after a few words of banter with the lasses, having still half the village to summon for the morrow. They too departed soon after, it being late.

Boryna said farewell to each one in particular, and even saw the elder women to the gate.

Yagustynka, on leaving, raised her voice, and said:

"God bless you for your good cheer; but all was not as it might have been."

"Indeed?"

"You need someone to keep house for you, Matthias: without such a one, how can things go right?"

"What's to be done, friend? What's to be done? . . . She died, it was God's will . . ."

"Have we no girls here? Why, every Thursday they all wait for you to propose to one of them," she said, cunningly trying to draw him out. But Boryna only scratched his head and smiled, looking instinctively towards Yagna, who was going out.

Antek expected her exit; so he dressed quickly and slipped out first.

Yagna had to return alone: her companions all lived in the direstion of the mill.

"Yagna!" he whispered, coming suddenly out of a hedge-side.

She stopped, knew his voice, and was at once seized with emotion.

"I'll see you home, Yagna!"—He looked round; the night was black, starless. Above them, the wind roared, sweeping over the tree-tops.

His arm enclosed her waist in a tight grasp; and, one close to the other, they both vanished in the gloom.

CHAPTER VIII

IT was on the following day that the news of the marriage arranged between Boryna and Yagna burst upon the village of Lipka.

The Voyt had gone over to her with the proposal. His wife, whom he had severely forbidden to breathe a single word about the matter until he had come back with the answer, waited till evening to visit an acquaintance, on the pretext of borrowing some salt; and as she went away, she took her good friend apart, and whispered:

"Do you know what? Boryna has just sent a proposal to Yagna, daughter of Dominikova. But beware and tell no one, for my husband has forbidden me to speak of it at all."

"Can this be?" she gasped in amazement. "Should my tongue wag of such a thing about the village? . . . So old a man, taking a third wife! . . . And his children, what will they say? . . . Oh, what a world it is!"

No sooner had the Voyt's wife withdrawn than, tying her apron over her head, she hurried through the orchard to the Klembas', "just to borrow a bit of tow to scrub with."

"Have you heard? Boryna is to marry Yagna, daughter of Dominikova! He has but now sent messengers with his proposal."

"Impossible! What do you say? Nay; he has full-grown children, and is himself stricken in years."

"True, he is not young. But they will not refuse him for that. . . . A farmer so reputable, a man so rich!"

"Ah, but that Yagna! she that has had dalliance, and with more than one! To be the wife of the first farmer here! Is there any justice in the world, say? And meanwhile, so many a girl is remaining unwedded—my younger sister, for example!"

"Or my brother's widow. . . . Or the Kopzyva girls. . . . Or Nastka, and many another.—No, it is not seemly, 'tis not meet, not right; what think you?"

"She will be mightily puffed up, and strut about like a peacock, will she not?"

"Great offence of God there must be: be sure that neither the smith nor Boryna's children will suffer her as a stepmother."

"Alas, what can they do? The land is as much his own as his will is."

"By law, yes; but in justice, it belongs to them as well."

"My dear friend, justice is always for him who has the power to get it on his side."

They continued thus, complaining and inveighing against the world and all its deeds, and went their way. And with them the news spread throughout the hamlet.

The little work there was to do was not urgent; so the people were all at home, the roads being as quaggy as so many sloughs; and the possible marriage was discussed in every cabin. All were eagerly expectant of what would take place, They well knew how headstrong Boryna was, and that he would not be turned away from a course he had chosen for himself, even were his Reverence to dissuade him. They knew, too, the unyielding pride of Antek's nature.

Even those men who had been drafted to mend the mill-side road where the dam had burst, stopped in their work to talk of so momentous an occurrence.

Various opinions were set forth; and at last, old Klemba, an intelligent and respected farmer, gave the stern judgment:

"The whole village will be the worse for this!"

"Antek will not suffer it," someone said. "What, another mouth to feed?"

"That would make no difference. But the inheritance! There's the rub."

"There will surely have to be a marriage settlement."

"Yes; Dominikova is shrewd, and will manage that."

"She is a mother," Klemba put in, "and even a bitch will defend her own puppies."

Thus, all the afternoon, the people in the village were talking the matter over. Which was no wonder, the Boryna family being of the very best stock of husbandmen, and Matthias holding land which had from time immemorial belonged to his people, being also endowed with hereditary keenness of wit, as well as riches; so that everybody, willingly or not, had to take him into account.

To none of his children, however, not even to the smith, durst anyone tell the news: the rage it would cause might be so great as to result in a sound thrashing for the teller.

All then was quiet at Boryna's hut; more so, indeed, than usual. The rain had ceased since morning, and the sky was clear. Antek, along with Kuba and the womenfolk, had been sent to the forest at once after breakfast, in order to get some dry fuel, and see whether they could not rake together some supply of pine-needles.

Boryna himself had stayed at home. Since early morning, he had been curiously ill-humoured and strangely irritable, always on the look-out for someone who should bear the brunt of the impatience and nervousness which had seized upon him. He had beaten Vitek for omitting to spread straw beneath the cows, which consequently had spent the night with their sides deep in dung; had quarrelled with Antek, and scolded Hanka, because her little boy had dirtied himself while playing outside the house; and had even spoken harshly to Yuzka.

When he was at last alone with Yagustynka, engaged overnight to see to the cattle the next day, he no longer knew what to do with himself. Again and again did he call to mind what Ambrose had related of his reception by Dominikova. Nevertheless he felt uneasy, and doubtful of the old fellow, who was able to tell any lie to get a glass of vodka. So he prowled about the hut, looking, now from the window, now from the porch, in the direction of Yagna's dwelling; and as a beggar waits for alms, so he awaited the coming of the night.

Many and many a time did he long to be off to the Voyt's and urge the man to start sooner: nothwithstanding, he remained at home, restrained by the look in Yagustynka's eyes, half closed and expressive of sarcastic amusement, which were continually fixed upon him.

"That hag!" he said to himself; "her eyes are gimlets."

She meanwhile went about the house and passage with her distaff under her armpit, seeing to things here and there. She span till her spindle whirred in the air as it turned; then she wound up the thread, and went out to the geese, the swine, the byre, while Lapa, drowsily and heavily, followed her steps. She spoke not a word to the old man, though she well knew what it was that tormented him so, and even drove him to put up stakes round the walls for the winter sheathing that was to keep the house warm.

Now and then, however, she made halt in front of him; and at last she said: "You seem not to be getting on with your work to-day."

"Devil take it! no, I'm not."

"Oh!" she thought, as she went away; "the place will be a hell . . . a hell!—But the old man is right to marry—quite right. If he did not, his children would be sure to give him board and lodging—as mine have done for me! . . . Yes, I made over a good ten acres of the very best land to them. And here I am!" She spat angrily. "I must go out now to work, and lodge in another's dwelling!"

At last the old man, unable to stand it any longer, tossed his ax away and shouted: "Curse this work!"

"There's something that troubles your mind."

"There is, there is!"

"And yet you have no reason in the world to be troubled."

"Much you know of it!"

Yagustynka came and sat down close by the wall, pulled out a long thread, wound it on the spindle, and said, slowly and not without trepidation:

"Fear nothing. Dominikova has a good head, and Yagna is no fool."

"What have you said!" he cried out delighted, and sat down by her side.

"I have eyes to see."

There was a long pause, each awaiting what the other would say.

"Just invite me to your wedding; and I'll sing you such a Hop-song [1] as will bring about a christening in the house in nine months. . . ." So she began; but, seeing the old man scowl, she changed her tone.

"Matthias, you are doing just what you should do. Had I but sought out another husband when mine died, I should not now have to lodge in a house that is not my own. Oh, no! . . . But I was a simpleton, I trusted to my children: they were to board me. I made over all I had to them: and now?"

"But I," he answered in a hard voice, "will give up not one single bit of ground."

"Right.—I had to drag my cause from court to court: the few *zloty* that I had went all that way, yet they got me no justice. And here I am in my old age, degraded to a woman of all work!—Last Sunday I went to them, only just to see my old place once more, and the orchard I had planted myself; and my daughter-in-law beshrewed me, saying I had come to spy on her! To spy, good heavens! . . . I thought I should fall down dead.—I went to his Reverence, that he might rebuke them from the pulpit for those words; but he told me that our Lord would make me amends for the wrong they had done. Aye, aye! of course. For him that has nothing in the world, even God's grace is worth having; but I would far rather have property here on earth, and sleep my fill in a warm room and a feather-bed, and eat much butter and fat, and divert myself!"

She continued holding forth against everything in the world, and with such violence that Boryna left her, and sallied out to the Voyt's: for twilight was at hand.

[1] *Hop-song*—a very primitive sort of nuptial song.—*Translator's Note.*

"Well, are you starting yet?"

"This very minute: Simon will be here at once."

Simon appeared and all three went to the tavern, to toss off a dram and get a flask of rum for the proposal-offering. . . . Ambrose, who was there before them, joined them directly; but they could not drink long, for Matthias was urging them to make haste.

"I shall be waiting here for you. If they drink back, then bring them hither.—And speedily!" he added, calling after them as they went out.

They walked along the middle of the road, splashing through the mud. The twilight deepened, covering the land with its gossamer web of sober grey; and soon the village was no more, save for the cabin lights that began twinkling through the dusk, and the barking of the watchdogs in the farmyards.

"My fellow-messenger!" said the Voyt, after a time.

"Well?"

"Boryna's wedding will, I fancy, be a grand one.'

"That's as it may be," the other returned, in surly fashion; he was a taciturn man.

"It will, I tell you—I, the Voyt, a man whom you may believe. We shall make such a match of it that . . . Ha! ha!"

"The mare may prove restive, if so be the stallion prove not to her liking."

"That does not concern us in any wise."

"But his children—they will curse us, sure."

"All shall be well: I the Voyt tell you so."

And they walked into Dominikova's hut.

The room was lighted, and carefully swept; they were expected.

The messengers "praised God"; then, greeting in turn everyone present, took seats close to the fire-place, and opened the conversation.

"The weather is cold; there seems to be a frost at hand."

"Very likely; it is not springtime, nor near it!"

"Have you gathered in all the cabbages?"

"All but a few that we cannot get in just now," the old dame replied indifferently, casting her eyes on Yagna, who was near the window, making up skeins of spun flax, and who looked so comely that the Voyt, a man still in the golden time of life, cast an eager glance at her, before he said:

"As the ways are foul and miry, and the night-air is dank, I and Simon the Soltys here thought we would enter your dwelling on our way. And seeing that you have received us with a kind and friendly welcome, perchance, Mother, we may even drive a bargain with you."

"A bargain may be driven only when there is something about which to drive it."

"Spoken truly, Mother, but that we have found already in your house: livestock, and of the best."

"Well," she cried, in good humour, "let us bargain, then."

"We would fain, for instance, bargain for a heifer of yours."

"Oho! that will be no small thing, and ye shall not lead her away with the first rope at hand!"

"As to that, we have for her a hallowed silver cord, and such that none can break it, he be strong as ten.—Well, how much, Mother?" And he pulled the flask of rum out of his pocket.

"How much?—Hard to say! She is young, will be nineteen in spring: good and hard-working. She might yet remain a year or two with her dam."

"Years without offspring, Mother; barren years!"

"Ah," Simon whispered, "were she other than she is, she might have offspring, even should she stay with her dam!"

The Voyt gave vent to a loud laugh. The old woman's eyes flashed angrily, and she made answer on the spot:

"Seek another, then! Mine can wait."

"She can; but we can find nowhere another so beautiful, or of so good a breed."

"Then what do you say?"

"I who speak am the Voyt: so believe what I tell you."—He took out a glass, wiped it on the skirt of his capote, filled it with rum, and said gravely: "Pay good heed, Dominikova, to what I say now. I am in office. A bird on the bough may chirp and twitter, and is gone: my word is not thus.—Simon too: all here know who he is; no man of straw, but a husbandman, the father of a family, and our Soltys! Mark well, then, who we are that come to you, and with what intention; mark this well."

"I do so, Peter, and most carefully."

"Now you, being a wise woman, must therefore know that, sooner or later, Yagna will surely leave your house for her own, as the Lord hath ordained. Parents breed up their children, not for themselves, but for the public weal."

"Ah, Mother, 'tis true, 'tis true!

> "'You may pet her and guard and caress,
> But give her you must none the less;
> Aye, and him that shall take her you'll bless!'"

"The world is made so, and there is no changing it.—Now, Mother, shall we drink together?"

"How can I say? I will not force her.—Will you drink, Yagna?"

"I . . . I don't know," she stammered in a thin voice, turning her burning face to the window.

"The lass is docile," Simon put in, with gravity. "'A docile calf, beyond all doubt, thrives, sucks much milk, and waxes stout.'"

"Well, shall I pass it on to you, Mother?"

"Drink ye, by all means; but we do not yet know who it is proposes," Dominikova remarked, attentive to the rules of etiquette that required her not to seem to know until told by the messenger.

"Who?" he exclaimed. "Why, who but Boryna himself!" and he lifted his glass.

"What, an aged man! A widower!" she objected, as in duty bound.

"Aged? 'Tis a sin to say so! Aged? and but now he was accused."

"I know: only the child was not his."

"How could it be? A man of such repute, was he to put up with any but the very best?—Come, here's to you, Mother!"

"Fain would I drink; but he is a widower.—Old, he may soon be in Abraham's bosom: and what then? Her step-children would thrust her out."

Here Simon interposed. "Matthias," he growled, "said there must needs be a settlement."

"Of course before the wedding."

The Voyt, having filled another glass, turned with it to Yagna.

"Come, drink, Yagna, drink to us! The swain we propose you is strong as an oak: you'll be his lady, the keeper of his household, the first of all in the village! See, I drink to you, Yagna: do not be shamefaced!"

She flushed scarlet, and turned away; but finally, throwing her apron over her face, she tasted a little, and threw the rest on to the floor.

The glass then passed round to all. The old dame produced bread and salt, and lastly some dried and smoked sausages as a relish.

Several times in succession did they drink, and in a little their tongues were loosened. But Yagna had fled into the inner chamber, where, she knew not why, her tears burst forth, her sobs becoming audible through the partition. Her mother would have followed, but the Voyt kept her back.

"Even calves, when weaned from their dams, shed tears: 'tis common. She is not to go away, no, not to the next village even: and you will still enjoy each other's company. It is I, the Voyt, who say it: she shall come to no harm: believe me."

"Aye, but I always thought to have grandchildren for my consolation."

"Let not that trouble you. The first of them will be here before the harvest!"

"The future is known to the Lord alone, not to us sinners. We have drunk to her betrothal, and yet my heart is heavy, as if 'twere a burial."

"Nothing strange. An only daughter, she ought to be duly mourned over. . . . Yet a little more, to drive your grief away.—Ah, do you know, let us all go to the tavern. There Yagna's future husband awaits us, boiling over with fierce impatience."

"Shall we celebrate such an occasion in a tavern?"

"As our fathers of yore. I, the Voyt, have spoken."

Yagna and Dominikova put on their best dresses, and all started off. But the Voyt remarked how disappointed her brothers were looking. "Are the lads to remain, then?" he said. "It is their sister's engagement-day: some pleasure is due to them."

"Can we leave the house to the care of Providence?"

"Then take Agatha from the Klembas; she will see to the place."

"She has gone begging. We shall get someone on our way. Well, Simon and Andrew, come; but put your capotes on. Would you come in your shabby everyday clothes?—And if either of you gets tipsy . . . he will never forget it!—The kine have not yet been cared for, and ye must mash potatoes for the swine.—See ye to it."

"We will, Mother, we will!" they both exclaimed, trembling with fear, though they were both big lads, as high as a small pear-tree, such as are planted along the fields.

And so presently they went to the tavern.

The night was murky and as dark as pitch, as is usual enough during the autumn rains. The wind roared overhead, swaying the tree-tops till they nearly lashed the neighbouring hedges.

When they arrived, the tavern had a gloomy look. A pane had been broken in the window, and the gusts that entered made the tiny lamp which hung above the bar by a cord swing there to and fro like a golden flower.

Boryna rushed to welcome and embrace and hug them warmly, knowing that Yagna was already as good as his own.

"Our Lord hath said: 'Thou worm, take unto thee a wife, that thou, poor wretch, shouldst not suffer loneliness!' So Ambrose said, or bleated rather: he had been drinking for more than an hour, and was good for little, either in the talking or the walking line.

The Jew instantly set before them rum, sweetened vodka, and "essence"; also salt herrings, saffron-seasoned cakes, and others (very dainty) made with poppy-seed.

"Eat ye, drink ye, dearly beloved brethren, true Christians!" cried Ambrose, taking upon himself to invite the guests. "I had a wife once—but cannot at all remember now where—In France, I think—no, in Italy! No, not there—but now I am bereft and a widower. . . . I tell you: our ancients used to cry thus: 'Attention!' "

Here Boryna interrupted him. "Drink deep, friends! . . . And you, Peter, give the example!" And then he brought Yagna a whole *zloty's* worth of caramels, and put them into her hand. "Here you are, Yagna, they are very sweet: here you are!"

She made as if she were disinclined to take them. "They cost so much money," she said.

"Fear not, I can well afford it. . . . You will see later.—Oh, if pigeon's milk were to be bought for any money, I would buy some for you, dear! Oh, how happy you will be with me!" And, taking her round the waist, he pressed her to partake of all that was there. And she did: accepting all, however, as coolly and indifferently as if it were someone else's engagement-day. She only thought: "Will the old man give it me before the wedding, that coral necklace he told me of at the fair?"

And now they began to drink in earnest—rum and sweetened vodka alternately, and all talked at the same time. Even Dominikova was not a little flustered, and she chattered and held forth about many a matter, so that the Voyt wondered at the wisdom she displayed.

Her sons were likewise in their cups, for again and again either Ambrose or the Voyt urged them to take some more. "Toss off your glasses, boys, 'tis Yagna's engagement-day!"

"Yes, yes, we know," they answered, and wanted to kiss the old sexton's hand.

It was then that Dominikova took Boryna apart to have a straight talk with the man,

"Yagna is yours—yes, yours, Matthias!"

"Thanks, Mother, for your gift of her." He put his arm round her neck and embraced her.

"You promised to make her a settlement, I understand."

"Why need there be any? All I have is hers."

"In order that she may look her stepchildren in the face and laugh at their curses."

"Woe betide them, if they interfere! All is mine, all is Yagna's."

"Kindly said. Only note this: you are somewhat elderly. Besides, we all are mortal. And, you know:

"'Death none can refuse:
He takes all he can,
Now a lamb, now a man,
Not caring to choose!'"

"Oh, but I am hale—good for a score of years yet. Never you fear!"

"'Never-Fear was eaten by the wolves.'"

"Well, I am glad you speak out! Would you have me settle on her the three acres I have, close to Luke's field?"

"'A hungry dog will try even to catch a fly,' as they say; but we are not hungry. Yagusia is to inherit five acres, besides one of forest-land, from her father. Settle six acres on her, you: those six where you grew potatoes last summer—close to the road."

"My very best fields!"

"Yagna too is the pick of the village."

"She is, indeed: therefore I sent you my proposers. But, mercy on us! six acres! It is a whole farm!" He scratched his head in perplexity; for his heart was sore at the thought of giving up so much of his best land.

"My good friend, consider, like the intelligent man you are, and you will see that the settlement is only a protection mained there but Boryna and his messengers, with Ambrose and the blind beggar, all now drinking at one table.

Ambrose was very mellow indeed. He stood up in their midst, now singing, now shouting very loud.

"He was quite black—black as that pot! He aimed . . . but where did he hit me? where? . . . And I—I thrust my bayonet into him, and twisted it: I heard his inside gurgle! —So we halt—halt! And the commander himself arrives with more men.—Ah! the commander! 'Boys,' he says, 'boys!' "

" 'Attention!' " the old man cried, in a voice of thunder. And he stood stiffly erect, and stepped slowly backwards, his wooden leg stumping along the floor: "Drink to me, Peter! to me who am an orphan!" he bleated out; but when close to the wall, suddenly he whipped out of the place. But they could still hear the braying of his voice, raised in song outside.

Just then the miller entered the tavern: a big burly fellow, red-faced, dressed town-fashion, and with small keen eyes.

"Drink, lads, drink together!—Ho, ho! the Voyt, the Soltys, and Boryna!—Is it a wedding?"

"No, it is not.—Sir miller, take a drink with us," Boryna said.

And once more the vodka went round.

"Well, now to you all three thus together, I shall tell some news that will sober you in no time."

All stared at him vacantly.

"Not an hour since, the Squire sold the clearing of Vilche Doly!"

"The hound! the miscreant! What, sell a clearing that belongs to our village!" Boryna shouted, smashing a bottle on the floor in a fit of rage. "Sold it, has he? But there is law—law both for the Squire and for all of us!" Simon stammered; he was completely intoxicated.

"It's false! I, your Voyt, have spoken: believe me, it's false!"

"Sold it! Ha!—But we won't let anyone take it: as

there's a God in heaven, we won't!" Boryna growled, and he brought his fist down upon the table.

The miller left them, and they stayed there far into the night, taking counsel together, and breathing threats against the manor-folk.

CHAPTER IX

IT was shortly after Yagna's engagement had taken place; All Souls' Day had dawned.

Ever since morning, the church-bells of Lipka had tolled incessantly, slowly; their doleful and sorrowful notes, floating over the desolate fields, called the people together with deep-sounding voices of sadness on this day, which rose pallid and swaddled in fog, as far as the far-off horizon —where the earth and the sky met, no one knew where, in a vague unfathomed abyss of vacuity.

Now, as soon as the sun arose in the east, which still glowed red as copper molten and cooling, hosts of crows and daws had been coming thence, winging their flight from beyond the lurid clouds.

They flew very high; so high that neither the eye could well make them out, nor the ear catch distinctly the wild and melancholy harshness of their croaking, which sounded like weeping in the autumn night.

And from the belfry, the tolling sounded continually.

The deep notes of that doleful hymn rolled heavily through the thick nebulous air—rolled all over the country-side, and men and fields and villages seemed as one vast heart, throbbing to the dismal dirge.

And still the flocks of birds increased, even to the dismay and stupefaction of the people; for now they flew lower, ever in vaster multitudes, sprinkling the sky as with scattered specks of soot; and the dull flapping and croaking was now louder, more boisterous, more turbulent—like a storm that is drawing nigh. They swept in circles over the village: and as a heap of dead leaves the blast plays with, so they wheeled over the ploughed lands, floated down to the woods, hung above the skeleton poplar-trees, took possession of the lindens round about the church, and perched upon the trees in the burial-ground.

"A severe winter it will be," people said.

"Snow is going to fall—they are flying towards the woods."

They now approached the huts in still greater numbers; never before had so many been seen together. People looked at them, sighing, in fear of an evil omen, and some made on their brows the sign of the Cross, as a protection from the evil to come, and put on their garments to set out for church. And continually the tolling sounded with a dull roar; from the neighbouring villages the people were already coming to pray.

An all-pervading sense of desolation filled every soul; in every heart, there reigned a strange distressful silence: the stillness of mournful reminiscences, the recollections of those who had gone before, gone to lie beneath the drooping birch-trees, and the darkly looming crosses, that stood slantwise in the churchyard.

"O my Jesus! O my beloved Jesus!" they would murmur, and then raise up their ashen-grey faces, and fear no longer, plunging into the mystery of futurity: and they calmly went forward to present their offerings and to say their prayers for the dead.

The whole village was as though lost in a sea of grave and heart-stricken quietude: only the whining singsong of the *Dziads* at the churchdoor now and then broke the stillness.

At Boryna's, the silence was especially deep: though indeed it was of that hell which reigned amongst them, and was on the point of bursting forth.

His children knew all by that time.

The day before being Sunday, the first banns had been published from the pulpit. On Saturday, Boryna had gone with Yagna to town, where he had settled six acres of land upon her in the presence of a notary. He came back late, and with his face scratched. Being the worse for liquor, he had behaved disrespectfully to Yagna; but had only got acquainted with the strength of her arm and the sharpness of her nails.

On his return, he said no word to anyone, but went to bed as he was—in his boots and sheepskin coat; and when Yuzka next morning complained that he had soiled his feather-bed with mud:

"Let me alone, Yuzka, let me alone!" he answered her merrily. "Such a thing may happen sometimes, even to one who has not been drinking."

In the morning he had gone over to Yagna, and stayed all day: at home, dinner and supper waited for him in vain.

This day, too, he rose late, considerably after dawn, put on his best capote, ordered Vitek to smear his Sunday boots with grease and line them with fresh-cut straw, was shaved by Kuba, girt himself, and, taking his hat, slipped out through the fence, and was seen there no more that day.

Yuzka cried all the time. Antek was in the grip of tortures, even sharper and more agonizing, and could neither eat, nor sleep, nor busy himself in any way. He felt dazed as yet, and could not wholly realize what had come to pass. His face had grown sombre, but his eyes seemed larger, and flaming glassily—full of hardened tears, as it were. He had to clench his teeth lest he should cry out and curse aloud, and was continually walking about the cabin, or around it, or about the enclosure, or in the road; and on coming back, he would throw himself on a bench in the porch, and sit there motionless for hours, racked by sufferings that were ever growing more intolerable.

The house was dreary, and within it there continually resounded the sound of weeping, as sobs and sighs resound in a house wherein someone lies dead. The doors of the byre and the sties stood wide open, the cattle and swine wandered about at liberty in the orchard, some even looking in at the windows. No one attempted to interfere with them but old Lapa, who barked and tried to drive them in again, but unsuccessfully.

Sitting on his truckle-bed in the stable, Kuba was clean-

ing a gun, while Vitek, gazing at him in wondering awe, took care to keep a look-out on the yard, for fear someone might drop in.

"Oh, what a noise it made! Lord! I thought it was the Squire or the keeper shooting."

"Ah, yes. I had not shot for ever so long, and the charge I put in was too big: it roared like a cannon."

"Did you go in the evening at once?"

"Aye, to the manor lands close to the wood. The roe-bucks are fond of coming that way to crop the sprouting blades in the sown fields. It was very dark, and I had long to wait. Just at dawn, a buck came by. I was so well hidden that he was only five paces away from me. But I did not shoot. He was as big as an ox, and I knew I could not carry him off. So I spared him; and after the space of a few Paters, some does appeared. I chose the finest, and took aim. What a report there was! I had put in a heavy charge: it kicked so, my shoulder is one bruise still. And the doe fell; but she still kicked, and made such a fearful noise that I was afraid the keeper might hear, and I had to cut her throat."

Vitek was full of enthusiasm.

"And—did you leave her in the wood?"

"Where I left her, I left her: it's no business of yours. And if you say a single word about this to anyone . . . you'll see what I shall do to you!"

"I won't, if you forbid me; but may I not tell Yuzka?"

"The whole village would know directly. No.—But here is a five-kopek piece, for you to buy something with."

"Without that, I'd hold my tongue.—But, O dear, dear Kuba! take me with you some day!"

"Breakfast!" Yuzka was in front of the cabin, calling to them.

"Be easy, Vitek, I shall take you."

"And you'll let me shoot—once, only once?" he entreated.

"Silly one! think you they give gunpowder for nothing?"

"But I have money, Kuba, I have. Master gave me two

zloty for the last fair, and I was keeping them for the Memorial offering. But . . ."

"Very well; I shall teach you how to shoot," he whispered, patting the boy's head, and touched by his appeal.

Almost as soon as they had finished breakfast, they went together to church. Kuba limped along as fast as he could; but Vitek lagged a little behind: he was ashamed to have to go barefoot, for he had no boots.

"Is it right to go into the vestry without boots?" he queried in a low voice.

"You are foolish. Does our Lord consider a man's boots, not his prayers?"

"True; but are not boots more respectful?" he whispered sadly.

"Oh, you will get boots one of these days."

"That I shall! Let me but grow up to be a farm-hand, I shall directly go off to Warsaw and get a place in some stable. In the town, they all wear boots, don't they, Kuba?"

"They do.—Can you remember anything about Warsaw, Vitek?"

"Of course. I was five when Kozlova brought me here; so I recollect perfectly. . . . Yes, we went on foot to the station, and there I saw no end of glowing lights . . . and houses all one close to another, and as big as churches."

"Nonsense!" cried Kuba, disdainfully.

"But I remember quite well. I could not see the roofs, they were so high. Windows, too, to the very ground. Whole walls of windows! And everywhere bells were ringing continually."

"No wonder; there are so many churches there."

"Else whence could the ringing have come?"

And now they were silent, having entered the churchyard and begun to push their way through the dense throngs that filled all the space round the church, not being able to get in.

There the *Dziads* had formed a lane from the church to the road, crying out, screaming, uttering prayers, or asking alms, each in his own way; some were playing on fiddles, and droning out hymns in mournful voices; others on flageolets or concertinas; and all together causing such a racket as almost to make one deaf.

The vestry, too, was full of people: so full that they were sorely squeezed against the tables, where the organist and his son (the one who had been at school) were taking down the names given for the Memorial offerings.

Kuba got through the press, and rolled off a long list of names to the organist, who wrote them down, and received for each soul three kopeks, or as many eggs (in case one had no ready cash).

Vitek was not able to push forward so fast, for his bare feet were sorely trod upon, but he got on as well as he could, clutching the money in his hand. When, however, he found himself in front of the organist at the table, he felt suddenly overwhelmed and tongue-tied with confusion. What! only farmers and farmers' wives round him—almost all those of the village . . . ? Even the miller's wife was there, wearing a hat like the wife of the Squire!—And the blacksmith and the Voyt, with their dames—all giving the names of those whose souls they wished remembered; some as many as a score of them—all the family, and their fathers and forefathers.—And he . . . what name could he give? His own father, his mother—what names had they? Could he tell? For whom, then, should his offering be made? . . . "O my Jesus, my little Jesus!" he cried in his soul; but his mouth remained wide open, and he stood there like a witling. His heart was wrung with an agony of grief, he could hardly draw his breath, and he felt so faint that he was like to drop down as one dead. But he could not stay there; the crowd shoved him aside into a corner, beneath the holy water stoup: and, in order not to fall, he crouched down with his head against the tin basin, while tears gushed forth and fell, like the beads of some rosary of desolation. It was in vain that he tried to keep them back; he was so shaken, so unnerved in every limb, that he had not even the strength to clench his teeth and stand up. So he crept into a corner out of sight, and wept abundant tears—the bitter tears of a fatherless, motherless boy.

"Mother, O Mother!" something within him was crying, and tearing his heart to pieces. . . . He could not think why each of the other lads had his father and his mother, while he alone was without either—bereft—and how bereft—of both!

"Jesus, my Jesus!" he sobbed, crying out like a poor bird strangling in a snare. . . . It was then that Kuba came upon him and said:

"Vitek, have you given in your Memorial offering?"

"Not yet," he returned; and, suddenly drying his eyes, he forced his way back to the table. Yes: he would give names. Did it concern anyone that he had no parents he knew? If he had none, it was his own affair. If he was a foundling, a foundling let him be.—He therefore took heart, wiped his eyes, and boldly gave the names Josephine, Marianna, Anthony—the first that occurred to him.

He paid, took the change, and went with Kuba into the church to pray and hear the priest read the names of his dear departed!

A catafalque, bearing a coffin at its summit, had been raised in the centre of the church. Round it many tapers were burning, while the priest read aloud from the pulpit an interminable list of names. Now and then he stopped, and the whole congregation said the Paters, Aves, and Credos that should relieve the souls of the faithful departed.

Vitek knelt down by the side of Kuba; the latter took out a rosary, and counted thereon all the prayers which the priest had recommended. Vitek too recited a few prayers; but the monotonous sounds soon made him drowsy, and, worn out by the heat of the place and his recent fit of tears, he presently rested his head against Kuba and went to sleep.

. . . .

In the afternoon, all the Boryna family were present at the Vespers which were sung once a year in the churchyard mortuary chapel. Antek and his family, the blacksmith and his, Yuzka accompanied by Yagustynka, and Vitek, and Kuba dragging himself in the rear, had come, determined to make the most they could of All Souls' Day.

As a man shuts his weary eyelids, and plunges into dark unfathomable shadows, so evening was closing in; the wind sounded with a dreary voice, long drawn out, and wafted the odours of many a mouldering leaf, redolent with unpleasant effluvia.

The country-side was serene, with the strange and sombre calm of that anniversary of sadness. The crowds went about their way—as it were, in painful silence; their trampling boots echoed with dull dead sounds: the roadside trees waved their boughs restlessly, and swayed overhead with a sad sullen murmur.

In front of the lich-gate and about the graves along the wall, stood rows of barrels, and many a *Dziad* was close by. It was by this road that the people came along to the burial-ground. The twilight had already covered the world, sprinkling it with its ashen greyness, although there twinkled athwart its folds many a rustic lamp (fed with butter for oil!), with yellow flickering flame. Each one, on entering the churchyard, took from his wallet either bread, or cheese, or a piece of bacon or of sausage; or a skein of thread, or else a handful of combed flax; sometimes even a string of dried mushrooms. These they deposited piously in one of the barrels that stood open there; they formed offerings for the priest, for the sacristan Ambrose, for the organist—and, lastly, for the *Dziads*. Such as had no offerings in kind to give, put a few kopeks into the outstretched hands of the latter, whispering the names of the dead for whom they asked them to intercede.

About the lich-gate, then, there was a continuous cadence of names called out, and prayers, and chants, in broken and unequal rhythm. The people went on and soon disappeared, vanishing among the graves. Presently, like so many glow-worms, tiny lights began to shine and tremble in the dusky thickets and the dry grass.

Breaking the stillness, which, as it were, exhaled from out of the earth, prayers were everywhere audible, in low quavering tones of awe. Now and again there would come from some grave a heart-broken sigh; sometimes a thrilling lament would rise from the winding paths around the crosses; and then a sudden short shriek of despair would burst forth, rending the air like a flash of lightning; or the faint weeping of children would be heard among the murky bushes, like the chirping of unfledged birds in their nests.

From time to time, there would creep over the churchyard a dull and dreary silence, when only the trees were audible, murmuring ominously, as the sound of human miseries and sorrows and clamorous agony floated up to Heaven.

They went about the graves noiselessly, and terror-struck they stared into the dim and unknown distance.

"All must die!" they muttered, in tones of torpid palsy-stricken resignation, and went on further, to sit by the graves of their fathers, and either recite orisons, or remain motionless, in a reverie that deadened both love of life and fear of death—aye, and even abhorrence of pain. They were like trees, bowing low in the blast; and, like them, their souls quivered slumberously: dismayed, yet benumbed.

"O my Jesus! O merciful Lord! O Mary!"—such were the ejaculations which burst forth from their tormented souls. They raised their faces—now expressionless with grief—and fixed their hollow eyes on the crosses, and on those trees in drowsy yet perpetual motion: and falling on their knees at the feet of the crucified Christ, they laid before Him their fear-stricken hearts, and shed tears of resignation and self-surrender.

Kuba went with Vitek in the same direction; but when it became quite dark, the former crawled further on—away to the old burial-ground. There the forgotten ones lay—those whose very memory had perished long ago, with their days, and the times they lived in, and all the past. There, only ill-omened birds uttered hoarse croakings, and the bushes rustled mournfully near some cross of rotting wood that still remained standing here and there. In this forgotten nook lay side by side whole families, hamlets, generations: no one came there to pray, to shed tears, to light lamps any more. The gale alone blew fiercely through the boughs, tore off the last of their leaves, and tossed them away into the night, to be lost therein. And voices howled that were not voices; and shadows moved—but were they only shadows?—striking at random against the trees, as though they had been blinded birds, and seeming to moan and beg for pity!

Kuba took from his bosom several pieces of bread that he had put by. Kneeling down, he broke them, and threw the morsels about among the tombs.

"Food for you there is, O Christian soul!" he whispered, very earnestly. "I forget you not at eventide.—Food for you, O sufferer that was mortal!—Food for you!"

"And will they take it?" Vitek asked in terror.

"Beyond doubt!—Our priest forbids it.[1]—The others put the food into those barrels, and these poor creatures get nothing. But what? Shall the priest's and the *Dziads'* swine have to eat, and Christian ghosts stray starving!"

"Ah! will they come hither?"

"Yea, all who suffer the cleansing fires—all. Jesus lets them back to earth for to-day, to visit their people."

"To visit them!" Vitek repeated, shuddering.

"Fear not. On this day, nothing evil has any power to harm: the Memorial offerings have driven him away—him, the bad Angel! So have the lamps. And our Lord comes in person about the world, and He, the beloved Shepherd, goes counting how many souls are His yet, and choosing from amongst them."

"Oh, does our Lord Jesus come to the earth to-day?" Vitek said faintly, looking around.

[1] Because it was a superstition: a very old one, no doubt, come down from prehistoric times, and now all but dead in Poland, if not quite so. Mickiewicz's poem "Dziady" deals with something similar which he came across in Lithuania, about a century ago.—*Translator's Note.*

"Do you think to see Him? That only Saints can do—and persons greatly wronged."

"See, see, lights are there; and there are people too," Vitek cried out in alarm, and he pointed to a long row of graves close to the hedge.

"Ah, there lie those slain during our insurrection. Yes, my master lies there; aye, and my mother too."

They forced their way through the underwood, and knelt down by the graves. These had fallen in, and were so level with the rest of the ground that they could hardly be traced. They were marked by no crosses, overshadowed by no trees. Only barren sand was there, and a few dry stalks of mullein: all was stillness, oblivion, death.

Ambrose, together with Yagustynka and old Klemba, were kneeling beside those perishing graves. A few lamps glimmered, fixed in the sand; the winds made them wave and tremble, and carried away the supplications into the blackness of the night.

"Aye; there lies my mother," Kuba said, rather to himself than to the boy, who had crept close to him, chilled to the very marrow.

"Magdalena was her name. My father had land of his own: he served as coachman to the manor, but never drove out, save with the old Squire, and stallions to the coach! . . . After that, he died. . . . His uncle inherited the land, and I became swineherd to the manor. . . . Yes, Magdalena was my mother's, and Peter, my father's name: surname, Soha, and I bear it. . . . Then the Squire set to making me coachman, to drive with his stallions, as my father had done. . . . I was continually going to the chase, with Master and other gentlemen; and I learned to shoot pretty well myself; and the son of the Squire gave me a gun. . . .

"I remember perfectly. . . . When they all went out for the insurrection, they took me with them too. . . . I fought for a whole year: killed more than one Russian grey dog . . . more than two, even. . . . Then the Squire's son was shot in the belly. His bowels gushed out. He was my master, and a good man; so I took him on my shoulders and carried him away. . . . Later, he got off somewhere to a warm country, but first gave me a letter to take to his father. Well, I went. I was weary of all, dog-tired . . . got shot in the leg on my way, and it would not heal; for I was always out of doors, sleeping under the stars. . . . Then came snow, and a terrible frost:—I remember well! . . . So I got there . . . at night . . . and looked about for the place.—Oh, what a thunderstroke!—No more manor—no more barns—no more hedges, even. All had been burned down to the ground. . . . And the old Squire . . . and his lady . . . and my mother too . . . and also the girl Yosefka, who was chambermaid there . . . all lay in the garden, slaughtered!—O Jesus! Jesus!—Aye, I remember.—O holy Mary!" These last words he uttered very low; great tears that he did not care to hide ran down his cheeks in floods, and he heaved deep sighs, as that night rose again before him.

The darkness grew more and more intense; the blast caught more and more fiercely at the trees; the long tresses of the birch-boughs thrashed the graves about them, and their trunks, white as sheeted ghosts, loomed dimly through the gloom. The folk were leaving the place, the lamps going out, the hymns of the *Dziads* dying away. A solemn silence, disturbed only by weird rustlings and thrilling whispers, now reigned among the tombs. The graveyard seemed filled with shadowy forms, the bushes bore questionable shapes; there were melodies of lulled soft moans, oceans of eerie tremors, movements of shapeless things in the dark, bursts of dread hushed sobs, mysterious and horror-breathing alarms which made the heart sink. Throughout the village, the very dogs were howling with long despairing howls.

On this holiday alone, Lipka was hushed. The roads were deserted, the inn-doors closed. Through the tiny mist-blurred window-panes of a few huts, lights were seen to shine, and holy hymns heard to quaver timidly forth, with loud supplications to God for the souls of the faithful departed.

Outside the cabins, the folk glided about in fear; in fear did they listen to the quiet sighs of the trees; in fear did they look towards the window, lest there should appear to them one of those who, on this day, wander by God's decree and their own yearning—lest they should be heard lamenting where four roads meet—or be seen looking sorrowfully in through the window.

Outside certain huts, the husbandmen—following ancient customs—set the remains of the evening meal for the hungry ghosts to partake of and, crossing themselves, breathed some such invitation: "O Christian soul that still abidest in the place of cleansing, lo! here is refreshment for thee!"

And thus, in stillness and sadness, amidst memories and fears, did the evening of All Souls' Day come to an end.

On Antek's side of his father's cabin sat Roch, the pilgrim to our Lord's sepulchre, reading and telling many a pious and holy legend.

People were there not a few: for both Ambrose and Yagustynka and Klemba had come, Kuba and Vitek, Yuzka and Nastusia: the only one absent was old Boryna, who remained at Yagna's till late in the night.

Save for the crickets that cried and the pine-knots that crackled on the hearth or in the fire, the cabin was still as death.

They all were sitting on benches round the fire; Antek alone sat looking out of the window. Roch now and then drew the red embers together with his staff, while he spoke thus, in a soft hushed voice:

"It is not terrible to die.—Oh, no!

"As birds in winter fly to a warmer land, so do our weary little souls long to fly to Jesus.

"Though the trees stand bare in winter, yet are they clothed in spring by the Lord with green leaves and scented blossoms: thus, O thou soul of man, dost thou go to Jesus to find with Him joy, and spring, and gladness, and vesture eternal!

"As the sun caresses our weary earth, fatigued with fruit-bearing, so doth our Lord caress each soul, and make it forget the past winter of anguish and death.

"Ah me! for in this world there is naught but trouble, and wailing, and woe!

"And evil increases and multiplies, as doth the thistle in the woodlands!

"All things are vain and to no purpose . . . like tinder-wood, and like the bubbles which the wind maketh on the water and driveth away.

"And there is no faith, nor hope, save in God alone!"

CHAPTER X

"I SPEAK of this, both from the pulpit, and to every man in particular . . ."—The wind put an end to the rest of the sentence by blowing violently down the priest's throat, making him fall into a fit of coughing. Antek was silent.

The gale was growing fiercer, sweeping down the road, lashing the poplars, storming through them, and causing them to bend and moan and shriek aloud with rage.

"Man, I have told you," the priest went on to say, "that I myself took the mare down to the pond. . . . Blind as she is, she may go astray in some coppice, and perhaps break a leg."—The very thought made him turn pale, and he continued looking under every tree, and seeking in every field.

"Well, but she always went about freely."

"She knows well her way to the pond. Anyone might find a pail for her to drink from, and then turn her round: she would have come back by herself. . . . Valek!" he suddenly cried, thinking he saw someone among the poplars.

"I saw Valek on our side of the pond; but that was before twilight set in."

"Gone perhaps to look for her: a little too late! . . . A mare twenty years old! She was foaled soon after I came here, and deserves to be fed for mercy's sake . . . As much attached as any man can be. . . . Good Heavens! if any harm should have befallen the poor beast!"

"What on earth can happen?" Antek growled, in a surly mood. He had come to his Reverence to complain and get counsel; and he had been, not only reprimanded, but asked to seek the lost mare besides! No doubt the mare, so old and blind, deserved pity; but ought not a fellowman to come first?

"As to you, you are to master yourself; do you hear? And curse him not! he is your father!"

"Oh, that," said Antek very bitterly, "that I know well."

"It were a grievous sin and offence against God. And no blessing will there be for him that in anger raises his hand against his father, to break the commandment!"

"I want justice: no more."

"No, 'tis revenge you seek. . . . Am I wrong?"

Antek was at a loss for an answer.

"Now I will tell you one thing more: 'A docile calf, beyond all doubt, thrives, sucks much milk, and waxes stout.' "

" 'Docile!' The word sticks in my throat, I have so much of it. Shall I allow a man to do me every wrong in the world, simply because he is my father? Are children forbidden to seek justice for the wrong done?—Good God! if that's the order of things, I had as lief bid it farewell, and go anywhere to get away from it."

"Go, then; what is it prevents you?" cried the priest, taking fire on a sudden.

"Well may I go: what—what is there left to me here now?" he muttered, almost in tears.

"You are simply talking nonsense. Others have not one bit of land: yet they stay on, and work, and thank God that they have work to do. You had far better settle down to do something, and not complain like a woman. You are strong and able, and have something to lay your hands to besides. . . ."

"Yes, indeed; three whole acres!" was the ironical reply.

"And a wife and child, who belong to you too: do not forget it."

They were now in front of the tavern; the windows were all aglow, and from the road where they stood they could hear voices inside.

"What! another drunken bout?"

" 'Tis the recruits who were chosen during the summer, drinking to keep their spirits up. Next Sunday the Russians will take them away to somewhere at the back of the world: so they are seeking comfort."

The priest had taken his stand near the poplars, from where he could look through the window, and see how thronged the place was. "Why, the tavern is well-nigh full!" he exclaimed.

"They were to have a meeting and advise together to-day, about the forest clearing which the Squire has sold to the Jews."

"But he has sold only the half."

"Till we have agreed to the sale, not one bush shall be sold!"

"What do you say?" the priest inquired, in a tone of anxiety.

"We don't give leave: that's flat. Father would go to law; but Klemba and the others with him won't have it. They forbid a single tree to be cut down; and if the whole village has to rise, rise they will—aye, and ax in hand, too. What is theirs, they never will give up."

"Merciful heavens! Pray God there may be no violence!"

"No, no! only a few of the manor-folks' heads split in two: that will be but justice!"

"Antek! has anger made you mad? My good fellow, this is senseless talk!"

He would not listen, but turned on his heels and vanished in the gathering dusk; while the priest, who heard the rumble of wheels and a mare's whinny, hastened back to his dwelling.

Antek passed by the mill on the other side, wanting to avoid going near Yagna's hut.

She was fast in his bosom: a festering wound of which he could not rid himself.

Afar, the light shone bright from within her cabin. In there it was joyful. He stopped to look once more, were it but to curse her in his rage. And suddenly something fell on him like a hurricane, and tore him away.

"She is my father's now!—My father's!"

He went round to his brother-in-law, the smith, though expecting no advice from the man, and only wanting to remain a short time away from his father's dwelling, and in somebody's company.—Ah! the priest would preach work to him, would he? Preaching to others was an easy thing for those who have nothing to trouble them!—"Remember your wife and child!"—Was he likely to forget them? Her! . . . whom he loathed so, with her wailing and her meekness and wistfully glancing eyes! Were it not for her . . . were he but single! O Lord! He groaned deeply; a wild fit of anger swept over him, and he would have liked to take someone by the throat—strangle him—tear him to pieces! . . .

But whom? He knew not. His fury passed away as suddenly as it had come. He looked blankly out into the night and hearkened to the whistling blasts. Then he walked on, trudging heavily, scarce able to drag himself; for now he felt weighed down by a mountain of sorrow, lassitude, and such a sense of prostration that he no longer knew whither he was going, nor for what purpose.

"Yagna is my father's—my father's!" he repeated again and again, each time in a lower key.

In the smith's shop, a boy was working the bellows with might and main, and the draught that poured on to the flaring roaring embers made them burst into blood-red flames. The smith stood at the anvil, grimy-faced, girt with a leather apron, his arms bare, his cap on the back of his head, beating a red-hot iron bar till the anvil resounded, while showers of sparks flew from beneath the hammer, and fell hissing into the moist ground of the forge.

"Well?" he asked, after waiting a moment.

"Well, what?" Antek mumbled, leaning against a basket-wagon frame, several of which were standing by to have their iron-work repaired; and he gazed into the fire.

The smith went on, working hard at the incandescent iron, and beat away, keeping time as he smote upon the anvil with his hammer; or, when a yet more powerful blast was needed, helping the boy to blow; but ever and anon stealing a glance at Antek, while a malicious smile peeped from under his red moustache.

"Well, so you have been to his Reverence again: and what has come of it?"

"And what should come? Nothing. I might have heard just the same in church."

"What else did you think to get?"

"Why, he knows a great deal," Antek replied in self-defence.

"As to taking, yes; as to giving, no."

Antek was in no mood to contradict him.

"I am going to your cabin," he said after a pause.

"Go; I shall join you at once, for the Voyt is to be here. You will find tobacco on the top of the press: help yourself."

Antek had not so much as heard him, as he made straight for the house which stood opposite.

His sister was kindling the fire, and her eldest boy, at the table, learning out of a spelling-book.

"Is he studying?" he asked; for the boy spelt aloud, pointing to each letter with a sharp stick.

"Yes. He began at potato-digging-time. The young lady from the mill is teaching him, for my husband is too busy."

"Roch, too, began teaching on Father's side of our cabin yesterday."

"I wanted to send our Johnny to him, too: but Michael will not have it. He says she knows more, because she has been at school in Warsaw."

"Oh, yes. Yes," he answered, in order to say something.

"Johnny gets on so fast with his primer that the young lady is astonished."

"Oh, of course. It's the smith's blood, you see—being the son of so clever a man . . ."

"You are jeering. And yet was he not right to tell you that Father can, so long as he lives, withdraw any settlement made?"

"Aye, try to snatch its prey from out of the wolf's mouth! . . . Six acres of land! My wife and I are both as good as his farm-servants; and see, he settles the land on the first strange woman he comes across!"

"You will wrangle, and fall foul of him, and ask for advice against him; and the end will be that he will drive you from his house into the bargain!" She spoke thus, looking timorously towards the door.

"Who told you that?"

"Hush, hush! That's what people are saying."

"He shall not! Let him get me out by force, if he can! I'll go to law. But as to giving way, never, never!"

"Yes, you'll butt your head against a stone wall, like a ram, but never get it smashed, eh?" the smith said, coming in.

"Then what's to be done? You give clever advice to everybody; advise me."

"It will never do to run counter to the old man's will." He lit a pipe, and set about explaining matters, excusing Boryna, and smoothing things over, till all at once Antek saw his drift, and cried out:

"You—you are on his side!"

"I want to be fair."

"You have been well paid for this."

"Not out of your pocket, at all events."

"My property is not yours to give up in my place. You no doubt have had a good instalment already, and are in no hurry to get more."

"I have had no more than you."

"Oh, no more? And what about your share of the cow? And all the pieces of linen, and odds and ends you have sneaked out of Father? Have I forgotten the geese, and the young pigs . . . and . . . and . . . there's no end of them! Ah, and the calf he gave you the other day? Is that nothing?"

"You might have got it just as well as I."

"I am not a gipsy, nor a thief!"

"A thief! Do you call me that?"

They both rushed forward, ready to spring at each other. But they stopped, for Antek went on more calmly:

"I was not speaking of you. But never will I abandon my rights, even to be saved from utter ruin."

The smith interposed, with a jeer: "It is not the land, I fancy, for which you would go to such lengths."

"For what then?"

"It is Yagna you want, and rage to lose her now!"

"Did you ever see . . . ?" he cried; the shot had hit the mark.

"There be those who have seen . . . and not once only."

"May their eyes drop out of the sockets!" But he said this curse very low; for just then the Voyt entered the room. Probably he too was aware of the reason why they quarrelled, for he at once set to justifying and defending the old man's behaviour.

"That you stand up for him is no wonder: he has given you drink and sausages in plenty!"

"No careless talk, pray; I, the Voyt, am speaking to you."

"For your Voytship I care as I care for this broken stick!"

"What!—what has the man said?"

"You have heard; and if not, you shall hear other things which will go yet farther."

"Say them, then, if you dare!"

"I will.—Behold, you are a drunkard, a Judas, a dissembler; one that squanders in revels the money the village has entrusted to him, and takes abundant pay from the manor, to let the Squire sell our forest land. . . . Will ye I say more?" he added furiously, snatching at a stick. "So I will, but with this cudgel, not with my tongue."

"Take care you rue not what you are doing, Antek; I am a man in office!"

"And do not fly at anyone under my roof! This is no tavern!" the smith shouted, placing himself in front of the Voyt. But Antek, now wrought up to exasperation, poured a volley of abuse on them both, slammed the door, and left them.

"Now," he was saying to himself, while breakfasting the next day, "now they will all be against me!" when, to his stupefaction, he saw the blacksmith come in. They met on their usual terms.

When Antek went to the barn afterwards to chop straw, the smith followed him, and said in confidential tones:

"I'll be hanged if I know why we quarrelled . . . some silly word dropped, belike. So I am first to come to you and shake hands."

Antek shook hands indeed, but grunted, with a look of mistrust:

"Yes, some hasty words passed between us; but I felt no grudge against you. That Voyt made me frantic. . . . Let him mind his own business, and keep himself to himself, or . . ."

"So I told him, when he wanted to follow you out. . . ."

"To fight me?—I would have given him such a dressing as I gave his cousin, who has been smashed up ever since harvest-time!"

"Of that, too, did I remind him," the smith observed, with a demure look and a sly leer.

"But I will settle with him yet . . . with that great man, that Jack in office! He will remember me!"

"He is not worth your notice: let him be.—I have had an idea, and have come now to tell you about it. This is what we have to do. . . . This afternoon my wife will come here. You will go with her to old Boryna, and talk the matter over thoroughly. . . . Of what use is complaining in holes and corners? Speak your mind out to him face to face. Perhaps you will succeed, perhaps not; but at all events we shall have threshed the matter out."

"But what is to be done, now the settlement has been made?"

"You see, by wrangling we shall get nothing at all. Yes, he has made it. But, so long as he lives, he has the power to revoke it. Do you understand? That is the reason why we must not irritate him. He wants to marry: well, let him. And to enjoy himself: why not?"

At the mention of marriage, Antek turned white, and shook so that he paused in his work.

"Do not oppose him openly. Approve him. Say he was right to make the settlement, since he chose to do so: only ask him to promise us the rest—that is, to you and me, and in presence of witnesses," he added, with a sly after-thought.

"Yes, but what of Yuzka, what of Gregory?" Antek inquired reluctantly.

"They shall get money instead. Gregory has been receiving not a little every month, ever since he has been in the army.—But just listen, and do as I tell you; you will not regret it. My management of things will make all the land ours in the end, my life on it."

"'To sew the sheep's skin do not strive, furrier, while the sheep's alive.'"

"Listen.—Let him but make a promise in presence of witnesses: we shall then have something to lay hold on. We can still fall back on the courts of justice. And there is another point besides: the land he got as your mother's dowry."

"A great thing, forsooth: four acres for me and your sister . . . four whole acres!"

"But these he has not given to either; and for so many years he has sown therein and garnered therefrom! For these he must pay you well, aye, and with percentage too! . . . I tell you once more: oppose the old man in nothing. Go to the wedding; do not grudge him fair words. We shall manage him, you will see. And if he is after all unwilling to give the promise, the law may then come in and force him. You are on very familiar terms with Yagna, and she may be very useful to you: only speak of this to her. No one could better succeed in bringing the old man round.—Well, is it agreed? For I must be stirring."

"Agreed!—That you get out quick, or I will smite you in the face and drive you out of doors!" Antek hissed through his clenched teeth.

"What . . . what has come over you?" the blacksmith

stammered, appalled by the looks of the other, who dropped the straw-cutter and came on, with eyes terribly gleaming and face as pale as a sheet.

"Thief! carrion! traitor!" He spat the words out, his mouth was foaming with hate as he advanced, and the smith fairly ran for it.

"Has the man lost his wits?" he said, as soon as he was out in the road. "I was giving him good counsel . . . and he—Oh, that's your game, is it? You would have struck me, driven me out, because I wanted to share the land with you, and came to you as to a friend and a brother! Is that your game . . . to have all to yourself? Ha! you will not live to see the day, my man! Though you wormed my thoughts out of me so cleverly, I will give you such a shaking, the worst ague will be nothing beside it!" He grew angrier and still more angry, as he reflected that Antek had taken him in so, and would inform old Boryna of all this intrigue.—The very thing he feared most of all!

"But that must at once be prevented!" He swiftly came to a decision, and though in bodily fear of Antek, went back to Boryna's.

"Is your master at home?" he asked Vitek, who was opposite the house, throwing pebbles at the geese in the pond to make them land.

"Over there at the miller's: gone to invite their people to his wedding."

"I shall go that way: perhaps we may meet," he thought, and made for the miller's; but he went home first, and told his wife to dress her best, take the children with her, and go round to Antek's at the first stroke of the noonday Angelus.

"He will tell you what to do. . . . Do nothing by yourself, for you are not clever; only fall a-crying at the right time, embrace your father's knees and beseech him, and all that. But give good heed to what Antek shall say and your father reply." And so he went on instructing her for some time.

"Now I shall look in at the mill: perhaps our meal is

ground." He was too uneasy to stay any longer in the house and, going out, walked on slowly, often halting to consider.

"The man threatened me; yet he'll do as I told him, I think. Better my wife should be there, and not I.—What else can he do but what I say?—Quarrel—and be expelled!"

He smiled in triumph, set his cap straight and buttoned up his capote, for a chill piercing wind came from the pond.

"There will be frost, surely, or else dirty weather," he predicted, standing on the bridge and looking into the sky, where a scud of driven clouds was passing, not unlike a flock of muddy unwashed sheep. The pond uttered a low murmur, now and then beating upon its shores, along which, scattered about amongst blackened drooping alders and weeping willows, the outlines of women washing linen appeared, traced in red, and the obstreperous clatter of their bats rose on either bank. The roads were empty, save for the numerous flocks of geese, soiled with stiffening mire, that were waddling in and out of the ditches, now filled up with dead leaves and rubbish. Children outside the houses squealed and screamed; and the cocks crowed in the hedges —weather-prophets telling of a change.

"Better wait for him at the mill!" he growled and walked down the slope.

Antek, when the smith left him, had set to chopping straw so frantically that he forgot everything but his work; and Kuba, returning from the wood, cried out aloud:

"Mercy! there will be enough of it for a week's fodder!" And then Antek woke up from his musings, threw the straw-cutter aside, stretched himself, and went into the hut.

"What must be will be," he reflected, "and I must speak to my father this day.—That blacksmith fellow is a lying traitor; his advice may be good, for all that. Nay, there must be something in it." He peeped in at his father's door, and at once drew back; a score of urchins were sitting there. Roch was teaching them, and paying great heed to their behaviour; going round with beads in hand, hearing their lessons, correcting them at times; at others pulling one boy's ear or patting another's head, but for the most part sitting patiently and explaining the printed matter, or putting questions, which the children hastened to answer in chorus as fast as they could, gobbling like a troop of little turkeys when excited.

Hanka was getting dinner ready, and having a talk with her father, old Bylitsa, who seldom came, because he was always ailing and could hardly move about.

He sat close to the window, his chin and hands on his staff; hoary-headed, with a twitch of the lips and a treble voice like a bird's, accompanied by thin wheezing sounds in the windpipe.

"Have you breakfasted?" she inquired.

"To say true, Veronka forgot me."

"Oh, she even starves her dogs! they often come to me for food," she cried. Her elder sister and she had been on bad terms ever since last winter, when their mother had died, and Veronka seized on all she had left, refusing to give anything up; which had estranged them.

He took her part in a feeble voice. "They have not too much for themselves. Staho threshes at the organist's, where he gets food and a score of kopeks daily besides. And there are many mouths to feed in the cabin: the potato-patch cannot suffice for all. True, they have a couple of milch-cows and take butter and cheese to town, and get a few coppers; but she often forgets to give me my meals. Yet I do not want much . . . only a little every day, and at the right hour . . ."

"Then come to us in spring, since you are so ill off with that jade!"

"But I make no complaint, no fuss; only . . ." His voice died into silence.

"With us, you could tend the geese, and see to the children."

"Hanka," he said under his breath, "there is nothing that I would not do."

"There is room for you here; I should put up a bed for you and make you cosy."

"Oh, if I could but be with you, Hanka, and never go back to them, I would sleep in the cowhouse or the stable," he answered in a husky beseeching voice. "They took my feather-bed from me; she says the children have nothing to sleep on. It is true that they were cold, so I had them with me. But my sheepskin is all torn, and does not keep me warm at all; and where I sleep there is no fire, and she will not let me have any wood, and counts every spoonful that I eat, and sends me out a-begging, and I am so weak I can scarcely crawl to your house."

"Good God! and you never told me this was so!—Why?"

"How could I? she is my daughter!—And he is a good-hearted man, but very little in the house.—How could I?"

"She is a hag! She took half the land and half the cabin, and the other things. . . . So that's the board and lodgings she promised to give you! We must go to law: they were bound to let you have food and firing, and clothing too.—And we were to give twelve roubles a year: have we not kept our promise, say?"

"Surely! For you are upright folk.—But those few *zloty* that I have saved for my burial—I had to give them up too, I could not help it." He said no more but sat crouching in his place, more like a heap of rags than a human being.

After dinner, when the smith's wife came with her children and greeted Hanka, the old man took up a bundle prepared for him by his daughter, and vanished unnoticed.

Boryna had not come home to dine.

The smith's wife was determined to see him, nevertheless, though she should have to wait till nightfall. Hanka had set up a loom near the window, where she set to work, drawing the woof of hempen thread across the warp assiduously, and but seldom and timidly taking part in the talk between Antek and his sister. His conversation with her about their grievances did not last long, however; for Yagustynka dropped in, saying in a casual tone:

"I have just come here from the organist's, where they need me for the washing. Matthias was there only just now, together with Yagna, to invite them to the wedding.

They are coming. Yes, everyone to his people: the rich to the rich. They have asked the priest also."

"What! have they dared His Reverence!" Hanka exclaimed.

"Is he, then, so sacred a being? They asked him, and he said he might possibly come. Why not? Is the girl ill-looking? will the food be bad? and will there be little to drink? The miller and wife and daughter have promised. Ho, ho! There will not have been such a wedding since Lipka was Lipka!—I know, for I shall be cooking with Eva—her from the miller's. Ambrose has killed a pig for them, and sausages are making now . . ." She broke off abruptly, noticing that no one asked any questions, or spoke at all. She looked round at them as they sat gloomily there, and, eyeing them attentively, cried out:

"I say! there is a storm brewing here!"

"Storm or no storm, what is that to you?" the smith's wife answered, so tartly that Yagustynka was offended, rose, and went over to Yuzka in the other lodgings, who (the children having just departed) was setting chairs and benches in order.

"Father is not likely to grudge himself anything," the smith's wife remarked, in an aggrieved tone.

"Oh, he can well afford it!" Hanka rejoined, and broke off abruptly, seeing Antek look fiercely at her.—They sat waiting in almost complete silence. From time to time a word was said; then that dull, crushing, ominous speechlessness came over them once more.

"He must have cash enough: he is always selling things, and never spending."

Antek's only rejoinder to his sister's words was a wave of the hand; and he went out of the room to get some fresh air. He was feeling ever more and more uneasy; nor could he tell why. He now expected his father, and felt impatient at the delay, yet glad in his heart not to have met with him yet.—"It is not the land you are angry about, it is Yagna!"—Those words, uttered by the smith the day before, now suddenly came back to him.—"He is a lying dog!"

was the cry of rage which burst from his lips. And he set to work at the outer wall which was to protect the hut from the side of the courtyard. Vitek brought him litter from the heap; Antek drove in the laths to form the wall, and rammed the litter down inside it; but his hands were trembling, he had to stop working more than once, and lean against the cabin walls, and look out through the bare leafless trees over the pond to Yagna's hut.—No, it was not love that was now growing within him, but anger and hatred in numberless billows! She, the jade—she, the hateful one!—They had thrown her a bone, and off she went after it!

Such were his thoughts. But then there swept over him remembrances coming up—whence, he knew not—laying siege to his heart, clinging to his mind, even visible to his senses . . . and the sweat bedewed his brow, his eyes flashed, a thrill ran through him.—Ah, there in the orchard! Ah, then in the forest! And again, when they once were coming from town together!

All at once he reeled; he again saw that burning face, those deep-blue eyes, those wondrous full red lips; and he heard her quick-drawn breaths of passion, and her voice, low and husky with love and rapture, calling to him: "Antek! Antek!" And she was again bending towards him, very close—he felt her touch him with all her throbbing self! . . . But he rubbed his eyes to drive away that too sweet phantom, and his implacable resentment again oozed icily from his heart, as the drops fall from the icicles under the eaves, when the spring sun shines upon them, and love awakens once more; within his soul, agonized yearning lifted her thorn-crowned head once more—a yearning so bitter that he would fain have eased it by clutching at any pain whatsoever, or by shrieking to rouse the dead!

"May a brimstone thunderbolt strike her!" he cried out; but, suddenly recollecting himself, he cast a sharp glance round, fearing lest Vitek should have understood whom he meant.

He had spent those three last weeks in a fever of expectancy, awaiting the happening of some miracle. As for him, he could do nothing, prevent nothing!

And of late, insane thoughts had often surged up in his mind, insane resolves. Often had he gone out to meet her, and many a night had he watched outside her cabin, in the rain and the cold. But she had not come out.—She shunned him!

No, no, no! Every instant he grew more angry against her, against the whole framework of things. She was his father's!—A strange woman, an adventuress, a thief who had robbed him of his land, the most precious of all possessions! Smite her he would—aye, beat the life out of her!

More than once he had determined to confront his father, and tell him to his face: "You cannot have Yagna; she is mine!" But the very thought made his hair stand on end. —What would his father, what would all the village say?

So now she, that same Yagna, was to be his stepmother—his mother . . . of a sort! How could that be? Was it not a sin, a most grievous one? He was afraid to think of it: the thought of some awful judgment of God at hand made his heart die within him. . . . And yet, to say nothing —to bear all this within himself, as one bearing in his bosom coals of fire that burned to the bone—that was beyond the endurance of man!

And the wedding was but a week away!

"Master is coming," Vitek cried; and Antek felt he was shaking with dismay.

It was getting dark,

It was getting cold, too; the ground was freezing, the air eager and nipping, but clear as usual when a frost is setting in, and wafting sound so well that the bellowing and trampling of the cattle driven to water, the creaking of the gates and bucket-dippers, the noises of the children and the dogs, were all heard distinctly across the pond. From some windows, there gleamed lights already, throwing athwart the waters their long, broken, quivering reflections; while, from behind the woods, the huge red full moon was slowly ascending.

Boryna, attentive to farm matters, came into the yard, and rated Kuba and Vitek soundly for having let the calves stray from their stalls and wander to the cows' mangers; so, when he entered the house, his visitors were awaiting him. They said nothing, but just gave one glance, and looked down, as he stopped short in the middle of the room, eyed them, and asked scornfully:

"All here? What, come to sit in judgment, hey?"

"No, indeed," the smith's wife returned, timorously; "we only come to you with a petition."

"But why is your goodman not here?"

"He was very busy, and could not come."

"Aha! Busy . . . yes." He smiled knowingly, threw his capote aside, and pulled off his boots. All remained tongue-tied the while, uncertain how to begin. The smith's wife cleared her throat and drew her children closer; Hanka, on the threshold, was suckling her little boy, and casting uneasy looks at Antek, who sat by the window thinking what he should say, and shaking all over with emotion. Yuzka alone was calm, peeling potatoes by the fire-place.

"Now, then, say what you have to say," the old man cried sharply, irritated by the silence.

"Better you, Antek, should speak first—about that settlement: we shall follow," the smith's wife stammered.

"The settlement? It is made, and the wedding is to be on Sunday: that I can tell you."

"We know, but we came for another reason."

"What is it?"

"You have settled six whole acres!"

"I chose to: if I choose, I can settle everything on her, and this instant!"

"You may, if all belongs to you," Antek retorted.

"And whose else is it—whose?"

"Your children's. Ours."

"That's nonsense. Mine the land is, and I can do with it as I please."

"Or not yours, and not to do as you please."

"Will you prevent me—you?"
"I shall . . . we all shall; and if not, we have the law to protect us." He could no longer control himself, and was raging.
"Ah! you do threaten me with the law, forsooth?—Hold your peace ere I am angered, or you'll rue it."
"Wrong us ye shall not!" cried Hanka in a loud voice, rising to her feet.
"And what is't she wants—she?—She brought us three acres of sand, and one piece of canvas cloth: and she dares wag her tongue here!"
"You have given Antek still less: not even the land, his mother's dowry; we are as your farm-labourers!"
"But in return for your work you get all that three of my acres yield."
"For work that is worth the yield of more than twenty."
"If unfairly treated, go elsewhere and fare better."
Here Antek shouted: "We will not! The land is ours, come down from our grandsires and forefathers."
Old Boryna glared at him, but answered nothing. He seated himself by the fire and, taking up a poker, used it on the brands till the sparks flew on every side. He was flushed with passion; his hair again and again came tumbling into his eyes, phosphorescent like a wildcat's; but he had some self-control still left.
A long pause ensued, and the stillness of the room was broken only by the hurried breaths drawn there.
"We have naught against your marrying; marry, if you like."
"And if you have aught, much difference will it make to me!"
"Only revoke that settlement!" added Hanka, in tears.
"Oh, that peevish mother of dogs! Always chattering like a fool!" And he poked the fire so furiously that the sparks flew all about the room.
"Take heed! She is no wench of yours, that you should speak such words to her!"

"Why should she prate, then?"

"She has a right to speak!" Antek shouted; "she stands up for what is our due."

"If you will," the smith's wife murmured, "let the settlement stand, but settle the rest of your property on us."

"Look at that simpleton! Going to divide my land, eh? No, I'll never take board and lodgings from you.—I have spoken."

"We will not give in! We will have justice!"

"If I but take my stick to you, I'll give you justice!"

"Try but to touch us!—You'd not live till the wedding!"

And now the squabble began in earnest; they rushed forwards, threatening; they beat the table with their fists, they shouted aloud all their grievances, all their injuries. Antek, in his anger, forgot himself so far as again and again to clutch his father by the shoulder, even by the throat, so furious was he; but the old man was yet master of himself. He wished to have no fight, and merely pushed him aside, seldom replying to insults, and unwilling to have the whole village taking part in his affairs. But the noise and confusion in the room waxed louder and louder; for both the women were weeping and pouring forth invectives alternately, while the children screamed so that both Kuba and Vitek came round from the farm-yard and peeped in at the window.

Hanka, leaning against the chimney penthouse, here burst into a torrent of tears and words:

"Yes, we shall have to go out into the world and beg our bread! O Lord, good Lord! . . . we that have toiled like oxen! . . . What have we now of our labour? . . . Ah, God will avenge this wrong of ours! . . . His judgment will be upon you! . . . Six whole acres settled—and mother's clothing and beads given away . . . everything! And to whom, great God? . . . To that swine! . . . Oh! wanton and harlot as you are! For the wrong you are doing us, may you end in a ditch some day!"

"What do you say?" the old man shrieked, darting furiously towards her.

"That she is a harlot and a wanton—as all the village and all the world knows!"

"Woe betide you! I'll beat your foul mouth to pulp!" He seized and shook her; but Antek leaped forwards to protect her, and shouted in his turn:

"And I say it too: she is a wanton, a harlot, and anyone may know her that cares!"—But he said no more. Boryna, in a paroxysm of rage, struck him such a blow in the face that he fell with his head breaking the pane of a glazed press, which he brought to the floor with him. Springing up instantly, streaming with blood, he charged his father.

They both rushed at each other like mad dogs, with a mutual clutch, driving and being driven backward and forward about the room, pushing and hurling one another against the bed, the great trunk, the walls, till their heads rang again. A horrible outcry arose: the womenfolk tried to separate them, but they rolled down upon the floor, so closely gripped in hatred that they turned over and over, each strangling each, each crushing the other, as best he could.

By great good fortune, the neighbours ran in while it was time, and separated them.

Antek was hustled away to the other lodgings, and water dashed over him; he was faint with exhaustion caused by loss of blood, for the glass had gashed him very deep.

The old man had no hurt at all; only a slight tear in the short jacket he wore, and a few scratches on his face, that was livid with rage. . . . He swore at the folk who had come, shut the front door on them, and sat down by the fire.

But nothing could avail to calm him.

He could not put out of his memory the words uttered about Yagna: they stabbed him like a knife.

"That hound! I will never forgive him, never!" was the oath he then swore to himself. "My Yagna! how could he?"—But then he recalled what he had heard said of her in former times and disregarded. He turned hot, he felt as if he were choking, and a wretched sense of dejection came over him. How, if his own son said such things, were people's mouths to be stopped? Oh, that villain! The very recollection of those words burned him like fire.

After Yuzka had cleaned away all the traces of the struggle, and given him his supper, though late, he attempted to eat, but could not, and laid his spoon down. "Have you given the horses their provender?" he inquired of Kuba.

"Of course."

"Vitek—where is he?"

"Gone for Ambrose, to see to Antek's head. His face is swollen like a pipkin," he added, hurrying out; for he had chosen this moonlight night to go out shooting.

" 'When dogs have too much bread, each flies at t'other's head,' " he grunted.

The old man stumped down into the village, but refrained from visiting Yagna, though the light was gleaming bright from her window. He turned away just outside her door, and went round to the mill. It was a chilly star-besprinkled night, and so clear that the whole mill-pond shone like glittering quicksilver. Over the deserted roads the trees cast long swaying shadows. It was late; they were putting the lights out in the houses, whose white-washed walls now stood out more distinctly among the skeleton orchard trees. Silence and darkness had swallowed up all the hamlet: only the mill-wheel and the water clattered and babbled monotonously. Matthias walked on, crossing to the other side. As he went, his anger grew stronger, together with his hatred. When he got to the tavern, he sent for the Voyt, and they both drank till midnight. He could not, however, drown the gnawing pain within him. Only he then registered a resolve.

No sooner had he risen the next morning than he went round to the other lodgings. Antek was in bed, his face bandaged with a bloodstained rag.

"Get out of my home this instant!" he said, "and let no trace of you remain! If you want war, if you will go to law, then do so; bring an action, and get back your property! What you have sown of your own grain, you may reap, when summer comes. And now, away with you! Let me set eyes on you no more! Do you hear?" he roared. Antek set about dressing slowly.

"By noon, you will have to be off!" he added, calling out to them from the passage.

Antek remained as dumb as though he had not heard.

"Yuzka, call Kuba: let him put the mare to the cart, and take them whither they want to go!"

"But there is something the matter with Kuba. He lies groaning on his pallet, and says he cannot rise at all, his lame leg hurts him so."

"A sluggard, who only wants to lie abed!" And Boryna saw to the farm-duties by himself.

Kuba nevertheless was seriously ill, but would not say what the matter was with him, though pressed by his master. As he lay, he uttered such groans that the horses came up to him, sniffed at his face and licked it, while Vitek brought him water in a pail, and secretly washed certain blood-smirched rags in the river.

Boryna, intent as he was on the departure of Antek and his family, noticed nothing of all this.

They departed.

Without clamour or disturbance, they packed everything, carried their belongings out, and made up their bundles; Hanka well-nigh swooning with distress; Antek refreshing her with drinks of water and hurrying her on, that they might be away—out of that father's house—as quickly as ever they could.

He would take no horse from his father, but borrowed one from Klemba, and took everything over to Hanka's parent, at the very end of the village and beyond the tavern.

Several peasants had come in from the hamlet, along with Roch as their leader, desirous of reconciling them; but to this neither father nor son would agree.

"No," said the old man; "let him try how he will enjoy his freedom, and bread of his own!"

Antek answered no word to their solicitations; but, lifting

his fist, he uttered such horrible maledictions that Roch turned pale and withdrew amongst the women, who were in numbers about the premises; partly to assist Hanka, but for the most part to air grievances aloud, and babble, and give advice.

When Yuzka, all in tears, gave dinner to her father and Roch, her brother and his family were off the place, together with all they had. Antek never even looked back at his hut; he only crossed himself, heaving a deep sigh; and whipping up the horse, put his shoulder to the cart, it being very heavily laden. He went plodding along, his face white, his eyes blazing with stubborn resolve, his teeth chattering as one in an ague: but never said one word. Hanka walked languidly after the cart, her elder son holding to her skirt and roaring, her younger one clasped to her bosom. Before them she drove a cow, a flock of geese, and two lean swine: and her voice was so loud in imprecations and mourning that folk came out of their houses, and followed her as in procession.

At Boryna's, the meal was eaten in sombre silence.

The old dog Lapa barked in the porch, ran after the cart, returned and howled. Vitek called it; but it paid no heed. It smelt the farm-yard, entered Antek's empty rooms, ran round them one or twice, rushed into the passage, barked again, whined, fawned on Yuzka, and again tore about as though distracted: then it sat down on its hind quarters with a strange air of imbecility—and finally made off, with its tail between its legs, on Antek's trail.

"Even Lapa has gone after them!"

"Do not fear, Yuzka," her father answered tenderly; "Lapa is coming back soon. They will have no food for him. Come, no silly puling, but prepare the other rooms: Roch is to live in them. Call Yagustynka to help you. . . . You must take household matters in hand now; being housekeeper, you'll have many a care on your head. . . . No, no! no whimpering, dear!" He took her head in both his hands, and stroked it, and drew her caressingly to his heart.

"When I go to town, I'll buy you a pair of shoes."

"Oh, will you, will you, Father?"

"Yes, I will indeed, and many another thing besides. Only be a good girl, and take care of the place."

"And will you buy me a caftan like Nastusia's?"

"Certainly, dear, I'll buy you one."

"And ribbons too?—But long ones . . . such as I shall want for your wedding-day."

"Say but what you need, little one, and you shall have it . . . all you want!"

CHAPTER XI

"ARE you sleeping, Yagna?"

"How can I sleep? I woke at dawn . . . with the thought that I am to be married to-day."

"You are sorry, darling, are you?" she whispered; there was in her heart a mingling of hope and fear.

"Wherefore? Shall I be sorry that I must leave your home, and go to my own?"

Dominikova, crushing down the pang which suddenly seized her at the words, did not reply at once. She rose from her bed, dressed herself carelessly, and went out to wake up the lads in the stable. These had overslept themselves somewhat, the "Unbinding of Hair"[1] having taken place in the cabin the evening before. It was broad daylight, and the morning, clad in hoarfrost, flooded the world with silvery splendour.

Dominikova washed her face in the passage, and went quietly about the house, ever and anon peeping at Yagna, whose face was scarcely discernible in the shades of the bedroom, dark as yet.

"Lie there, darling! lie there still! Lie for the last time in thy mother's home," she murmured, love and sorrowing pain contending within her many a time. What she had coveted so ardently, she had now: yet she felt such anguish that she could not but wince at the smart of it, and sat down upon the bed.—Boryna . . . a kind man, who would treat her daughter with due respect. . . . And Yagna could do whatever she liked with this man, who saw nothing in the whole world but her!

[1] As Polish peasant-girls' tresses are cut after the wedding, they have a little domestic party the evening before, to which only girls are invited, and the tresses are then unbound, ready to be shorn. —*Translator's Note.*

No. It was not he that she dreaded, but the stepchildren. —Ah, why had he driven the Anteks from his home? Now, if ever, would they brew mischief and seek revenge. But yet, if he had not done so? . . . Antek at Yagna's side! —A sin against God might have ensued.—Well, there was no help for it now. The banns were published, the guests invited; the pig was killed, the settlement safely stowed away. . . . No, no, no! What would come of it had to come; and while Dominikova lived, she would suffer no wrong to be done to her daughter.—Having come to this final decision, she went out to rate the lads for their sloth.

When she returned, she thought to rouse her daughter too; but Yagna had fallen asleep again, and the quiet regular breathing of slumber was heard from her bed. Once more did the mother feel anxieties and uncertainties swoop down upon her, like hawks with talons tearing at her heart, screaming distrust, and predicting some vaguely awful impending doom. But she dropped on her knees by the window and, with red bleared eyes fixed upon the flushed dawn, prayed very hard for a long time. And she rose, full of strength to meet any fate that might come, no matter what!

"Now, Yagna dear, get up; it is high time. Eva is coming at once to cook, and we have so much to do still!"

"Is the weather fine?" the girl inquired, raising her heavy head.

"So fine that all the country round is glistening over with hoarfrost. The sun will rise presently."

Yagna, aided by her mother, was soon dressed. Then the latter, after due consideration, spoke thus:

"What I have told you before, I will repeat again. Boryna is a good, kind man; but you must take great care . . . not to make friends with any chance acquaintance, or let tongues ever again wag against you. People are curs: they love to bite.—You hear me, dear?"

"I hear, yes; but you speak as though I had not any judgment at all."

"No one is the worse for good advice.—See well to this:

Boryna must never be set at naught, but always treated with tender respect. An old man cares much more for that sort of thing than a young one does. . . . And who knows whether he may not settle all his land on you? or perhaps give you a big sum—from hand to hand?"

"For that I care nothing," she interrupted impatiently.

"Because you are young and inexperienced. Look round you: what is it men quarrel for, work for, and make every attempt to get? Why, what but property, property alone! —The Lord never, never made you for toil and suffering.— Whom have I laboured for all my life, if not for my Yagna? —And now I shall be alone—quite alone!"

"But the lads will not quit your side; they will always be with you."

"Of them I have as much joy as of the day that is no more!" She wept, and added, wiping her eyes: "You must also live in harmony with your husband's children."

"Yuzka is a kindly girl. Gregory will not be back from the army for some time yet. And—and . . ."

"Beware of the smith!"

"Why, he is on the best of terms with Matthias."

"If so, it is for some reason of his own: be sure of that.— The Anteks are worst of all; they will not be reconciled. . . . His Reverence wanted to make peace yesterday, but they would none of it."

"Oh, but Matthias is a wicked old man to drive them from his house!" Yagna burst out passionately.

"What's that—what do you say, Yagna? Do you know that Antek would have taken back the land from us—that he cursed you, and said of you things unfit to repeat?"

"Antek against me? Antek? They lie who told you so. . . . May their foul tongues drop out of their heads!"

"Oh! And what is it sets you so strongly on his side? Say!" she asked with a threatening look.

"Their being all against him! I am not a begging dog that fawns on all who toss him bread. He is ill-used, and I know it!"

"You would like to return the deed of settlement to him, would you not?"

Yagna could speak no further; a stream of tears fell from her eyes; she rushed into the inner room, bolted the door, and cried there for a long while.

Dominikova did not try to interfere. The scene had awakened new feelings of anxiety in her mind, but she had no time to brood over them. Eva came; the lads slouched into the passage; the last preparations and arrangements were now to be made.

The sun was up, and the morning-tide rolling on.

The frost of the previous night had been hard enough for the roadside pools and the borders of the pond to be coated with ice, and the quagmires to bear the weight of the lesser flocks.

Now it was growing warmer, though in the shadow and under the hedges the frost still reigned. The thatches dripped with crystal drops, and wreaths of smoke-like vapour were curling up from the marshes.

Not the least little cloud floated in the dark azure of the sky.

Nevertheless, crows hovering about the cabins, and cocks frequently crowing, foretold bad weather to come.

It was Sunday; and though the bells had not yet begun to ring, the whole village was like a hive of swarming bees. Half the inhabitants were smartening themselves up for the wedding of Boryna with Yagna.

In every cabin, turmoil and racket prevailed; everyone was getting ready, trying things on, and dressing carefully; and out of many an open window and door came the sounds of merry voices.

On Dominikova's premises, of course, everything was in seething tumult, as usual on such a day.

The cottage, freshly whitewashed, was noticeable from afar, having been decorated with green boughs in Whitsuntide fashion. Already the day before, the boys had come to fix pine-branches on the thatched roof and where possible along every chink in the wall. From the fence to the porch, fir-tree boughs had been likewise set up, so that the fragrance was like that of the woods in the springtime.

Within, the arrangements made were very fine indeed.

On the farther side of the house, generally used as a storeroom, a great fire had been made, and Eva from the miller's was cooking there with some neighbours and Yagustynka to help her.

All the furniture had been removed from the other side, the room whitewashed afresh within, the chimney-piece veiled with a great piece of blue drapery. Nothing remained but the holy images on the walls; but the lads had carried in stout benches and long tables, which they set up along the sides. The ceiling, with its age-darkened rafters, had been adorned with paper figures that Yagna had herself cut out. Matthias had fetched her coloured paper from town, out of which she had snipped many a fringed and variously coloured circle, and imitating flowers, and curiosities of different descriptions—as, for instance, a dog running after sheep, its master following it, staff in hand; or a church procession, with priest, banners flying, and images borne aloft—and so many other marvels of the same kind, it was impossible to remember them all! And all were well-shaped and artistic in appearance, and had been greatly admired the evening before, when they were unplaiting Yagna's tresses. She knew how to make many another thing besides—anything that caught her eye or fancy; and in all Lipka there was not a cabin without some cutting made by her hands.

Having partly dressed herself in the other room, she came out to paste the rest of her cuttings upon the walls beneath the holy images, there being no room anywhere else.

"Yagna! will you have done with those fancy things of yours? The people are assembling, the band is marching through the village: and that girl is amusing herself with drolleries!"

"Plenty of time, plenty of time," she returned briefly; but she now stuck no more cuttings, and busied herself strewing the floor with pine-needles, laying the tables with fine linen cloth, exchanging a few words with her brothers, or strolling about the place and looking out at the scenery. But she felt no pleasure in all this: not the least. She was going to dance and hear the band play, and was fond both of music and of dancing: that was all. Her soul, like the present day of autumn serenity, was cloudless and radiant, but lifeless. Were it not that all things reminded her it was her wedding-day, she might even have forgotten that. At the "Unplaiting," the day before, Boryna had put in her hands eight strings of coral beads—all that his wives had left at their death. And now they lay at the bottom of her trunk: she had not even put them on. To-day she felt no interest in anything. Willingly would she have flown away somewhere—but where, she knew not! Everything teased her; and what her mother had told her about Antek recurred persistently to her mind. What! *he* speak evil of her? She could not, would not believe it: the very thought made tears start.—Yet, it might be! . . . Yesterday, she was washing linen; he had passed by, and never looked her way! In the morning, she was going with Boryna to confession. Antek, coming in their direction, had turned back as from a savage dog. . . . Well, then, let him snarl at her if he would; let him snarl!

She began to feel herself in indignant revolt against him. But a sudden flash of memory brought that evening back to her, when they had returned together from plucking cabbages at his father's. The recollection went to her head, her mind was wrapped and plunged in flames all over; it revived so intensely that it was not to be borne. Thereupon, to make a diversion, she cried point-blank to her mother:

"I'll have you know I won't let my hair be cut off after the wedding!"

"Here's a clever one for you! Who ever heard of a girl whose hair was not shorn after the wedding?"

"At manors, and in towns."

"Certainly. Yes, they—*they* have to keep their hair, to cheat the folk, and pass for what they are not.—Why would you bring in a new order of things, you? Let the manor girls make laughing-stocks of themselves by all means; let them go about, hairy as Jewesses. They are fools, and they may. But you—no town rubbish, a daughter of the soil from grandsire and greatgrandsire—you have to do as has ever been done amongst our peasantry!—Ah, I know them, those town conceits and fancies!"

Yagna, however, stuck to her point. Eva, an experienced woman, who knew many a village, and year after year went on foot to Chenstohova with the pilgrim companies, tried her best to persuade the girl; so did Yagustynka, though according to her way seasoning her advice with jests and bitter railleries. At last she said:

"Keep your tresses, do; they will serve Boryna, when he beats you. He'll twist them round his hand, and so use his stick better upon you. And then you will cut them off by yourself. . . . I knew a woman . . ." But here she broke off. Vitek had come to call her. She was staying with Boryna since Antek's expulsion, Yuzka proving too young for a housekeeper. Now helping Eva in the cooking, she would once in a while run round to the house to see to things there, as the old man's brain was topsyturvy that day. Ever since morning, Yuzka had been at the blacksmith's, smartening herself; and Kuba lay continually ill in bed.

The lad had come in a hurry. "Kuba wants you sorely: pray come this instant."

"Off at once!—Good friends, I shall just see what it is, and be back here directly."

"Hurry, Yagna; we are expecting the bridesmaids," said Dominikova warningly.

But she made no haste at all, seemingly in a drowsy fit. . . . Her work fell from her fingers, and she would stand sometimes gazing vacantly out of window. Her soul was as though turned to water within her—water that flowed hither and thither, and now and again splashed and broke on some rock of memory.

In the cottage, the hubbub was ever increasing, with the

constant arrival of many a dame—now a kinswoman, now a housewife: these, according to ancient custom, bringing Dominikova fowls, or a loaf of wheaten bread, cake, salt, flour, pieces of bacon, or a silver rouble wrapped up in paper—all these things as thank-offerings for the invitation, and to make up for the heavy expenses incurred.

Each of them drank a little nip of sweetened vodka, chatted a few minutes with the old dame, admired everything, and hurried away.

Dominikova herself superintended the cooking, cleared things away, and saw that everything was duly done; not omitting to scold her sons for laziness; and, indeed, they dawdled much, and each of them slipped out whenever he could into the village to the Voyt's, where the musicians and the bridesmen had gathered already.

Few people attended High Mass, and this vexed his Reverence, because folk had forgotten the Divine Service on account of a mere wedding. Which was very true; but people also said to themselves that such a wedding was not to be witnessed every Sunday.

All those invited came driving in at once after the noonday meal from the neighbouring villages.

The sun, shedding a dim hazy splendour over the autumn fields, had begun to roll westward; the ground seemed shiny and glistening as if with dew, the pond shimmered tremulously, the roadside ditches had a glassy gleam; the whole landscape was soaked in the dying light and the cooling heat of the last autumn days.

Burning down like a candle, the day was slowly approaching extinction.

The village of Lipka, however, was inspired with all the animation of a fair.

No sooner had the Vesper bells rung for the first time than all the musicians at the Voyt's sallied forth into the road.

First came the fiddlers, each marching abreast with a flutist; then the bass-viol-players, and the drummers, to whose instruments there were little bells attached: all adorned with flying ribbons, and advancing with elastic steps.

After the musicians walked a troop of eight: the two "proposers," who had arranged the match, and the six bridesmen. These were all handsome young fellows, slender as pine-trees, slim-waisted, broad-shouldered, enthusiastic dancers, audacious of speech, fond of a fray, and great sticklers for their rights: such were they all six, and all of good families, pure farmer's blood.

Together they marched, shoulder to shoulder, down the middle of the road, the ground echoing under the tramping of their boots: with such merry daredevil looks, and so gayly adorned, that they killed the whole scene—a vision of striped trousers glancing in the sun, of scarlet jackets, hats decked with bunches of floating ribbons, and white capotes, open and flapping in the breeze like wings.

Uttering shrill cries, and humming joyful tunes, on they dashed, tramping noisily in measure—a young pine-grove in motion and rushing with the blast!

The musicians played polonaises, going from hut to hut to call the wedding guests; here vodka was offered them, there they were asked in; elsewhere a song would answer to their tunes; while on all sides the folk came out, dressed in their best raiment, and went swelling the main body. And under the windows of the bridesmaids all sang in unison the following verse:

Lasses, lightly treading,
Come ye to the wedding—
　　Hear our gleeful tune!
Hear our voices' chorus
Join with flute sonorous—
　　Hautboy and bassoon!
Let the tankard clink now:
Who is loth to drink now—
　　He's a scurvy loon!
Oy ta dana dana,
Oy ta dana dana,
　　Oy ta dana da!

And then they shouted so loud that they could be heard throughout the whole village, and beyond in the fields and the forests.

The folk had come out in front of their houses, into the orchards. Many who had not been invited joined the party, merely to look on and listen; so, before it had reached its destination, pretty nearly the whole village was round them, pressing and surging on every side, while the children ran on in front: a dense crowd, a swift and a noisy one.

Having brought the guests to the bridal cottage, playing them in with a joyful strain, they returned to fetch the bridegroom.

Vitek, who, brave in his short jacket adorned with ribbons, had accompanied the bridesmen, now ran fast before them.

"Master!" he cried through the window. "They are coming!" And off he ran to where Kuba lay.

They played a good while there before the porch. Boryna came out directly, threw the door wide open, and would have had them all in; but the Voyt and the Soltys took him by each arm and led him straight away to Yagna; for it was high time to go to church.

His gait was full of mettle, and he looked surprisingly young. Clean-shaven, with hair newly cut, and his wedding-suit on, he made a rarely handsome figure; besides which, portly and broad-shouldered as he was, the dignified expression both of his features and his whole outer man made him conspicuous from afar. He smiled and talked pleasantly with the young men who had come; especially with the smith, who managed to be always close to him.

They brought him in ceremony to Dominikova's, where the crowd made place for him; and, with tumultuous cries, and sounds of many instruments and songs, he entered the cabin.

Yagna was as yet invisible: the women were arraying her in the inner room, carefully watched and strongly bolted. For the young fellows knocked and battered at the door; they cut narrow slits in the partitions, and made careless jests with the bridesmaids: whereupon rose great screaming, much laughter, and of old women's scolding not less.

The old dame, with her sons, received the guests, offered vodka, conducted the elders to the places reserved for them, and in short had an eye to everything.

All the guests were of high condition: no common men, but only men of property and of good family; and of these only the wealthiest. All were connected with the Borynas and the Paches by ties of family and friendship, or were at least acquaintances who had driven over from distant villages.

None of your Klembas, or your Vincioreks, none of your one-acre starvelings were there: nor any of the small fry that eked out their existence by working for others, and were the closest adherents of old Klemba!

"No dainties for dogs, and no honey for hogs," says the adage!

Presently the door opened; and the organist's wife and the miller's ushered Yagna into the big room. The bridesmaids formed a circle round her—a wreath of human flowers they were, all so beautifully dressed and so fair to see. And she—she stood in their midst, like a rose, the most fearless of them all; with head-dress of plumes and ribbons and silver and gold lace, she was like one of those images they carry in church processions; and they all stood mute before her.

Ah! since the Mazur was first danced, no one was ever more splendid!

Then did the bridesmen lift up their voices, growling from the depths of their throats:

> Resound, O violin, resound!
> (Yagna, now ask pardon of your mother!)
> Resound, O flageolet, resound!
> (Yagna, now ask pardon of each brother!)

Boryna came forward and took her hand. They both knelt, and Dominikova made the sign of the cross over them with an image, and then sprinkled them both with holy water. Yagna, bursting into tears, fell at her mother's knees, embracing them, and the other women's too, as she begged pardon and took leave of them all. The women gathered her into their arms, passing her from one to another, and all wept much: Yuzka the most, thinking of her dead mother.

They all formed up before the house and marched off on foot, for the church was but one field away.

Then the bridesmen took possession of Yagna. She walked on with delight, smiling through the tears which still trembled in her lashes. She now was gay to see as a spring-blossoming bush, and riveted every eye. Her hair, braided over her forehead, bore above it a rich pile of gold spangles, and peacock's eyes, and sprigs of rosemary. Therefrom, down to her nape and shoulders, fell long ribbons of every hue; her white skirt was gathered at the waist in abundant folds; her corsage, of sky-blue velvet, was laced with silver; she wore great puffed sleeves to her chemise. Round her throat there was an abundant frill, embroidered with designs in dark-blue thread, and necklaces of coral and amber, row upon row, hung covering half her bosom.

Matthias was being led by the bridesmaids.

As the stalwart oak may be seen rising behind the graceful pine in the woods, so did he appear after Yagna's figure. There was in his gait a certain jaunty swing, and he shot glances on either side of the road: he fancied he had beheld Antek in the ruck.

Following him came Dominikova, with the "proposers," the smith and his family, Yuzka, the miller's and the organist's people, and all the persons of any note.

And following these came the whole village.

The sun was now hanging above the woods, red, enormous, flooding all the road, and the pond, and the huts, with its blood-red glow.

In the midst of this crimson conflagration they walked on slowly. It made the eyes blink to see them as they went —with ribbons and peacock plumes and flowers; gay in red trousers, petticoats of orange tints, rainbow kerchiefs, snowy capotes: just as if a whole field full of flowers in bloom had arisen and moved forward, swaying in the wind!

Aye, and singing too! For again and again the high treble of the bridesmaids' voices would strike up the ditty:

On the clattering wagons go,
And my heart is full of woe,
Alas!
Round you while our songs rise glad,
You, O Yagna, you are sad,
Alas!

All the way, Dominikova was in tears, her eyes fixed upon Yagna alone.

Ambrose was already lighting the tapers in church when they came.

They formed in ranks—two and two—and proceeded toward the high altar, just as the priest was coming out of the sacrisy.

The wedding was soon over: his Reverence had to visit a sick man in haste. When they left the church, the organist played them out with Mazurs, Obertases, and Kuyavy dances, till their feet beat time of themselves; and more than one was on the point of singing aloud, but luckily remembered where he was.

They returned pell-mell, and very noisily, for bridesmen and bridesmaids were singing together.

Dominikova got to her home first and, when the company arrived, was there to welcome the newly married couple on her threshold, and offer them the hallowed bread and salt; then she had to receive the whole company a second time, embrace them all, and ask them in once more!

In the passage, the music was striking up. So, on passing the threshold, everyone made a partner of the first woman he met, to perform the stately polonaise that was being played. At once, like a many-coloured serpent, a chain of couples, following each other about the room, waved and twined, twisted and turned back decorously, struck the floor with dignity, swayed to and fro in graceful undulation, placed, swam, wheeled about, one after another in serried ranks, Boryna with Yagna leading off!

The lights placed on the chimney penthouse flickered, and the very walls seemed like to fall asunder with the forceful gravity of this solemn dance, performed with such dignified grace.

This was the introduction, and lasted but some minutes. Then began the first dance, in honour of the bride, and according to the usages and customs of old days. All present squeezed themselves into corners, or huddled against the walls; and the young men made a wide circle, within which she danced. As she stepped out, she felt the blood tingling in her veins; her dark-blue eyes shone; her white teeth gleamed; her face was flushed; she danced persistently, and for a long time, for she was obliged to give each partner at least one turn round the room, and dance with all.

The musicians worked hard—worked till they felt worn out: but Yagna seemed to have but just begun. The flush on her face deepened, she turned and whirled more impetuously than ever; her ribbons fluttered and rustled as she went by, lashing those near her on the cheek; and her skirt, expanding to the streaming air, spread out and bellied wide around her.

The young men, delighted, beat time on the tables, and shouted in eager excitement.

It was only after all the others that she chose her bridegroom. Boryna, who had been waiting so long, now leaped forward, pouncing on her like a forest lynx, seized her waist, whirled her round like a hurricane, and cried to the players:

"Now, boys, the Mazur—and with a will!"

All the instruments sounded with might and main; the whole room was in a fever.

Holding Yagna in a strong grip, Boryna lifted the skirts of his capote over each arm, settled his hat upon his head, clicked his heels together, and set off, swift as the wind!

Ah! but how he danced! Now turning round and round, now with a backward step, now bringing his foot down as if he would stamp the floor to shivers—then sidling with Yagna, and sweeping her on, and whisking her hither and thither, and whirling her so that they twain formed but one indistinct mass, looking for all the world like a spindle full of yarn, spinning about a room; and from each of them there came forth a full blast of power and force.

Furiously, unceasingly, the players went on playing the Mazur dance!

The crowds in the corners and at the door looked on in silent wonder: Boryna was so indefatigably active, and ever at higher and higher pressure, that he instilled not a few with riotous boisterousness, even to beating the measure with their feet; and some of the hottest heads, no longer restrained by decorum, seized a girl and danced about with her.

Yagna, though brawny and well-knit, soon had to give in; he felt her weakening in his arms, and immediately ceased from dancing, and led her to the inner room.

"What a splendid fellow you are!" the miller cried out. "Henceforth you are my brother!—Ask me to be godfather at the first christening, I pray you!" And he put his arm round Boryna's neck. Soon they were on very familiar terms, for the music had stopped and refreshments were handed round.

Dominikova and her sons, with the smith and Yagustynka, now glided swiftly about, bearing bottles and clusters of glasses, and drank with each one. Yuzka and the friends of the old dame carried pieces of bread and cake about in sieves to the guests.

And the tumult grew and increased.

On a bench near the window sat the miller, with Boryna, the Voyt, the organist—all the notables in the place besides; and there a bottle of rum—not of the worst—was circulating among them.

Many were also standing about the room in groups, talking loudly to anyone they met, as they felt inclined; and the vodka glasses were in requisition.

The inner room was lit by the organist's great lamp, lent

for the occasion. The housewives, with the organist's wife and the miller's at their head, had gathered there, and sat on chests and benches strewn with pieces of woven wool. They held their heads up with great dignity, sipped their mead by tiny droplets, crumbled the sweet cake with dainty fingers, and very rarely threw in a word or two, but listened attentively while the miller's wife told them all about her children.

The very passages were quite full. Some tried to invade the other side; but Eva drove them out. They proved too greedy for the dishes, the appetizing scent of which had filled the house, and was making many a mouth water.

The young people then dispersed all about the premises, in the yard and the orchard. The night was chilly, but serene and starlit. Here they strolled, disporting themselves in merry guise; and all the place echoed with laughter, shouts, and running to and fro, one chasing another among the trees. So the elders cried a warning to them from the window:

"Are ye seeking flowers by night, girls?—Beware lest ye lose what is more than any flower!"

But who paid heed to them?

Yagna and Nastusia were now walking about the big room, their arms round each other's waists, whispering together, and ever and anon bursting into laughter. Simon, Dominikova's eldest son, was watching them, with eyes glued to Nastusia, and frequently going to her with vodka and attempting conversation.

The blacksmith had dressed up most grandly, having on a black capote, and trousers over which the boots were drawn. He slipped about with great activity, was everywhere, drank with everybody, walked to and fro and talked; and his red head and freckled face were never long on the same spot.

The young people danced several times, but not long, nor with much animation. They were looking forward to the supper.

The old men, on their side, were deep in debate, the Voyt

raising his voice higher and higher, striking the table with his fist, and laying down the law:

"I, the Voyt, have said it: you may take it from me. I, a man in office, have received a paper commanding me to call a meeting, and order half a kopek per acre to be voted by every landowner for educational purposes."

"You, Peter, may vote even five kopeks an acre if you like: we won't!"

"No, that we will not!" one of the men roared.

"But I am making you a statement as an official!"

"We do not care for such schools as those," Boryna remarked; and the others assented in chorus.[1]

"In Vola," said one, "there is a school which my children attended for three winters running. What is the result? They cannot even read in a prayer-book.—Devil take such teaching!"

"Let the mothers teach prayers at home; prayers have naught to do with studies. I, the Voyt, tell you this!"

"Then what are schools for?" grumbled the man from Vola, rising.

"I will tell you, I the Voyt: but listen . . ."

Here he was interrupted by Simon, who cried aloud to them all that the trees of the clearing sold to the Jews had already been branded by them, and that they would have them cut down as soon as the sledges could run.

"Brand the trees they may: to fell them will be harder!" Boryna put in.

"We shall complain to the commissary."

"Who is hand in glove with the Squire?—No: let us go in a body and drive the woodmen off."

"They shall not hew down one single sapling!"

"Matthias, drink to me! Now is no time for holding councils. A tipsy man will even defy God!" So cried the miller, filling Boryna's glass. The talk was as little to his

[1] The reader should bear in mind that this book was published before the War, when only schools where Russian was taught were permitted by the government, and Polish was not learned except in secret.—*Translator's Note.*

taste as the threats were; for he had an agreement drawn up with the Jews, and the trees were to go to his sawmill.

They drank and left their places; the tables were now to be laid for supper, and all the needful things were being brought in.

The farmers, however, still stuck to their forest grievance, which was a great wrong done to them. They formed a group, and with lowered voices (so that the miller might not overhear them) determined to thresh the matter out at Boryna's.

At this juncture, Ambrose came in, and went straight to them. He had come late, having had to go with his Reverence to a sick person three villages away, in Krosnova. So now he set to drink energetically, to make up for lost time. Vainly: for at that very moment a chorus of elderly women struck up the song:

> Bridesmen, about, about! With you it rests
> Round the spread tables now to bring the guests!

To which they replied, having given the signal by striking on the benches:

> Lo, we have called them: they are ready here
> Your spread to taste, if it be but good cheer.

The guests, now straggling in to table, took their seats on the benches.

The newly married couple had the first places, and all the others sat about them in order of precedence, as they were higher in standing, in possessions, or more advanced in age—from the elders to the girls and children. Tables had been set up along three of the walls, and yet there was scarce room for them all. The bridesmen and the musicians remained standing, the former to serve the guests.

There was a hush. The organist stood up and said a prayer aloud; after which, a glass went round, with the sentiment: Health and enjoyment!

The cooks and bridesmen then bore in a huge and deep dish of smoking food, singing the while:

Friends, we bring you dainty food:
Fowls in rice-soup boiled and stewed!

And, carrying in the second dish:

Tripe with pepper, spiced and hot:
He's a fool that likes it not!

The musicians, stationed near the fire-place, played various tunes very softly, to give more savour to the food.

All the company ate with becoming refinement, and deliberation; few spoke at all, and for some time the room resounded only with the sound of munching and the clatter of spoons. When they had to some extent slaked their appetites, the smith set another bottle in circulation; and now they began conversing (though in low tones) to one another across the table.

Yagna ate scarcely anything at all. In vain did Boryna urge and coax her, entreating her as one entreats a child to eat. She could not even swallow the meat before her; she was so hot, so tired!

"Yagna, are you content, sweet? Most beautiful Yagna, you will be as happy with me as ever you were with your mother. . . . Yagna, you will be a lady—a lady! I'll hire a girl, that you may not be overworked."—He spoke in hushed tones, and looking with love into her eyes, caring not for what folk might say; and they began to make fun of him openly.

"He looks like a cat after bacon!"

"How the old fellow flaunts his wantonness! Beside him, a cock is nothing at all."

"Oh, he is enjoying himself, Grandfather Boryna is!"

"As a dog does out in the frost," old Simon here muttered spitefully.

All held their sides with laughter, and the miller laid his face down on the table and beat it with his fists for sheer joy!

Once more the cooks entered, proclaiming:

Here is a dish of Turkish wheat,
Cooked with plenty of lard, for lean folk to eat!

"Yagna, just bend over to me, I'll tell you a thing," the Voyt said, plucking at her dress behind her bridegroom, whose next neighbour he was.

"I would be your child's godfather," he cried, laughing, and gloating over her with greedy eyes.

At this, she grew very red; and the women, seeing this, fell a-laughing and jesting yet more facetiously, some setting to explain to her how she ought to behave to her husband.

"You'll have to warm a feather-bed for him every evening before the fire, or he'll be cold as ice."

"And especially see he has much fat to eat: it will keep him in good condition."

"And pet him well, with your arms round his neck."

"And drive him with a gentle hand, that he may not know he is driven at all!"

So they babbled on, each sentence freer than the last, as happens when women have taken too much, and let their tongues run away with them.

All in the room were shaking with merriment, and things at last went so far that the miller's wife set to lecturing them on their duties towards the girls and little ones present; and the organist pointed out how grievous a sin it was to cause others to offend by evil example.

"What? is this bellows-blower forbidding people every pleasure in life?"

"Being close to the priest, he thinks himself a saint!"

"Let him stop his ears, an it like him not." And more unpleasant cries began to be heard, for he was disliked in the village.

"We have a wedding to-day, and therefore, my good people, I, your Voyt, assure you it is no sin to enjoy yourselves, laugh at things laughable, and make merry."

"And our Lord Himself used to go to weddings and drink wine," Ambrose added seriously; but no one made out what he said, as he was now tipsy, and sitting by the door besides. Then all fell to talking, joking, clinking glasses, and eating more and more slowly, in order to get more compactly filled up; some even, to make room for the most food possible, undid their girdles, and sat straight and stiff.

Again the cooks entered, with the following couplet:

> It grunting, squealing, rooting once about the garden ran:
> But now, for all the harm it did, 'twill pay the husbandman!

"Well, they have done the thing grandly!" the people declared.

"Truly, this wedding must come at least to a thousand *zloty!*"

"Oh, she can well afford it: has she not got six acres of land thereby?"

"Just look at Yagna! Is she not gloomy as night?"

"As a set-off, Boryna's eyes are shining like a wildcat's."

"Say, like tinder, my friend—rotten tinder!"

"Aye, the man will weep over this day yet."

"No. He is not of the weeping sort. Of the cudgelling, rather."

"Just what I said to the Voyt's wife, when she told me the marriage had been settled."

"Ah, I wonder why she is not here to-night."

"Out of the question. Her child may be due any day."

"But I'd lay my head that in no long time—say, before the Carnival begins—Yagna will be again running after the lads."

"Matthew is only waiting for that."

"I know. Vavrek's wife overheard him say so in the tavern."

"Because he was not asked to the wedding."

"Yes. The old fellow would have had him, but Dominikova was against it.—All the folk know why, do they not?"

"Well, all say so; but what has anybody seen?"

"Bartek Koziol saw them in the wood last spring."

"He is a liar and a thief: Dominikova accused him of stealing a pig, and what he says may be mere spite."

"But others too—there be others that have eyes."

"All this will end ill . . . you will see. 'Tis no affair of mine, but to my mind, Antek and his family have been unjustly dealt with."

"Of Antek, too, people talk—say they have been seen together here and there."—The voices dropped lower as the spiteful talk went on, leaving no shred of reputation on any of the family, and the more unmerciful for their hostess as they had more pity for her two sons.

"Is't not a sin?—Simon, a man wearing mustachios—thirty, if a day—and she will not let him marry, nor leave the house: and for the slight fault she raises a tempest!"

"It is indeed a shame: such strapping lads, and doing all the woman's work!"

"So that Yagna, forsooth, may not soil her hands!"

"Each of them has five acres of his own, and might marry at his ease!"

"With so many unmarried girls around them!"

"Yes, yes; your own poor Martianna, waiting for ages, and the land quite close by Paches'!"

"You let her alone! See rather to your girl Franka, lest she come to grief with Adam!"

"Those great oafs!—Afraid to leave their mother's apron-strings!"

"They are beginning: Simon has been all the evening staring at Nastka."

"Their father was of the like mould: I remember well.—'Aye, and the old woman was in her time no better than Yagna."

"As the root is, so the boughs; as the mother, so the daughter."

The music ceased, and, supper being over, the musicians went to refresh themselves in the kitchen. But after a time the noise waxed even louder than before, and the whole place seethed with uproar: all talking, ranting, shouting away one to the other across the tables, and no one able to make out what was said.

At the close of the meal, the most select guests were offered a drink compounded of mead and spices, while the others got strong vodka and beer in abundance.

By this time, but few were well aware of what they were drinking, being too far gone and in a blissful state. They made themselves comfortable, and unbuttoned their capotes to be cooler; beat the tables with their fists till the dishes jingled, embraced each other, either round the neck or clutching at the shirt-collar; and they talked freely, unbosoming themselves and telling all their sorrows as if they had been brothers.

" 'Tis ill living here on earth! Things are out of gear with mankind, and we have naught but grief!"

"Aye, men are like dogs, snapping at one another for a bone."

"No consolation, save when neighbour meets neighbour over a glass, and they take counsel, and make complaint; and if any has wronged or been wronged, he is forgiven and forgives!"

"As even now, at this wedding-feast: but, ah! for one day only!"

"Ah! To-morrow will come, though we call him not! You'll not shun him, save in God's hallowed Acre. . . . Yea, he will come and seize you, and lay on you his yoke, and smite you with the whip of poverty; and you, O man! must pull . . . even till the yoke be bloodstained."

"What is't aggravates our misery, setting men one against the other, like dogs quarrelling for a fleshless bone?"

"Not poverty alone, but an Evil Power; and they then are blinded by him, discerning not good from evil."

"Truly so; and he bloweth upon our souls as one bloweth on half-quenched embers; and he causeth greed, malice, and all wickedness to burst out into flame!"

"Yes; for he that is deaf to the commandments hath a quick ear for the music played in hell."

"It was otherwise of old days.—Then was there obedience, and respect for old men, and concord."

"And each man had land, as much as he could till; and pastures, and meadows, and the forest."

"Who in those days ever heard of taxes?"

"Or was there anyone that purchased timber? He had but to drive to the wood and take all he needed, though it were the best pine or oak. The property of the Squire was the peasants' property too."

"And now it belongs to neither, but to the Jews, or to men still worse."

"The foul carrion! (I have drunk to you: drink you to me! . . . They are now established as on land of their own! (Your health, Brother!) . . . To drink vodka is not a sin, if only at the proper season and with brothers: this is a wholesome thing, it cleanses the blood and drives away distempers."

"Who drinks at all, should drink one quart complete—likewise, who makes merry, should do it all Sunday long. —But have you work to do? Man, do it with all your might, grudge not your force, but put forth all your strength. And if ill things come to pass—if your wife be taken, if your cattle die, or your home burn down—why, 'tis the will of God. Do not rebel: what will it avail you to lament, poor creature as you are? Be patient, therefore; trust in God's mercy. Aye, and if the worst should hap, and should grim Cross-Bones stare you in the face and clutch your throat, attempt not to escape, which is more than you can do; all is in the hand of God!"

"Verily, who is to know the day when the Lord shall declare: 'Thus far, O man, is thine: what is beyond is mine?' "

"It is so of a truth. As lightning flashes, so are the decrees of God: and none, be he a priest, be he a sage, can know them till they fall, as ripe corn falls out of the ear."

"Man, you have to know but one thing—to do your duty, live as God commands you, and not look too far ahead.—Surely our Lord prepares the wages of His servants, and pays most strictly what is due to each."

"By these laws did the Polish people stand of old; and they are for ever and ever, Amen."

"Aye, and by patience shall we prevail against the gates of hell."

Thus they discoursed together, with not infrequent libations, everything pouring out all he felt in his heart, all that had long stuck in his throat and stifled him. Ambrose talked the most of all and the loudest.

At the very end, Eva and Yagustynka came in with great ceremony, bearing in front of them a large ladle, tricked out and beribboned. A musician who followed accompanied them on his fiddle, while they sang:

> Ere you quit us, here come we;
> 'Fore you both your cooks you see:
> Pray forget us not, good men:
> For each dish give stivers three;
> For our seasoning stivers ten!

The company had eaten plentifully, and drunk yet more; their hearts were warmed by good cheer, and many a man tossed even silver coins into the ladle as it passed.

They then slowly rose from table, and went out, some to breathe the fresh air, some to resume their conversation in the passages or in the great room; some gave way to enthusiastic demonstrations of friendship; and more than one reeled about, running his head against the walls or some other man, butting like rams.

Only the Voyt remained at the board with the miller, both quarrelling with intense fury, and about to fly at each other like two hawks, when Ambrose came to reconcile them, offering more vodka.

"Back to your church porch, old beggar," the Voyt snarled at him, "and hold yourself aloof from your betters."

So Ambrose walked off in dudgeon, hugging the bottle to his breast, stumping noisily and seeking someone to drink and talk with as a friend.

The young people had dispersed about the orchard, or were walking arm-in-arm along the road, with much horse-play, and chasing of one another, and shouting. The night was serene; the moon hung over the pond, which glittered so bright that the feeblest circles tremulous on its surface were distinctly visible, moving like snake-coils in silence, responsive (as it seemed) to the light that struck on them from above. The frost was pretty hard, the road-ruts were crisp underfoot, the roofs rime-crusted and hoary. It was in the small hours, for the first cock-crow had already been heard.

Meanwhile they set the great room in order for dancing again.

Rested and refreshed, the players now again, in subdued strains, called the guests together.

Yagna had been taken to the private room by the matrons, Boryna sat with Dominikova close to the door, the elders took seats on benches and in corners, where they discussed various matters, and only the girls stood about the room besides, giggling together: a pastime which soon tired them, and they decided on starting some games, "to stir the boys up a little."

First there was the game, "Fox goes out to make his round; both his hands and feet are bound."

Yasyek, nicknamed Topsy-turvy, was dressed up as Fox, in his sheepskin turned inside out. He was a silly fellow, a simpleton, and the laughing-stock of them all. Though a full-grown man, he played with children, and was in love with all the girls and foolish beyond measure: but, being an only child with ten acres of his own, he was invited everywhere. Yuzka Boryna was his quarry, the Hare. And they laughed; Lord, how they laughed!

At every step, Yasyek stumbled and fell down, sprawling, with a thud like a log. The others, too, put out their feet to make him fall; and Yuzka got out of his way with perfect ease: she sat up quite as a hare does, and imitated to perfection the way its lips move.

Then came "Quails."

Nastka was leader, and so nimble that no one could catch her till she let them (in order to dance a measure with someone).

Finally, Tomek Vahnik was made up for a Stork, having a sheet over his head and a long stick which he held under it for beak; and he clack-clack-clacked like a real stork, so well that Yuzka, Vitek, and all the youngsters ran after him, calling (as they do to the live bird):

> Klek, Klek, Klell!
> Thy mother's in hell!
> What does she there?
> Cook children's fare!
> What was her sin?
> That her little ones' bellies had nothing in!

And the hullabaloo was great; for he ran after them, and pecked with his beak, and flapped his wings violently.

These games lasted but an hour, when they had to make way for other observances.

Now the married women brought Yagna out of the private room, covered all over in a white wrapper, and seated her in the centre, on a kneading-trough on which a featherbed had been put. The bridesmaids thereupon rushed forward as though to snatch her away, but the men kept them off: and at last they formed a group opposite, intoning a sad and plaintive chant:

> Where is your wreath, oh, where
> Your bridal wreath so fair?
> Henceforth, to man's will bowed,
> A cap, your locks to shroud,
> You on your head must bear!

The matrons then uncovered her.

She was seen wearing the cap of the married women over the thick plaits of her tresses; yet in this disguise she appeared still more fascinating than before.

To the slow strains of the band, the whole assembly, young and old, struck up the "Hop-Song" in one grand unison of gladness. This ended, she was taken over by the matrons alone, to dance with them. . . . Yagustynka, by this time much heated, set her arms akimbo, and flung this impromptu verse at her:

> Oh! had I known this day would see
> My Yagna wed a widower,
> A wreath I would have woven thee
> Of naught but prickly juniper!

After which came others, yet more biting than the first.

But little note was taken of them; for the musicians had struck up for the greatest performance of all; and forward now came the dancers, and the trampling of many feet was heard. They crowded thickly, couple close to couple, cheek by jowl, moving ever more swiftly as the dance went on. Capotes flew open and flapped wide, heels stamped, hats waved—now and then a snatch of song burst forth—the girls hummed the burden, "da dana," and tore on more quickly still, and swayed in measure in the mighty, swirling, headlong rush! No one could any longer distinguish his neighbour in the throng; and when the violins burst forth in quick sharp volleys of clean-cut separate notes, a hundred feet echoed on the floor at once, a hundred mouths gave tongue, a hundred dancers, seized as by a cyclone, whirled round and round; and the rustling of capotes, skirts, kerchiefs waving about the room, was like the flight of a flock of many-coloured birds. On they went, on continually—dancing without the slightest pause for breath, the floor clattering like a drum, the walls vibrating, the room a seething cauldron. And the rapture of the dance waxed greater, greater yet.

Then came the moment to perform rites which are always gone through when the bride puts aside her crown of rosemary.

First, Yagna had to pay toll, on entering the matrons' set!

Immediately afterwards, another ceremony was gone through. The men had a long rope, woven of the straw of unthreshed wheat, of which they made a large ring, carefully held and guarded by the bridesmaids, Yagna standing up in the middle. Whoever wished to dance with her was obliged to creep under it, tear her away by force, and tread a measure, though they scourged him all the time with cords, wherever they could. Finally, the miller's wife and Vahnikova made a collection, for "The Cap." The Voyt came first; he tossed a gold piece into the plate; after that, silver roubles tinkled like hail; lastly, paper ones, as leaves in autumn.

More than three hundred roubles were thus collected!

Dominikova, quite overcome to see so large a sum offered for Yagna's sake, told her sons to bring more vodka, with which she herself pledged her hosts, kissing her friends and weeping at their great kindness.

"Drink, my good neighbours, drink, dear friends, beloved brothers of mine. . . . I feel spring back in my heart again . . . ! Yagna's health . . . drink once more . . . once more . . ." And when she gave over, the smith drank with others, and her sons too, each separately; for the throng was very thick. Yagna too, thanking them heartily for their kindness, embraced the knees of the elders present.

The room was humming, the glasses circulating freely from hand to hand; everyone exhaled ardour and joy. Faces were crimson, eyes resplendent; hearts went out to hearts. They stood in knots about the room, drinking and talking blithely, each saying his say very loud, unheard by any, but not caring for that!—All felt at one; one joy united and penetrated them all! "Ye that have troubles, leave them for the morrow; take your fling to-night: enjoy friendly company, solace your soul! Our hallowed land, its summer spell of fruit-bearing over, is given rest by the Lord: even so is it meet that men should rest in autumn, when their field-work is done. Man, that have your cornstacks piled and your granaries full of grain worth heaps of precious gold—rest you now from summer labour and toil gone by!"

So spake some, while others again revolved in their minds their troubles and their griefs.

To neither of these classes did Boryna belong. His eyes saw only Yagna, his heart swelling and throbbing with the pride of her beauty. Again and again would he throw *zloty* to the musicians, that they might not spare catgut: for the sounds were growing weak, as their zeal was flagging.

On a sudden, then, they thundered out an Obertas that made one quiver to the backbone. Boryna leaped to Yagna's side, caught her in a mighty grasp, and at once started such a dance as shook the planks beneath them. He wafted her down the room—back again—clanged on the floor with his horseshoe heels—knelt suddenly to her, and sprung up again in a flash—bore her about from wall to wall—roared out a solo which the instruments took up and accompanied, and still led the dance, while other couples imitated him, leaping, singing, stamping, and all with ever-increasing rapidity: as if as many spindles full of particoloured wools were together on the floor, turning, twisting, twirling, faster than the eyes could make out their hues; so that no one could discern lad from lass in the swift rush—only rainbow masses, flying about, driven as by a goal, with ever-changing tints, turning always with greater and more impetuous speed! At times the rush of air even blew out the candles: the music went on in the dark, and the dance as well, lit by the faint white beams of the moon shining in through the window. Then, athwart the seething dimness, were seen quick shadows, flying fast, chasing one another in the mingled darkness and silvery mist; foaming waves of pale glimmering and melodious din surged up out of the black night, in dusky harmonies of colour and sound—as in a vision or a dream—fading back into impenetrable murk, to loom once more distinct against the pallid wall, from which the glazed images of the saints reflected the moonbeams with crinkled flickers; and again they plunged and vanished into the shadows, and only the sounds of heavy breathing, and quick steps and cries, made their presence vaguely known in the entangled confusion of the unlit room!

One dance followed another in rapid succession, and with no interval between them. As each new dance was struck up, new dancers directly sprang forward, erect as a forest, swift of advance as a gale of wind; and loudly the stamping feet thundered afar, and shouts of merriment echoed through the house, while the onset went on, wild, mad, stormy, and earnest as a struggle for life and death!

Ah! how they danced!

Those Cracoviennes, with their frolicsome hop-skip-and-jump measures, and the quick lilt of their clean-cut, tinkling, metallic tunes; and the terse ditties, full of fun and freedom, with which, like the spangled girdles of the peasantry who made them, they are so brightly studded—those tunes welling with joyous dashing melody, redolent of the strong, abounding, audacious savour of youth in sportful pursuit of the sweet thrilling emotions that tell of the heyday in the blood!

And those Mazurs, long-drawn-out as the paths which streak the endless plains, wind-clamorous and vast as the endless plains they streak: lowly, yet heaven-kissing; melancholy and bold, magnificent and sombre, stately and fierce: genial, warlike, full of discordances, like that peasants' nature, set in battle array, united as a forest and rushing to dance with such joyful clamours and wonderful strength as could attack and overcome ten times their number, nay, conquer, sweep away, trample down, the whole of a hostile world, nor reck though they themselves be doomed, and fall, but still carry on the dance after death, still stamping as in the Mazur—still crying out aloud: "Oy dana dana!"

And oh, those Obertases!—short of rhythm, vertiginous, wild and frantic, warlike and amorous, full of excitement mingled with dreamy languor and notes of sorrow; throbbing with hot blood, brimming over with geniality and kindliness, in a sudden hailstorm: affectionate voices, dark-blue glances, springtime breezes, and fragrant wafts from blossoming orchards, like the song of fields in the young year; making tears and laughter to burst forth at the same time, and the heart to utter its lay of joy, and the longing soul to go beyond the vast fields around her, beyond the far-off forests, and soar dreaming into the world of All Things, and sing ecstatically the burden, "Oy dana dana!"

And all these dances, beyond the power of words to describe, thus followed one after the other, that our peasantry might make merry in season!

And thus did they take their pleasures at the wedding of Boryna and Yagna.

The hours slipped away in clamour and din and uproar; in noisy merry-making and dances fast and furious: they did not note that the dawn was spreading in the East, that the daybreak's streams were slowly pouring their pallor into the night's black gloom. The stars grew wan, the moon sank; a wind that sprang up beyond the woods passed by, chasing the dark that waxed thinner and thinner: the gnarled tufted trees looked in at the windows, bowing yet lower their slumbrous frost-crowned heads, but the folk within were singing and dancing still!

The doors had been thrown wide open; so had the windows; the house, brimming and boiling over with lights and tumult, trembled, creaked and groaned, while the dance went on, now in utterly uncontrollable and rapturous excitement. It seemed to those within—such was their state! —that trees and people, earth and stars, and the hedges and the time-honoured cabin itself, were all wrestling and writhing together, united in one inextricably whirling cluster, blind, intoxicated, raving, and in utter oblivion of all; reeling and rolling from room to room, from wall to wall, from passage to passage, and out into the road and the enormous world, caught in a round that filled the universe—fading away in the long unbroken chain of crimson lights now glowing in the East!

And the music led them on—the tunes played and the songs.

How they kept time in their growling, the gruff bass-viols, uttering their broken humming sounds, like huge humblebees! And how the flutes led the band, merrily whistling and twittering, as in mockery of the drum's joyful thuds and strokes, swelled by the jingling of its bells that shook with laughter, and floated lightly like a Jew's beard in the wind! And then how the fiddles took the lead and came to the front, like girls leading the ballet, and sang out loud and shrill at first as though to try their voices—then played with wide, sorrowful, heart-rending sweeps of the bow—the lamentations of orphans driven from their homes—and then again, with an instantaneous change, fell into a lilting tune—short, trilling, sharp, like the tripping of a hundred dancers' heels, at which a hundred full-throated lads shouted themselves out of breath, and quivered all over, and set once more to turn and sing and dance mincingly, laughing and rejoicing, heat rising anew to the head and desire to the heart, lie strong vodka . . . when they fell again into the slow long notes of sorrow and weeping—as dew upon the plains!—uttering the notes of our own beloved tune, most near to the heart, instinct with mighty yearning tenderness, and making all dance deliriously to the strains of our Mazovian air!

. . . .

The candles were growing dim, so near was the day; a dingy ashen twilight pervaded the room where they danced. But they still took their enjoyment as heartily as ever. If any found the liquor now flowing too scantily, he sent to the tavern for more vodka, sought out companions, and drank with them to his liking.

Some had withdrawn; some were tired and resting awhile; some, overtaken by drink, were sleeping off its fumes in the passage or by the door: others, still more intoxicated, were stretched under the hedges. All the rest danced on, danced ever.

At last, some of the more sober made up a group by the porch and, beating the floor in measure, sang thus:

O wedding-guests, come home!
Already sings the lark;

The wood is deep and dark,
And ye have far to roam:
Come home!

O wedding-guests, come home!
There's danger in delay:
Athwart our weary way
The loud floods roll and foam:
Come home!

But no one cared to listen to them and their song!

CHAPTER XII

IT was grey dawn when Vitek, tired out by the merry-making and driven home by Yagustynka, hastened to Boryna's hut.

A little watch-light was burning there, like a glow-worm. Vitek looked in at the window, and beheld the old *Dziad*, Roch, sitting at the table, where he was singing hymns.

The boy silently glided away to the stable, and was fumbling at the door-catch, when he jumped back with a cry of astonishment. A dog had leaped upon him, uttering a whine.

"What, Lapa, Lapa? 'tis you back again, poor wretch!" he cried, and sat down on the door-step, overcome with joy. —"Hungry and starving: is it not so?"

He had put by a bit of sausage, saved from the feast, which he now took out of his bosom to offer the dog. But it did not care for food just then: it barked, laid its head on the lad's breast, and whined for sheer delight.

"Did they starve you, poor thing? did they drive you away?" he whispered, opening the cow-byre door, and at once throwing himself on his straw bed. "But now I shall defend and take care of you." With these words he nestled deep in the straw; and the dog, lying down beside him, growled gently and licked his face.

They were both asleep in an instant.

From the stable close by, Kuba called to him in a voice weakened by illness. He called for a long time; but Vitek was sleeping like a dormouse.

After a time, however, Lapa recognized his voice, and fell to barking furiously and pulling the boy's coat.

"What's the matter?" Vitek asked sleepily.

"Water! The fever is pulling me to pieces. . . . Water!"

Vitek, peevish and drowsy though he was, brought him a pailful, and held it to his lips.

"I am so ill, I can hardly breathe! . . . What's growling round here?"

"Why, Lapa!"

"Lapa is it?" Kuba groped to touch the dog's head in the dark; and Lapa leaped about, frisked, and tried to get on to the bed.

"Vitek, give the horses their hay; they have been gnawing the empty mangers a long time; and I cannot move. . . . Are they still dancing?" he asked a little later, when the lad was filling the racks with hay.

"They are not like to have done till noon; and some are so drunk, they are lying by the roadside."

"Ah, they are enjoying themselves, the masters are!" And he sighed deeply.

"Was the miller there?"

"Aye, but he left rather early."

"Many people?"

"Beyond counting. Why, the cabin was overflowing with them."

"Plenty for all?"

"Like manor guests! They brought them meat in such huge dishes! And vodka and beer and mead were poured out in floods! Of sausages alone, there were piles enough to fill three troughs."

"When is the bride coming?"

"This afternoon."

"They are rejoicing and feasting still. My God! I thought I'd gnaw a bone at least, and eat my fill once in my life! . . . And here I am, lying, sighing, and hearing about other people's good cheer!"

Vitek returned to his bed.

"If I could but feast my eyes on those good things!"

He said no more, feeling weary, sad, and tormented by a sort of faint timid querulousness that gnawed at his heart now. At last, however, he spoke, patting the dog's head.

"Well, well! may they all be the better for it! Let *them* at least get some pleasure out of this life!"

The fever, increasing, began to confuse his thoughts; to drive it away, he applied himself to prayer, offering himself to the mercy of the Lord Jesus; but he could not remember what he was saying; he was dazed with sleep coming over him, and only a string of ejaculations that were prayers mingled with tears, trickled from his consciousness —the told beads of a crimson rosary!

Now and then he roused himself, but only to look around him blankly, recognizing nothing, and fall back into deathly and corpselike unconsciousness.

Again he woke, now to groan so loud that the horses pulled at their bonds and snorted to hear him.

"O God! that I may but hold out till day!" he moaned in terror; and his eyes wandered through the window, staring out at the world and the approaching dawn, seeking the sun in that sky yet grey and lifeless and studded with paling stars.

But the day was a long distance away still.

In the stable, plunged in turbid mistiness, the horses' outlines were growing dimly visible; and the racks beneath the window slits showed like ribs in the pale glimmer.

Fall asleep again he could not: the pains were torturing him anew; they felt like sharp gnarled sticks thrust into his legs, piercing, boring, stabbing in and in; and the agony became so unbearable that he started up, screaming with all his might, till Vitek woke and came round.

"I am dying! . . . Oh, how it pains! . . . How the pain swells! how it crushes me! Vitek, run for Ambrose . . . O Lord! . . . Or else call Yagustynka. . . . Perhaps she can help. . . . I am not able—my last hour is here . . ." He burst out weeping terribly.

Vitek, all sleepy as he was, ran to the wedding feast.

The dancing was yet at its height; but Ambrose, being completely tipsy by now, had taken his station on the road opposite the cabin, where he kept reeling and singing between the road and the edge of the pond.

Vitek implored him to come, and tugged him by the sleeve, but to no purpose; the old man heard nothing, understood nothing around him, singing the same song over again with obstinate repetition.

Vitek then applied to Yagustynka, who was not ignorant of healing. But she was in the private room, sipping *krupnik,*[1] talking and chattering with her good friends so intently that she would listen to no one else. And as the boy was importunate, begging her with tears to come at once, she in the end drove him from the room. So he went back crying to the stable, having accomplished nothing.

When he returned, Kuba was asleep again; and he too, burrowing deep in the straw and covering his head with a clout, went off to sleep.

It was long after breakfast-time when he was waked by the noise of the hungry unmilked cows, and by the fierce scoldings of Yagustynka, who, having overslept herself just like the others, now made up in clamour against them for what she had neglected herself.

It was only after she had got the work somewhat in swing that she went to see Kuba.

He said in a feeble voice: "Pray help me and do something."

"Just you marry a young wench, and you'll be well in a trice," she began cheerily; but, seeing his livid swollen face, grew serious at once. "You need a priest more than a physician. . . . What on earth can I do for you? . . . So far as I can see, you are sick unto death, aye, even unto death!"

"Must I die?"

"All's in God's hand: but you'll not escape Cross-bones' clutches, I'm thinking."

"I'm to die, say you?"

"Tell me: shall I send for his Reverence?"

"For his Reverence?" Kuba cried, in amazement. "His Reverence to come here—to a stable—to me?"

[1] *Krupnik*—a drink made of vodka, hot water, honey and spices. —*Translator's Note.*

"What of that? Think you he's made of sugar, and would melt if he came near horse-dung? It's a priest's business to go wherever they call him to a sick man."

"O Lord! how could I dare?"

"You are a silly sheep!" She shrugged her shoulders and left him.

"The woman knows not what she says," he muttered, greatly scandalized.

And now he was quite alone, all the others seeming to have forgotten him.

From time to time, Vitek looked in to give the horses provender and water. He gave him water, too; but presently went back to the wedding. At Dominikova's they were preparing to bring the bride home.

Often Yuzka would rush in noisily, bring him a bit of cake, prattle of many things, fill the stable with racket, and run out in a hurry.

Yes, and she had something to run for. Hard by, they were amusing themselves fairly well: the band, the shouting, the singing were to be heard through the walls.

Kuba lay motionless. A strange feeling of desolation had come over him. He merely listened, and noted how well they enjoyed themselves, and talked to Lapa, his never absent companion. They two ate Yuzka's cake together. Then the sick man called to the horses and talked to them also. They neighed with pleasure, turning their heads round from their mangers: the filly even managed to slip her halter and come to his pallet, where she caressed him, putting her warm moist nose close to his face.

"Poor dear, you have lost flesh, you have!" He patted her tenderly, and kissed her dilated nostrils. "As soon as I am well, you will fill out, even if I have to give you nothing but oats!"

Then he lapsed once more into silence, and stared at the blackened knots in the timber walls, oozing with dark drops of resin—as it were, tears of congealed blood.

Dumb, and with feeble sunbeams, the day peeped in

through the chinks, and a flood of shimmering motes appeared at the open doorway.

Hour after hour dragged by at a snail's pace, like lame, blind, and dumb beggars, crawling painfully through toilsome beds of deep sand.

Only, now and again, a few chirruping sparrows, swooping down on the stable in a noisy band, would boldly make for the mangers.

"Ah, the clever little ones!" Kuba said. "And God gives those tiny birds understanding, to find out where they can get food.—Be still, you, Lapa! let the poor things feed and keep up their strength: winter will presently be with them too."

The pigs now began to squeal and poke their muddied noses in at the door.

"Drive them off, Lapa! The beggars, they never have enough!"

After these, a lot of fowls came cackling to the threshold, and one large red cock was so bold as to pass over it to the baskets of provender. The others followed, but had no time to eat their fill, when a flock of gaggling geese drew near, hissing on the threshold, flashing their red bills, stretching and swaying to and fro their straight white necks.

"Out with them, Lapa—out with them! All those fowls—as bad as women for quarrelling!"

Suddenly there was an uproar—screaming, flapping, feathers flying as out of a torn bed. Lapa had entered well into the spirit of the chase, and came back breathless and its tongue lolling out, but uttering cries of delight.

"Be quiet now!"

From the house there came a torrent of angry words, a sound of running, and the dragging of furniture from one room to another.

"Ah, they are making ready for the bride's coming!"

Someone, though rarely, passed along the road: this time it was a lumbering creaking cart, and Kuba, listening, tried to guess whose it was.

"That's Klemba's wagon. One horse—ladder framework; going to the woods for litter, I dare say. Yes, the axle rubs against the nave, so it creaks."

Along the road there was a continual sound of footsteps, talk, and noises scarcely to be heard at all; but he caught them, and made them out on the spot.

"That's old Pietras, going to the tavern.—Here comes Valentova, scolding: someone's geese have gone on to her field, belike.—Oh, she's a vixen, not a woman! . . . This, I think, is Kozlova, shouting as she runs—yes, it is! . . . Here is Peter, son of Raphael . . . when he talks, his mouth always seems full.—This is the priest's mare, going for water. . . . Now she stops . . . cart-wheels blocked by stones.—One of these days she will break a leg."

And so he went on, guessing at every sound he heard, going about all the village with quick thoughts and lively mental vision, and entering so into the whole life and troubles and worries of the place, he scarce noted that the day was declining, the wall darker in hue, the doorway dimmer, and the stable quite obscure.

Ambrose arrived only when evening had set in. He was as yet only partly sober; he staggered a little, and spoke so quickly it was hard to follow him.

"Hurt your leg, eh?"

"Look and see what it is."

Silently he undid the bloodstained rags; they had dried and stuck so fast to the leg that Kuba could not help shrieking as he pulled them off.

"A girl in childbed would not cry as you do!" Ambrose muttered scornfully.

"But it hurts so! How you tear me! O God!"

And Kuba all but howled.

"Oho! you have caught it finely! Was it a dog that tore your leg like that?" Ambrose cried, wondering. The leg was horribly mangled, and swollen with matter to the size of a water-can.

"It was—but pray tell no one—the forest-keeper that shot me. . . ."

"Yes, I see.—And hit you from afar, eh? Well, well! your leg will never again be of any use. I feel the splinters of bone rattling about. . . . Ah, why did you not call me in at once?"

"I feared . . . lest they should know I had been after a hare. . . . But I was out of the forest, when the keeper shot at me."

"Once, in the tavern, he complained; someone was doing mischief, he said."

"The foul carrion! Is a hare, then, the property of anyone? . . . He laid a trap for me. . . . I was in the open field, and he let fly with both barrels.—Oh, the hell-hound! —But say nothing; they would take me to the lawcourt; the gun, too, is not mine, and they would seize it at once. . . . I thought it might heal by itself.—Oh, help me! It pains so! it is tearing me to bits!"

"Ah, you cunning trickster, you! with your sly games and your forbidden quests, sharing the forest hares with the Squire!—But, you see, this partnership will have cost you your leg!"

He examined it again, and looked sorely distressed.

"Too late, ever so much too late!"

Kuba was terrified. "Please do something for me," he moaned.

Ambrose, without replying, turned up his sleeves, whipped out a very keen clasp-knife, grasped the leg firmly, and set about extracting the shots and expressing the matter.

Kuba roared like a beast at the slaughter-house, till the other gagged his mouth with his sheepskin, and then he swooned with the agony of it. After dressing the wound, and applying some ointment and fresh bandages, Ambrose brought him to.

"You will have to go to the hospital," he said in a low voice.

Kuba was still dazed. "To the hospital?" he asked, not knowing what was said.

"They would cut off your leg, and you might get well."

"My leg?"

"Of course. It is good for nothing: black—decayed—rotten."

"Cut it off?" he asked, still unable to understand.

"Yes. At the knee. Fear nothing: mine was cut off almost at the thigh; and I am alive yet."

"Then I shall get well again, if the wounded limb is cut off?"

"Even as though one should take out the pain with the hand . . . but you must go to the hospital."

"There . . . there they cut and carve living men's bodies!—Cut it off, you: I'll pay whatsoever you will, but cut it off!—To the hospital I will not go: I prefer dying here!"

"Then here you will die. None but a doctor can cut it off for you. I am off to the Voyt's at once; he will send you to town in a cart to-morrow."

"No use: I will not go," he replied, stubbornly.

"Fool! do you think they will ask your leave?"

The old man went out, and Kuba said to himself: "When it is cut off, I shall be well."

After the dressing, his leg had ceased to pain. But it was numb as far up as the groin, and he felt a tingling all along his side: this he did not notice, plunged in thought as he was.

"I should recover.—Yes, I surely should. Ambrose has nothing left him of his leg: all he walks on is wooden. And he said: 'As though one should take the pain out with his hand. . . .'—But then, Boryna would turn me away. . . . Aye, a farm-hand with but one leg—such a one cannot plough, nor do aught else.—what would become of me? I should have to tend cattle . . . or beg my bread! Wander about, or sit at some church-door.—O Lord, merciful Lord!" And on a sudden his position flashed clearly upon him; and under the horror that now assailed him, he even sat up. And then he uttered a deep cry of impotent agony, his mind rolling in an abyss from which he saw no issue. "O Jesus, Jesus!" he repeated in a fever of excitement, quaking in every limb.

Long did he shriek and struggle thus in his anguish; but in the midst of those tears and that despair, a certain resolve was slowly shaping itself, and he brooded more and more deeply. Little by little, he grew calmer, more at peace, thinking so profoundly that he heard nothing around him, though surrounded by the din of instruments and songs and clamour; just as if he had been in a deep sleep!

It was then that the bride and the wedding guests arrived at Boryna's house.

They had led away a goodly cow, and sent Yagna's box and feather-bed, and various articles that she had received as wedding presents, before her in a cart.

And now, just a little after sundown, the procession left Dominikova's cabin, as darkness was falling and the mists rising up.

Playing lustily, the band marched in front; then Yagna went on, still in her wedding dress, and conducted by her mother and friends: last of all, and without any order, came the ruck of guests, each in the place he had chosen.

Their way wound along by the pond, now darkened, its gleaming quenched in the ever-thickening folds of the fog; the silence and obscurity growing blacker and more dead, the tramping and music sounding muffled and, as it were, from underneath the water.

From time to time one of the younger folk broke out into song, or a matron took up a stave, or one of the peasant lads cried: "'Da dana!" but it was only a short outburst.

They were as yet in no merry mood, and, besides, they were chilled to the marrow by the bleak damp air.

Only when they turned in to Boryna's enclosure did the bridesmaids lift their voices in a sad farewell:

> Wending her way to her wedding,
> The maiden wept.
> Then lit they tapers four,
> And played upon the organ.—
> Didst fancy, maiden,
> That they would play for ever?
> —A little yesterday, to-day a little,

And after, thou shalt weep for all thy life!
Da dana! . . . All thy life!

Before the threshold, and under the porch, Boryna was waiting along with Yuzka and the young men.

Dominikova came forward first of all, carrying in a bundle a piece of bread, a pinch of salt, a little charcoal, some wax from a Candlemas taper, and a handful of ears of corn, blessed on Assumption Day. As Yagna passed the threshold, the matrons cast behind her threads plucked from cloth seams, and the peels of hempstalks, that the Evil One might find no entrance, but all things thrive with her!

They greeted, kissed, and pledged one another in cups of mead, with wishes of luck, health, and all good gifts and blessings; then they entered and filled the whole room, every bench and nook and corner.

The players tuned their instruments, and then strummed softly, so as not to interfere with the feast that Boryna was now giving.

He simply went from matron to matron with a full goblet in hand, offering, pressing them to partake, gathering them in his arms, and drinking to each of them; the blacksmith took his place with the others.

Yuzka was bearing on platters pieces of a cake she had baked with curds and honey on purpose to please her father.

All the same, the party was dull. True, they emptied their glasses as in duty bound, nor did they turn away from the sausages. Nay, they even drank plentifully and with due zest; only there was no mirth amongst them.

The women too, who as a class are inclined to diversions and pastimes, now only sat still on the benches, or here and there in corners, not even talking much amongst themselves.

Yagna went into the private room, where she undressed. Returning in her everyday costume, she would have done the honours of the cabin and treated her guests herself, but that her mother would not let her touch anything.

"Darling, enjoy your wedding-day now! You'll yet have work enough and enough toil!" And again and again did she weep over her most tenderly, and clasp her to her bosom.

The company found matter for laughter in this maternal sentimentality of hers: their jeers being all the sharper that now, on Yagna's arrival as mistress in her husband's home, owner of so much land and property of every sort, her new position was brought home to them. Many a mother, with yet unmarried daughters, felt very bitter against her; many a girl was choked with bile at the thought.

They went over to survey the other apartments, where Antek had formerly lived with his family. There Eva and Yagustynka had prepared a grand supper and made a roaring fire. Vitek had hardly been able to bring logs enough and place them under the enormous pots.

They examined all the premises besides, and ran their envious eyes over all that there was to be seen.

The house itself, to begin with, was the first in the whole village: large, conspicuous, tall, with rooms (they fancied) as good as those in a manor-house: whitewashed, and with boarded floors! Then how numerous the household articles and utensils were! In the big room, too, there were a score of holy images: and all of them glazed! And then, the byre, the stable, the granary, the shed! Five cows were kept there, to say nothing of the bull—no small source of profit. And the horses, and the geese, and the swine—and, above all, the land!

Eaten up with envy, they sighed deeply; and one said to another:

"Lord! and to think that all this goes to one that is undeserving!"

"Oh! they knew well how to bring their pigs to market!"

"Yes; he that goes to meet luck always finds it."

"Why should your Ulisia have missed this chance?"

"Because she fears God and leads an honest life."

"And all the rest do the same!"

"Oh, were she other than she is, folk would not stand it of her. Let them but meet her once at night in company with a lad, and all the world will know!"

"What luck this one has!"

"'Tis the fruit of shamelessness."

"Come along!" Andrew called out, interrupting their talk. "The music is playing, and not one petticoat is in the room—nobody to dance with!"

"A mind to dance you have, but will your mother let you?"

"So eager?—Beware and let not your trousers fall, boy: 'twere no fair sight!"

"Nor trip the dancers up with your legs!"

"Pair off with Valentova; you'll make a fine couple . . . of scarecrows!"

Andrew rapped out an oath, took hold of the first girl he came across, and led her off, paying no heed to the wasps humming behind him.

There were but few couples in the room as yet, and these danced but slowly and (it seemed) with little zeal. Nastka and Simon Paches were the only exception, and frisked about very willingly. They had arranged matters beforehand and, with the opening sounds of the music, had joined in close union, and bounced about in scrupulous fulfilment of their promise.

But no sooner had the Voyt come in (he was late, having had to go with the recruits to the District Barracks) than he began to make things look more lively; drinking deep, talking with all the farmers present, and cracking jokes with the newly-wedded couple.

"Why, your bride is as red as her skirt, and you are as white as a sheet!"

"You'll not say that to-morrow."

"Matthias, experienced as you are, you surely have not wasted a day."

"Nay, with all eyes upon him? Fie! the man is no gander."

"I would not bet half a quart that you say true. You know: throw but a pebble into the bush: out flies the bird! 'Tis the Voyt tells you so!"

Yagna made her escape from the room; which occasioned a loud guffaw.

The women then proceeded to wag their tongues very much at their ease, careless of what they said.

The hubbub swelled, and the guests grew more good-humoured in proportion. Boryna, bottle in hand, went several times the round of the company; the dancers, now more numerous, frisked with livelier steps, and began to stamp and sing, and circle about the room in wider rounds.

Then did Ambrose make his appearance and, sitting down (nearly at the threshold), follow the bottle with wistful eyes, as it went its way.

The Voyt cried to him: "You never turn your head, except towards the clinking of glasses."

"Because of that same clinking!" he answered. "And he has merit who gives to drink to them that thirst."

"You leather bottle! here's water for you!"

"What's good for cattle may be bad for man. They say: 'Water to drink is now and then not bad, but harm from vodka no one ever had!' "

"Here's vodka for you, since you discourse so well."

"You first, Voyt!—They say, too: 'Water for a christening, vodka for a wedding, and tears for a death!' "

"Well said: drink another."

"I should not even shirk a third. For my first wife I always take one, but two for my second!"

"Why so?"

"Because she died in time for me to seek a third."

"What! Still dreaming about women, and his old eyes see no more as soon as twilight comes!"

"It is not always necessary to see."

At this, they laughed uproariously, and the women cried out:

"For the love of vodka and of talk, they are both well matched."

"There's a saying: 'A wife good in talk, and a man strong in deed, have every chance in the world to succeed.' "

The Voyt had now sat down by Ambrose, the others crowding round, as many as could find seats, or, if they could not, standing about with little heed to the dancers' convenience.

And then began such a running fire of witty sayings, jests, comic tales, and joyous banter, that they all shook with laughter. In this field, Ambrose was the recognized leader, and chaffed his hearers to their very faces with so much humour and fun that they were like to split their sides. Amongst the women, Vachnikova yielded to none for drollery; she played first fiddle in that respect, with the Voyt for bass-viol, so far as his official dignity permitted.

The musicians sawed away as hard as they could, and scraped out the liveliest tunes they had; and the dancers were shuffling along as fast, and shouting, and screaming, and tapping with nimble heels. Blithe and delighted, they had forgotten the rest of the world, when one of them chanced to notice Yankel standing outside in the passage. At once they pulled him into the room. The Jew took off his cap, with amicable bows and salutations to all present, and taking no notice of the nicknames showered upon him.

"Yellow one!—Unchristened one!—Son of a mare!"

"You be quiet there!" cried the Voyt. "Let us treat him! Here, a glass of the best vodka!"

"I was passing along the road, and wanted to see how you husbandmen divert yourselves.—God reward you, Mr. Voyt.—I'll take a drop of vodka—why should I not?—to the health of the newly-wedded pair!"

Boryna raised the bottle and invited Yankel, who, after wiping the glass with the skirt of his capote, covered his head, and tossed off one glass, followed by a second.

"Stay a bit, Yankel: it will not make you unclean," they cried out in a merry vein. "Here, musicians, play us the Jewish dance, and Yankel will caper to it."

"Yes, I may dance; why not? 'Tis no sin."

But ere the players had understood what was wanted of them, Yankel slipped quietly into the passage, and vanished in the yard. He had come to get back his gun.

They scarce noticed his exit. Ambrose had all the time

gone on with his entertainment, to which Vachnikova contributed a violoncello accompaniment, so to speak. And he continued until supper-time, when the music ceased, the tables were pushed forward, and the clatter of dishes was heard: yet they still listened and he still held forth.

Boryna invited them to sup, but without effect. Yagna asked them again and again. The Voyt only got her into the circle, made her sit down by him, and held her by the hand.

It was Yasyek (nicknamed Topsy-turvy) who bellowed out: "Come, good folk, and set to: the dishes are cooling."

"Hold your tongue, blockhead, or lick the dishes with it."

"Old Ambrose! You are lying like a gipsy, and fancy we don't know it!"

"Yasyek, take what folk put into your mouth: you're good at that. But leave me alone, you are no match for me!"

"No match! Just you try, then!" the foolish lad shouted. He thought Ambrose meant fighting.

"An ox could do all you can . . . or more!"

"Because you bear his Reverence's night-vase, Ambrose, you think none has wit but you."

Ambrose was offended, and growled: "Let a calf into church, he'll come out just as he was.—Idiot!"

Yasyek's mother attempted to stand up for her son. He went off to table first of all, and soon the others took their places in a hurry; for the cooks had brought in the smoking dishes, and the odour filled the room.

They seated themselves in order of precedence, as was fitting for the bride's installation ceremony: Dominikova and her sons in the middle, bridesmen and bridesmaids together; Boryna and Yagna remained standing to serve the guests, and see that all was done properly.

A quiet interval succeeded, save that the brats outside made a noise at the window, fighting with one another, and Lapa barked in great excitement about the house and passages. The company were quiet and decorous, while they worked hard to put the eatables away: only their spoons tinkled about the rims of the dishes, and the glasses jingled going round.

Yagna was continually busy, setting some particular dainty before each guest: here it was meat, there some other very good thing. And she begged them all so courteously not to stint themselves, and behaved with such natural grace, conquering all hearts with her beauty and the pleasant words she said, that many of the men present could not but gaze on her in adoration, and her mother even laid down her spoon to look and rejoice in her daughter.

Boryna, too, noticed this, and when she happened to go to the kitchen, followed, caught up with her in the passage, gave her a mighty hug, and kissed her enthusiastically.

"Dear, what a housewife you make!—Like a manor-house lady—so dignified and so pleasing in everything!"

"Am I not, eh?—Now run away to the room: Gulbas and Simon are sitting apart, grumpy and eating little. Get them to drink with you!"

He obeyed, and did all she wanted. And Yagna felt now strangely blithe of heart, and full of affection. She knew herself the mistress of the house, knew that power had somehow got into her hands: and therewith she was aware of an accession of authority and serenity and strength. She walked about the place at ease, eyed all she saw with keen understanding, and managed things as though she had been married ever so long.

"What she is, the old man will find out soon enough, and that's his business; but to my mind there are in her the makings of a housewife—and a fine one, too!" was Eva's muttered remark to Yagustynka.

"A fool that's in favour will always be clever," the latter returned bitterly. "Things will go on as they are till she has had too much of the old man, and begins again running after young fellows."

"Aye, Matthew is lying in wait: he has not given her up."

"But give her up he will! Somebody else will make him!"

"Boryna?"

"Boryna?" She smiled a crafty smile. "No, someone yet mightier. I mean—no: time will show, and you will see.—Vitek! Drive that dog away: it barks and barks till my ears are aching. And drive those boys away too: they will be breaking the panes, or doing some mischief."

Vitek rushed out with a stick. The dog barked no more. But there were cries without, and the noisy footfalls of a crowd of flying urchins. He drove them into the road, and ran back, bent double to escape a shower of missiles that assailed him.

Roch showed himself in the shade at the corner of the yard. "Vitek, wait a little. Call thou Ambrose; say I want him very urgently indeed, and am awaiting him in the porch."

It was only after some time that Ambrose appeared, and in a detestable humour. His supper had been interrupted, and at the very best dish of all—sucking-pig with peas.

"What? what? Is the church on fire?"

"Do not raise your voice so. Come to Kuba: I fear he is dying."

"Oh, let him die, then, and not prevent folk from eating their supper! I was with him only this very evening, and told him he would have to go to the hospital, and get his leg cut off, and he would be well in a trice."

"You told him that?—Oh, then I understand. . . . I—I think he has cut off his own leg!"

"Jesu Maria!—His—his own leg?"

"Come instantly and look. I was going to sleep in the cow-byre, and had just entered the yard, when Lapa came barking to me, and jumping, and pulling me by my capote. I could not make out what it wanted; but it ran forward, sat down on the stable threshold, and howled. Thither I went and saw Kuba lying in the doorway, half in, half out. I thought at first he had gone to get some air, and fainted on the way: so I carried him back to his pallet, and lit the lantern to get him some water; and it was then I saw he was bloodstained all over—deathly pale, and with blood pouring from his leg."

They went in, and Ambrose did his very best to bring Kuba to; but the poor fellow was extremely weak. He scarce drew breath, and a rattling sound came through his teeth, clenched so fast that, to give him a little water, they had to prize them open with a knife.

The leg, which had been hewn off at the knee, and still dangled by a shred of skin, bled profusely.

A great pool of gore lay on the threshold, close to a bloodstained ax and the grindstone, usually placed under the eaves, now fallen near the doorway.

"Aye, he has cut it off himself. Afraid of the hospital. —A fool to think it would avail him: but dauntless and resolute all the same.—Good God! . . . his own leg! . . . it is simply incredible. . . . And the blood he has lost!"

At this juncture, Kuba opened his eyes, and looked round him with returning consciousness.

"Is it off? . . . I struck twice, but swooned——" he said feebly.

"Any pain?"

"None at all. . . . Weak as water . . . but not ailing."

Ambrose dressed, washed and bound the leg with moist rags, Kuba lay still meanwhile, uttering not the least sound.

Roch, on his knees, held the lantern, praying fervently the while; but the patient smiled—a faint tearful smile, as when an orphan babe, abandoned afield, knows only that his mother is not there, not that she has forsaken him, and enjoys the grass waving over his head, and the sunbeams, and stretches out his hands to the birds that fly past, conversing with all around him after his fashion: even so did he feel now. He was at ease, without pain and in comfort; so cheerful that he thought no whit of his ill, but felt secretly rather proud of himself. How sharp he had ground the ax! how well he had placed the limb on the threshold, and—one blow not sufficing—struck a second with all his might! And now the pain was all gone; so of course he had succeeded.—Oh, if he were but a trifle stronger, he would not lie rotting on that pallet any more, but be up, and go to the wedding . . . dance even—and eat a morsel, for he would fain eat!

"Lie you still, and do not budge. I will tell Yuzka, and you shall have something to eat presently." So said Roch, patting his cheeks; and he went out into the yard with Ambrose.

"He will drop off ere morning—fall asleep like a little bird: there's no more blood in him."

"Then, while he is conscious, the priest must be sent for."

"His Reverence has gone to spend the evening at the manor-house at Vola."

"I'll go and tell him: there must be no delay."

"Five miles on foot and through the forest! You would never be in time.—No: the carts of those guests here who leave after supper are ready; take one and go."

They got a cart on to the road, and Roch seated himself.

"Do not forget Kuba!" he called out as he started: "Have a care of him!"

"Yes, yes, I shall remember, and not leave him by himself."

Nevertheless, he did forget him almost directly. After telling Yuzka about the eatables, he went back to supper, and applied himself so close to the bottle that he very soon remembered nothing at all. . . .

Yuzka, being a kind-hearted little girl, at once brought him all she could get, piling it up on a dish, with half a quart of vodka.

"Here, Kuba, is something for you, that ye may eat and enjoy yourself."

"God bless you!—Sausage it is, I fancy;—a delightful smell!"

"I fried it for you, that you might find it more savoury." She put the dish into his hands, for the stable was dark. "But drink of the vodka first."

He drained the glass to the last drop.

"Will you sit with me a little? I feel lonely here."

He broke the food, bit and chewed it—but could swallow nothing.

"Are they in good spirits over there?"

"Oh, yes! and so many people! I never saw more company in all my life."

"Of course, of course," he said, proudly; "is it not Boryna's wedding?"

"Yes; and Father is so pleased . . . and always going after Yagna!"

"Indeed, for she is so beautiful—as fair to see as a Manor-house lady any day."

"Do you know, Simon, Dominikova's son, is taken with Nastka!"

"His mother will forbid him. There are only three acres of land at Nastka's, and ten mouths to feed."

"That's why she keeps strict watch and drives them apart when she finds them together."

"Is the Voyt here?"

"He is.—Talking a great deal, and—together with Ambrose—making the company laugh."

"And why not, being at so great a wedding, and with so great a man?—Do you know anything of Antek's doings?"

"Ah, I ran over to him at dusk, with cake and meat and bread for the little ones. But he turned me out, and threw the things after me. He is very resolute; and fierce. Oh, so fierce! And there is wailing and misery in their hovel. Hanka is always quarrelling with her sister, and they have well-nigh come to blows."

He made no reply, but breathed somewhat harder.

"Yuzka," he said after a while, "the mare!—I hear her moaning. Since evening she has been lying down: she must be near foaling-time, and ought to be looked after. Prepare a mash for her.—Hark how she moans! And I cannot help at all, so weak I feel—quite helpless!"

He was worn out, and said no more for a while, seeming to be asleep.

Yuzka rose and went out in a hurry.

"Ces, Ces, Ces!" he called to the mare, as he woke suddenly.

The mare uttered a low whinny, and tugged at her halter till the chain clanked again.

"So then, once in my life at least, I shall eat and be filled! Aye, and you too, good dog, shall get your share: no need to whine."

He attempted once more to swallow some sausage, but quite in vain: it stuck in his throat.

"Lord, Lord, such heaps of food . . . and I cannot so much as eat one mouthful!"

Yes, it was utterly useless: he could not. His hand fell powerless, and, still grasping the meat, he put it underneath the straw of his bed.

"So much! Never so much yet! And all for nothing!" —He felt rather sore.

"But let me rest a little now; and later, when I can eat, the feast shall begin."

He was just as unable afterwards, and slipped off into a coma, still holding the sausage, and unaware that Lapa was stealthily gnawing at it.

Suddenly his senses returned.—The supper was over, and such a blast of music burst on his ears from over the yard, that the stable-walls vibrated, and the frightened fowls fell a-cackling on their roosts.

The dance was in full and boisterous swing—and the laughter and the frolic and the fun. Again and again the trampling of feet resounded, and the shrill cries of the lasses pierced the night.

At first, Kuba gave ear; but presently he became oblivious of all things. A drowsiness seized upon him, and carried him off into, as it were, a clangorous darkness, as though beneath swift swirling murmurous waters. But when the dance grew noisier, and the tumult and hubbub of the stamping heels seemed about to beat all to shivers, he stirred slightly: his soul peered up out of the dungeon where it lay; roused from oblivion, coming back from infinite distances, it listened.

At such times, Kuba would endeavour to eat a little, or whispered low, but from the heart:

"Ceska, Ces, Ces!"

And now at last his soul was slowly withdrawing—winging its way through the universal frame of things. A new-fledged bird divine, it fluttered around uncertainly at first, unable to soar, and at times with a revival of attachment to that sacred earth, its body, where it fain would rest from the weariness of flight, and craved to soothe the pangs of bereavement in the haunts of men. Back it went on earth amongst his own, its loved ones, calling sorrowfully to its brethren, and imploring their aid: but after a time, strengthened by the Divine power and mercy, it was enabled to soar on high, even unto those mysterious fields of endless spring, those infinite unbounded fallows which God has made beautiful with everlasting sunbeams and eternal joy.

And higher yet it flew, and higher, yet higher, higher—yea, till it set its feet——

Where man can hear no longer the voice of lamentation, nor the mournful discords of all things that breathe——

Where only fragrant lilies exhale balmy odours, where fields of flowers in bloom waft honey-sweet scents athwart the air; where starry rivers roll over beds of a million hues; where night comes never at all——

Where silent prayers go up for ever, like smoke of incense, in odoriferous clouds; and the bells tinkle, and the organ plays softly; and the ransomed people—Angels and Saints together—sing the Lord's praises in the Holy Church, the divine and lasting City!

Yes, worn out and longing to be at rest, thither did the soul of Kuba fly away!

. . . .

But in the house they all were dancing—enjoying themselves with the heartiest mirth and the best goodwill. Better still than the evening before, the good cheer being dealt out more generously, and the hosts more pressing. And so they danced till they could dance no more.

The place was in commotion, like a cauldron set upon a great fire. Did the enjoyment show any signs of flagging, at once the band set to with renewed zeal; and the guests, like a field stirred by the wind and waving, sprang up and began to dance anew with fresh fire and song and din and tumult.

Now were their souls quite melted within them by the volcanic enthusiasm of their host; their blood seethed hot, reason was almost giving way, their hearts were beating with the wildest frenzy. For them, every movement now seemed a dance, every cry a song, and every look a glance of ecstasy!

And so it went on all night long, and even till morning. But the day rose, dull and still: the rays of dawn appeared together with dense dreary masses of clouds. Ere the sun had risen, the world grew very dark and dismal. And then the snow came down: at first whirling, fluttering, scanty—as when the needles fall from pine-trees on a windy day; until it set to falling in earnest.

Then, as though coming through a sieve, the snow descended in perpendicular flakes, straight down, equally dealt out, monotonous, noiseless, covering roofs, trees, and hedges, and all the land, as with an enormous covering of white feathers.

The wedding was really at an end at last. True, they were to meet again at the tavern in the evening, "to wind up"; but for the present they decided to return home.

Only the bridesmen and bridesmaids, with the band to lead them, drew up in the porch and sang in unison a short song, in which, declaring themselves the devoted servants of the wedded couple, they wished them good night—in the morning!

It was then that Kuba laid his soul at the sacred feet of the Lord Jesus. . . .

END OF PART I